MISSION ACCOMPLISHED:
High praise for *New York Times*
and *USA Today* bestselling author
CINDY GERARD
and her scorching alpha hunks!

"I'm hooked on Gerard's tough-talkin', straight-shootin' characters."

—Sandra Brown

"A true master!"

—*RT Book Reviews*

"Slam-bang romantic suspense."

—*Fresh Fiction*

"Kicks romantic adventure into high gear."

—Allison Brennan

"Just keeps getting better and better."

—*Romance Junkies*

KILLING TIME
**Book One in the thrilling new One-Eyed Jacks series
Nominated for the *RT Book Reviews*
Best Romantic Suspense Award!**

"Cindy Gerard writes such fun books. Full of tons of action, witty lines and plenty of sexual tension, *Killing Time* totally lived up to my expectations."

—*USA Today*

"A Gerard novel is always worth the time and money invested, and this one is no exception."

—*RT Book Reviews* (Top Pick!)

THE WAY HOME
A captivating stand-alone novel with some sizzling heroes you might recognize

"A story readers can't help but fall in love with."

—*RT Book Reviews*

"Smart, romantic, exciting, and so emotionally satisfying. I hugged myself for hours after reading it. Cindy Gerard really knows how to bring it home!"

—Robyn Carr

"A really sweet read about second chances, finding love, and the path that leads you to your happily ever after. Gerard continues to impress me."

—*Smexy Books*

"An interesting meditation . . . on the changing foundations of love. In many ways it challenges the first and only soul mate concept that is so prevalent."

—*Dear Author*

"I anxiously await every new Cindy Gerard release. I've always thought there was nobody who wrote romantic suspense better, able to seamlessly blend romance and action while creating strong heroines and macho yet caring heroes."

—*Fiction Vixen*

"Gerard is an author whose stories I always have an easy time falling into and thoroughly enjoying. . . . You can never go wrong with the Black Ops world."

—*Happily Ever After-Reads*

"Gerard simply excels when it comes to writing action-packed scenes that are highly detailed and infused with passion and fun. Similarly, her heroes have been some of the hottest in RS that I've read."

—*Under the Covers Book Blog*

Also by Cindy Gerard

CINDY GERARD

RUNNING BLIND

Pocket Books
New York London Toronto Sydney New Delhi

Pocket Books
A Division of Simon & Schuster, Inc.
1230 Avenue of the Americas
New York, NY 10020

This book is a work of fiction. Any references to historical events, real people, or real places are used fictitiously. Other names, characters, places, and events are products of the author's imagination, and any resemblance to actual events or places or persons, living or dead, is entirely coincidental.

First Pocket Books paperback edition March 2015

POCKET and colophon are registered trademarks of Simon & Schuster, Inc.

For information about special discounts for bulk purchases, please contact Simon & Schuster Special Sales at 1-866-506-1949 or business@simonandschuster.com.

The Simon & Schuster Speakers Bureau can bring authors to your live event. For more information or to book an event, contact the Simon & Schuster Speakers Bureau at 1-866-248-3049 or visit our website at www.simonspeakers.com.

Manufactured in the United States of America

10 9 8 7 6 5 4 3 2 1

ISBN 978-1-4767-3935-9
ISBN 978-1-4767-3952-6 (ebook)

To the loves of my life:
Kyle, Eileen, Kayla, Blake, Lane, and Hailey.
And, to Tom, for all the reasons I've told you and for
all the reasons I can't even put into words.

The price of freedom is eternal vigilance.

—Thomas Jefferson

Acknowledgments

If ever a writer had a guardian angel, it's me. Without my friend Joe watching over my shoulder and making sure I get all the technical "stuff" right, helping me manipulate the action part of my plot, and generally being there to aid in the creative process, this book wouldn't have been completed.

So thanks again to Joseph Francis Collins—a fine author in his own right—for being there with the wings and the halo, and for helping with the heavy lifting.

Monday

I think we consider too much the good luck of the early bird and not enough the bad luck of the early worm.

—Franklin D. Roosevelt

1

A trancelike calm kicked in, as it always did once she settled into her sniper's "nest." Oblivious to the cold, she peered through the scope of her rifle and smiled. From the sixth floor of the abandoned office building, she had a perfect sight line into Brewed Awakenings. And soon her targets would start to gather for their monthly breakfast.

She'd been called a well-tuned killing machine, her reputation acquired from fifteen years of kill shots. But this was no ordinary contract kill; this was the mother of all kills. Her reputation in the global "work for hire" community was on the line, for one. Her newfound standing with the Russians, for another; they would pay well when she performed to their satisfaction. Even more important, however, was her personal objective: revenge.

And she was primed and pumped to kill.

• • •

This early on a Monday morning was so far from Jamie Cooper's comfort zone he felt as if he'd landed in a different zip code. All because of a woman who wouldn't give him the time of day.

Disgusted with himself, he sat at the large table the hostess led him to. He was the first to arrive; the members of DOD's two off-the-books black ops teams weren't due at Brewed Awakenings for a good fifteen minutes. Opening a menu, he sized up the twenty or so other customers. He'd give it a 99 percent probability that none of them represented a threat. Even off the clock, he never dropped full alert status.

And right this moment, he was alert for one team member in particular: Rhonda "Bombshell" Burns.

The new head computer analyst and security expert had thrown him way off his game. In the six months she'd been on board, the woman had single-handedly elevated the stereotype of "computer nerd" to "computer sexpot." Taggart's term, not his, but he damn sure agreed. The woman was a walking, talking wet dream.

But God help the man who called her that to her face; her smackdown would be brutal. And hot.

Get your head out of your ass and recalibrate, Coop.

The Bombshell was strictly "look but don't touch." Not only was she his teammate, but she'd also made her total lack of interest in him crystal-clear.

Yet here he sat, waiting to set eyes on her. And the woman barely spoke to him.

How screwed up was that?

If Taggart and Mike knew he'd turned stupid over a woman, they'd laugh their asses off. Needle him about being a stalker. Want to check his temperature.

Maybe they'd be right. Maybe he was sick—in the head. He'd actually set his alarm so he could watch her make her grand entrance. It was *so* high school. But her entrances were always grand—so he cut himself a little slack.

Then he spotted her walking past the plate-glass windows. When she sashayed through the door, he nearly stopped breathing. It felt as if a combat boot had kicked him in the chest. Her cheeks were flushed pink with cold, her baby-blues sparkled, and her thick, glossy blond mane framed her face like the angel hair his mom used to drape on their Christmas tree.

Except Rhonda Burns was no angel. As she slipped off her coat and hung it on the rack by the door, her skintight pink sweater, ass-hugging skirt, and nosebleed-high heels conjured up thoughts that could send him straight to hell. He shifted in his chair because suddenly, his pants were a little too tight for comfort.

He didn't know where she got those soft, fuzzy sweaters, but he hoped she never ran out of them. And he hoped she never changed the way she dressed, the way she smelled, the way she walked, and the way she radiated confidence and sass and sensuality.

With her luscious curves and "look all you want, enjoy, but don't touch" attitude, she made his day every time she walked into a room. And now she was walking right toward his table.

He could handle her; he had no doubt about that. But beside the fact that the Department of Defense would frown on any type of slap-and-tickle between teammates, the oh-so-tempting Rhonda would undoubtedly prove to be a massive complication. And he liked his personal life just the way it was: pie simple.

But because he couldn't help himself, he did his best to get a rise out of her now and then, just to feel the afterburn of her explosion.

"Good morning," she said crisply.

To show that her frosty greeting hadn't fazed him, he flashed her a smile, which she didn't return.

She smoothed a hand over her hair and gave a toss of her head that sent her long golden tresses flowing over one shoulder. Sitting regally on the chair he'd pulled out for her, she crossed one long leg over the other, then made the monumental effort of glancing at him. "A little early for you, isn't it, Hondo?"

Bada-bing.

There was the needling he'd come to enjoy.

"Good morning to you, too, Buttercup." She hated cutesy nicknames as much as he hated being called Hondo.

She dismissed him like a used napkin. "Make yourself useful. When they bring coffee, pour me a cup. I've got to go powder my nose."

Pretty darn sure that she just wanted to get away

from him until more members of the team arrived, he deliberately cleared his throat. "Somebody forgot the magic word."

A disingenuous smile flashed, then disappeared. "Please."

"Your coffee will be my number one priority."

She turned away and, like every other man in the restaurant, he watched the sweet, deliberate sway of her hips as she walked toward the ladies' room.

2

A rush of icy February air blew in as Bobby Taggart arrived. He glanced around, spotted Coop, and did a comical double take. Coop grinned and prepared for the flack the square-jawed, tough-as-nails Bronx native was bound to give him. His brown hair was military-cut, his eyes were always watchful, and if the ink on his right forearm paying tribute to his fallen brothers hadn't pegged him as a warrior, his Ironman build left no question. One look from those hard green eyes sent grown men scattering and women wondering if they should be fascinated or fearful.

Yet Taggart could always make Coop laugh. Despite the fact that Coop was retired Marine and Taggart was retired Army Special Forces, they were best friends.

Taggart reached the table and pulled out a chair. "So who lit a fire under your ass?"

Coop gave his buddy the one-finger salute, grabbed one of the coffeepots the busboy had just brought, and poured them each a cup. "What? I can't be the first one here for a change?

"You? Early? It goes against all the laws of nature."
Taggart shrugged out of his worn leather jacket, hung
it on the back of the chair, and sat down across from
him. "And it hurts my heart to think that a pretty boy
like you might not've gotten all your beauty sleep."

Taggart's flack over Coop's past as a model got seriously old. "I know something else that'll make your
head hurt," Coop warned.

"Your fist in my face if I don't mind my own business?"

Coop lifted his coffee cup in salute. "There ya go."

Brewed Awakenings was one of several places the
two teams gathered once a month on an irregular rotation. Original brick walls, stained pine floors, and a
shabby-chic décor made the place comfortable—not
to mention that the coffee was the best he'd found
outside of his own kitchen. The general public had
no idea who they were or that their two units were
the first line of human defense for homeland and international terrorist threats. Even so, they still varied
venues and arrival and departure times as precau-
tionary measures. It was all about security, mixed in
with a healthy dose of Spec Ops paranoia, but come
hell or hurricane, they kept their monthly breakfast
date.

Because even though they worked together day
in and day out and all had lives outside of Uncle
Sam's domain, the deal was, they liked one another.
To a man and a woman, all of them had ties to one
another that only they could understand. And they

needed these out-from-under-the-umbrella gatherings to stay connected.

"Man, she's something, huh?" Taggart said.

Coop followed his gaze and saw Rhonda walking back toward the table.

Combat boot. Direct hit. Solar plexus.

Rhonda gave Taggart a big grin and an even bigger hug. "Aren't you a fine sight on a cold Monday morning?" she drawled in a Georgia peach voice she reserved for people she liked—which explained why Coop heard it only in mixed company.

"New shirt." Taggart shot Coop a needling wink over Rhonda's shoulder.

"I noticed, and I like it."

Taggart beat Coop to the carafe. "Let me pour you some coffee, darlin'."

"Good to know I can count on someone." The glance she shot Coop could have leveled a small building.

He gave her a mock salute.

Which she ignored, walking toward the door to greet more team members as they entered.

"God, I love how she busts your balls," Taggart said as they both watched Rhonda walk toward the new arrivals. "How does it feel to finally meet a woman who doesn't automatically worship at the altar of your bed?"

Coop cracked up. "Worship at the altar of my *bed*?"

"Can't decide if it's that ugly face of yours," Taggart speculated, slinging an arm over the back of his chair, "the smooth talk, or the sock you stuff in the front of your pants that attracts the ladies like sharks to chum."

So, okay. He didn't exactly have a face that broke plates. He got a lot of long, lustful looks from the opposite sex. And yeah, sometimes he took them up on their offers.

But he wasn't a dick about it. He didn't make promises he didn't intend to keep, and he sure as hell didn't invite most of the attention he got. But as he opened his mouth to tell Taggart to shove it, Rhonda and the others joined them.

When she had settled back in and picked up her coffee, Taggart poured on the charm, making it clear how much it amused him that she was unaffected by Coop's . . . sock.

"Careful, the coffee's really hot," Taggart warned her.

What was really hot was the woman who took pains to ignore him. And damn it, if she'd just flirt with him like she did with Taggart and the rest of the guys, he wouldn't be in this fix now. But no. She had to give him all kinds of crap all the time.

Well, she could pretend indifference until there were solar flares on the moon, but he'd caught her looking at him more than once. Looking a little perplexed, a little peeved, and maybe even a little turned on. He'd love to mine those cracks in her personal firewall to see what was going on inside her head — or maybe not.

The truth was, she wound him up as tight as a re-coil spring in a shotgun, which was a huge problem, because Mike had partnered them up next week to do security checks at a couple of Air Force bases.

A week with the Bombshell. Alone.

He glanced at her, all silken blond hair, big blue eyes, and tight sweater. He hadn't told her yet about the field assignment; he'd do that back at the office. But he'd told himself plenty: she was hands off, and not merely because DOD wouldn't approve. No, he'd keep his distance from the Bombshell because bombs exploded, and he didn't want to get blown to hell.

3

She shivered with anticipation as she sighted down the rifle's scope for perhaps the hundredth time since she'd set up the nest. The air was bitter cold, but adrenaline kept her blood pumping, sending heat to her extremities, keeping her fingers nimble as she made minute adjustments to the legs of the tripod mount.

The Ruger M77 bolt-action was her new personal favorite. She loved the irony that it shot ammo similar to the M16 rifle that the U.S. military loved so much. And regardless of the range of almost three hundred yards, the cartridges she'd hand-loaded would ensure maximum destruction.

She'd have made this hit free of charge, so it was icing on the cake that the Russians were paying her a king's ransom. And it was no accident that they'd contacted her to take out one of the Department of Defense's top covert tactical teams. She'd laid bread crumbs from Munich to Moscow, making certain they'd follow the trail straight to her and understand that she had the goods they needed and a product to sell.

Her intricate planning had paid off. Yet another thing she owed to her mentor. He'd left her the means to this end, and the thought of finally exacting revenge for his death had her shaking with excitement.

"Are you all ready to order?" a preppy young waiter asked Rhonda.

She didn't find it unusual that she'd been singled out as the spokesman for the group; it had always been that way. She'd been told that she had a look—social organizer, office administrator, corporate deity, boss lady, whatever—that drew others to assume she was in charge. She'd stopped fighting it long ago.

She glanced around the table. Her boss, Mike Brown, sat beside his wife, Eva. Then came Jamie Cooper. If he'd meant to annoy her by moving to a chair directly across from her, he'd done a good job of it. After him were two other team members, Enrique Santos and Josh Waldrop. Only Joe and Steph Green had made it from the other Black Ops team, rounding out the group.

"Anyone else coming?" she asked Brown. When he shook his head, she turned back to the waiter. "Why don't you start with the big guy here"—she patted Taggart's shoulder—"and work your way back to me?"

While the waiter took orders, Rhonda sat back, feeling the disbelief that sometimes hit her when she thought about her new job. These men were elite operatives. They made up the core group of the International Threat Analysis and Prevention Agency

(ITAP), along with Brett Carlyle, who hadn't made it to breakfast today.

Now she was one of them. A member of a covert antiterrorist team.

Never in her wildest dreams.

She'd thought long and hard before she accepted the position. She'd known from the get-go that it wasn't as innocuous as the name of the unit implied.

And after she'd signed so many confidentiality and security clearance documents that it made the NSA's requirements seem like hooking pinkie fingers and crossing hearts, Mike had briefed her on the unit's real mission.

"ITAP is a cover agency created to ensure we can operate with anonymity and complete autonomy," he'd said.

Yikes. Who in any government agency was granted autonomy?

"For instance," he'd added, "if someone starts snooping around DOD records, they won't discover anything, because we're listed as a private consulting firm, hired on a contractual basis for security and threat assessments."

"But that's not what you—I mean, we—do?" she'd asked him.

"Security assessment is one of our functions, yes. In fact, our first field assignment will most likely be a cyber-threat analysis of a high-value military facility. But our primary purpose is rapid response and deployment when a specific threat to national security is confirmed."

At that point, it had started to sound a lot like covert operations. And she'd been right.

The team could deploy to any U.S. military facility for the official reason of assessing potential security breaches, when, in fact, they might be there to take out an Al-Qaeda kingpin.

"So, we are and we aren't who everyone thinks we are," she'd concluded.

Mike had grinned. "Exactly."

It was really quite ingenious. With the security consultant cover, the team could get into facilities stateside and internationally that no one else could.

Rhonda looked around the table. In private, the team called itself the One-Eyed Jacks; she didn't know much about the story behind the name. She knew they all carried old, tattered jacks of hearts and spades like they were treasured club membership cards, cards that only came out of their pockets when they were drawing for who bought breakfast. She imagined there was a much bigger story there—just like ITAP had a bigger story.

"Big responsibilities," she'd said, after absorbing all the information Mike had fed her. "Why so few operators?"

"Because we run fast and lean. Only the best make the cut. I keep the unit scaled down for that reason, and it's going to stay that way."

She couldn't help feeling a twinge of pride that Mike considered her among the best at what she did. Turned out she was pretty good with weaponry, too. Passing her probation had involved time on the rifle range and in close-quarters combat drills. But even though her instructor said she was a natural, she had no interest in being part of any shoot-'em-up operations. She wanted to be on the front lines fighting cyber-terrorism with a unit that could make that happen.

Cooper was the only wrinkle in her game plan. She glared at him when she was sure he wasn't looking. If she had an Achilles' heel, unfortunately, he was it—which ticked her off. Not that anyone would ever know. She was not only good at finding secrets, she was also good at keeping them. Nope. No one would ever know that she'd spent far too much time wondering what was behind the pretty boy's face . . . and what it would be like to sleep with him.

"So, how's it going?" Stephanie Green asked, reminding her that this morning was about socializing.

"Good," Rhonda said with a firm nod, taking advantage of the ordering and male-to-male ribbing that gave them a moment of privacy. "It's going well."

Three years ago, Rhonda and Steph had worked together as cryptologists at the National Security Agency. Then Steph had left the stifling bureaucracy of the NSA for greener pastures. She'd turned in her secret decoder ring for a wedding ring, married Black Ops agent Joe Green, and adopted a street orphan from Sierra Leone who had been instrumental in saving their lives. Steph had also joined Nate Black's unit and, judging by how happy the pretty brunette looked, was loving every minute of it.

"So you're not sorry I talked you into applying for the ITAP position?" Steph asked.

Rhonda covered Steph's hand with hers and squeezed. "Are you kidding? You saved me from a life of endless boredom. I'm in the front lines now, chickie. I'm no longer a drone slogging through a maze of cubicles like a robot and praying for something big to happen."

Stephanie laughed. "In the first place, you could never be categorized as a drone. Drones don't look like you or get stared at the way you do. Speaking of which," she added quietly after a furtive glance across the table, "what's with Golden Boy over there?"

Rhonda glanced at Jamie Cooper, then quickly away. Damn. He *was* staring. And damn, he was . . . golden. From his skin—he clearly had some Latino blood—to the gold rimming his chocolate-brown irises, to the natural highlights that shimmered in the dark brown hair that was just long enough to make him look like a badass. A very sexy badass.

"We haven't quite figured each other out yet," she hedged.

"Really?" Steph's sparkling eyes smiled as she gave Rhonda an all-knowing look. "Seems clear to me. The man's got the hots for you, my friend."

Rhonda snorted. "What man doesn't?" She knew what she looked like, and she liked to maximize her assets. She had a passion for Manolo Blahniks and vintage angora sweaters, and she was on a first-name basis with the clerks at her favorite makeup counter. So sue her.

When she'd decided to take the position, she'd also decided that the team was going to have to take her as she was—blond and curvy and not shy about showcasing those curves. She enjoyed being a woman. She also had a smart mouth that she'd have to make a big effort to control; so far, that wasn't working out too well. She took way too much pleasure needling Cooper, who had the mistaken impression that he was God's gift to womankind.

"At least, until they get to know me and they figure out what a bitch I am," she added.

"You're not a bitch. You're protective of yourself. Nothing wrong with that."

Rhonda changed the subject, as she always did when it veered too close to her emotional space. "Better give the man your order," she said as the waiter reached them.

Steph was her dearest friend, but even she didn't know the reason Rhonda evaded, avoided, and even sabotaged budding romantic relationships. One day, maybe she'd tell her. In the meantime, she kept it to herself.

Feeling a tingle at the base of her spine, she glanced across the table again. And again, there was Cooper, that cocky smile on his face, his gaze lasered in on her, irritating the hell out of her.

She was going to have to do something about that

man. She didn't like the way he made her feel . . .
off her stride, a little bit out of control. And too often
unfocused—not something she could afford if she
was going to pull her weight on the team. She still
had a lot to prove before she won their complete confidence.

Cooper might want to play silly games, but she
didn't. Before they headed for work, she'd get him
alone and call him on it. By the time she finished with
the Golden Boy, he'd be looking for a new hobby—
one that didn't involve messing with her mind.

4

Setting up the nest had required mechanical precision, patience, time, and tolerance for extreme boredom. It had been well over an hour since the targets had started arriving. And still, she waited.

She peered through the Leopold 3x9 rifle scope and set it to minimum magnification. The scope made the targets appear to be only thirty feet away instead of three hundred yards, making long-distance kills almost as easy as close-ups. Jamie Cooper. Bobby Taggart. Mike Brown and his bitch of a wife. Their tightly knit group would soon be gone.

Calculating the wind speed with the help of a flag fluttering on a nearby building, she adjusted the scope. The Kestrel weather meter provided temperature and humidity, since both would affect the bullet's flight. As would the range and the thickness of the restaurant's plate-glass window. She consulted the range card again, then made another slight alteration so that the bullets would hit straight and true.

Satisfied that everything was properly set, she

made a final check of the defenses she'd put in place. If any of Brown's team attempted to enter this room, a little surprise awaited them. They thought they were cagey, alternating their meeting days and times and locations, but they weren't cagey enough. Her contact had told her they'd be at this restaurant this morning.

Predictability, thy name is victim.

Adrenaline shot through her veins, and she quelled the rapid beat of her heart with long, steadying breaths. Then she settled deeper behind the scope and savored the moment.

After two years of planning, another few minutes were nothing. Now wasn't the time to get jumpy and rush the shot. There could be no possibility that this job went wrong.

When they'd killed her mentor, they'd killed part of her, too. He would approve of her ensuring that those who mourned her targets would know exactly who'd pulled the trigger and why. They would know that this was about revenge.

"I still don't know what you see in this chump." Coop hugged Mike's wife, not only because it would get Mike all riled up but also because he had a special affection for her.

Eva, an attorney for the CIA, had hunted Mike down in Peru and forced him to fight the false charges that had ended all of their military careers in disgrace ten years ago. If not for her, Coop, Taggart, and Mike wouldn't have been reunited, exonerated, and working together today.

"Hey," Mike groused good-naturedly, as predicted. "Get your hands off my girl. And for your information, I have some very special qualities. Right, *chica*?"

Coop laughed when the unflappable Eva blushed, making it clear that Mike might have recently worked on perfecting those "special" qualities with her.

"Who's organizing next month's breakfast?" Eva asked, dodging the question.

"I think that would be me," Stephanie said. "I hope more members of Nate's unit can make the next gathering. In the meantime, I assume you'll be picking up Coop and Taggart's tab again?" she asked Mike with a grin.

"Har-har." Grumbling, Mike tossed his credit card onto the table with the bill, then scowled at the tattered jack of hearts he'd pulled out of his wallet with the credit card; a bullet hole pierced the playing card clean through the middle. "That *used* to be my lucky card," he said, tucking it away again.

"Better luck next time, boss." Taggart kissed his own one-eyed jack of spades, which had been sliced half through with a KA-Bar knife.

"Not a word out of you, Cooper." Mike gave him the evil eye.

"Wasn't going to say a thing," Coop said. "Certainly wasn't going to point out that your card has let you down the last nine out of ten times."

"Nope. Because you're not that kind of guy." Mike grunted.

"I'd never gloat." Coop grinned. "Sure did enjoy those pancakes, boss."

He glanced down at his own card, a faded jack of hearts that was burned around the edges. Every time he looked at it, or saw Mike pull his out of a pocket, or watched Taggart flip his over and over between his fingers, he was transported back ten years to Afghanistan, where all the men in their unit had carried one-eyed jacks as a symbol of solidarity, of brotherhood.

Mike, Bobby, and Coop were the only ones left, and they carried their cards in honor of their fallen brothers.

And because none of the three of them could resist a gamble, they always drew cards to see who paid for breakfast.

"I hate to be the one to break up this friendly sparring," Eva said as she shrugged into her coat, "but I've got a nine o'clock meeting I need to—"

A huge, booming crack cut off her words as the front window exploded, and flying shards of plate glass flew through the room like Hellfire missiles.

"Shooter! Contact front!" Coop yelled. He dived across the table and tackled Rhonda to the floor.

The rest of the team members scrambled for cover, reaching into concealed shoulder or waist holsters for their handguns.

"You okay?" he asked Rhonda.

She squirmed beneath him. "I'm fine. Get off of me!"

He rolled, scrambled up onto all fours, and, heart slamming, appraised the situation.

Stunned civilians, frozen in shock, sat with mouths agape. Then the restaurant erupted in terrified screams.

"Get down! Get the hell down!" Coop yelled. His 9mm in hand, he crab-crawled across the floor, sweeping glass aside with the heels of his hands. Mike was right beside him.

"Get down!" Mike dragged two screaming women to the floor. "Everyone hug the floor! Get as low as you can, and stay there!"

When people finally realized that they were the good guys, they scrambled to make themselves as small as possible. Behind Coop, tables slammed to the floor as the team flipped them over to use as shields. He crawled low over broken glass to get a fix on the shooter's position.

The eerie silence was broken only by soft, terrified sobs and the sounds of 911 calls flying out from cell phones. A cutting wind scuttled in through the shattered window.

"Did it stop?" a woman's voice sobbed.

"Just stay down," Coop repeated loudly, so everyone knew to stay cautious. "Is anyone hit? Anyone hurt?"

Silence among the sharp breaths and muffled sobs.

"Check your neighbor. Make sure everyone's okay!" Mike said from under the open window.

Taggart and Waldrop belly-crawled across the floor toward them, and the four of them made a quick check on the civilians.

Joe Green made a break to cover the back of the restaurant. Santos, hunched low, ran to support him.

Another shot rang out.

Santos spun in a circle and went down. "I'm okay," he assured everyone quickly as he scooted behind a downed table. "Just nicked my arm. I'm okay." To prove it, he scrambled toward the back door and got into position with Green, his gun trained outside.

"Mike," Rhonda said tremulously.

Coop looked over his shoulder. Her face was white. "Eva's been hit."

"Oh, Jesus, please," Coop prayed under his breath as Mike tore across the room to get to his wife.

Another shot sang through the air right behind him, missing its mark.

Coop left Taggart with the jumpy civilians and rushed after Mike.

Stephanie knelt beside Eva, who'd been lowered to the floor. She'd tucked her coat under Eva's head, and Rhonda covered her with her jacket.

"We need to stop the bleeding." Rhonda scrambled off in search of something to use.

Oh, God, Coop thought. Eva was so pale and still.

Mike carefully peeled back the jacket to see where his wife had been hit, and a horrible, gut-wrenching sound welled from deep in his chest. Coop made himself look and bit back a gasp. Eva's pale, delicate hand lay low across her ribs. A steady trickle of blood spilled between her fingers. Her eyes fluttered open, unfocused, then drifted shut again.

Mike folded her into his arms. "Call 911!" he yelled, knowing full well that several calls had already gone out. "Call 911!" he roared again desperately as Stephanie placed another call requesting an ambulance.

"How bad?" Coop whispered, glancing up at Stephanie, but he already knew the answer.

Grim-faced, Stephanie shook her head.

Eva was bleeding out. No one had their gear with them. No medic's kit, no QuikClot. No IVs. Nothing.

Rhonda crawled back to Eva's side with a thick stack of linen napkins that Mike pressed against the wound and applied pressure on the bleed.

"Get her flat, Mike," Steph said when he tried to hold Eva tighter in his arms. "She needs to be flat."

She needs a doctor, Coop thought, sick with helplessness and fear. Eva was semiconscious and fading fast. Her skin was so pale. He reached for one of her hands. Cold and clammy. Then he checked her radial pulse. Weak and thready.

He knew just enough medicine to treat field wounds and understood that her body was trying to shunt blood to her central organs. Not good. Not good at all. It meant things were shutting down.

"We need to locate the shooter," Taggart said, meeting Coop's eyes from across the room.

He was right. They were pinned down like ducks on a pond, with no flight options in sight. Too many lives were on the line to sit here. Someone was going to have to play cowboy.

He glanced at his friends. There was nothing he could do for Eva. Mike, Stephanie, and Rhonda were doing what they could. Taggart and Waldrop guarded the shattered window. Green and Santos covered the back.

He crawled up to join Taggart on the floor at the window and searched outside. The shots could have come from anywhere. The bank of office buildings to the east of the restaurant. An apartment building to the west. An abandoned building in the middle of it all. They had to find out.

"Toss me a coat. Any coat!" Coop yelled at Rhonda. "Taggart, Waldrop—keep your eyes peeled outside for a rifle flash."

Rhonda grabbed Taggart's jacket and, at Coop's nod, let it fly.

The shot was almost instantaneous.

"Muzzle flash. Vacant building, six floors up. One, two . . . wait, I've gotta count . . . thirteen windows in!" Taggart shouted after a brief, intense moment.

They had him—and he wasn't as smart as he thought, if he allowed anyone on the ground to see his muzzle flash.

"Taggart. You're with me." Coop headed toward the rear of the restaurant and shot out the back door.

5

Waldrop laid cover fire as Coop and Taggart sprinted the length of three football fields. Pumping blood and adrenaline kept them warm in the fifteen-degree weather; their breath escaped in frosty white puffs as it left their burning lungs. When they reached the target building, they drew their guns and took a few seconds to suck in some breath and assess the building. Ten stories of brick, it took up an entire block. Graffiti was scrawled across the walls and the few ground-floor windows that weren't broken out.

"I'll go left," Coop said, and Taggart immediately took off to the right.

When Coop reached the first corner of the building, he pressed his back against it, checked around the brick, then raced for the opposite end, stopping at every doorway to check for a possible entry point.

"Locked tight," Taggart said, breathing hard, when they met at their original point of contact.

"I didn't see any vehicles. You?"

Taggart shook his head. "Nope."

So either the shooter had already left, had a driver waiting for him somewhere nearby, or had arrived on foot. That gave them two chances out of three that he was still up there. And still shooting to kill.

"Ideas?" Coop asked as they bolted toward the closest door.

"A good, hard kick ought to do it."

Holding his pistol in a two-handed grip close to his body, Coop mule-kicked the door open and burst inside. He cleared the left side of the stairwell and felt Taggart at his back, clearing his sector.

They'd breached enough enemy strongholds together that their actions were a well-choreographed, deadly dance.

A hand clasped his shoulder, confirming that Taggart was ready to go up.

Stairways were a bitch to clear. The "fatal funnel." The bad guys could toss a grenade or fire a burst of shots and be guaranteed to hit something.

Quickly, but taking care, they cleared each stairway and landing.

Coop's pulse pounded in his head by the time they got to the sixth floor, where they figured the shooter had been hiding.

Office doors flanked either side of the hallway. They eliminated the side to the north and center of the building.

"Which window?" Coop glanced down the hall.

Taggart looked at the first door. "The thirteenth."

"How many windows in each room?"

"Guess there's only one way to find out."

"Cover me."

Two-handing his 9mm in front of him, Coop drew a deep breath. Then he hauled back again, kicked open the first door, and burst through the threshold, staying low and out of the kill zone.

Taggart rushed in low behind him.

The room was empty.

"Captain America couldn't have done it better," Taggart said, a weak attempt to cut the tension.

"Just count, smart-ass."

"Five."

Five windows in the room.

They hustled back to the door, checked out the hall, and, finding it empty, rolled out of the empty room together.

Taggart stopped by the next door. "What do you think?"

Though they both knew the room after this one held the thirteenth window, it never paid to assume.

"Clear it just in case."

Taggart went in first this time. And again, they found the room empty.

As they stepped back out into the hall, Coop heard the soft click of a latch on the next door down the hall.

Beside him, Taggart nodded. He'd heard it, too.

Rhonda hoped that everyone in the restaurant was asking whatever power any of them believed in to save Eva. With more pleas sent in Taggart and Cooper's direction. They were out there now, easy targets for whoever was doing the shooting.

"They'll be fine," Steph said, reading her mind. "They know what they're doing."

She might not like Cooper much, but her heart beat more for his and Taggart's safety than for her own.

And it beat more for Eva's.

She fought back tears. Her teammates weren't just battle buddies. They were good friends, including their wives and kids. To many of them, this extended family was the closest to normal that it got. And now she was one of them. Now she understood that when one of their own was in danger, they'd move mountains to remove the threat.

She felt so helpless. It seemed like an eternity since the first shot had been fired, though it had barely been four minutes since Eva was hit. Less than two minutes since Taggart and Cooper had raced out the back door after the shooter.

"Where are the police?" Mike demanded. "Where's the ambulance?"

She wanted to help him, to reassure him that Eva was going to be okay. But she'd seen the wound. She knew . . .

The sound of sirens cut into her dark thoughts and provided much-needed hope.

"Thank God, they're here!" She felt a rush of relief as the first wave of squad cars rolled to screeching stops in front of the restaurant, lights flashing. Uniformed cops piled out of the cars, guns drawn, and carefully approached the building.

"DOD!" Joe Green shouted, flashing his government credentials high in the air so the cops could see them clearly. The rest of them did the same.

"Take cover," Green warned them. "The shooter's still out there."

Half a dozen cops scrambled inside and tucked in low beside them.

"We've got two men out there looking for the shooter," Green said.

Normally, Mike would coordinate the action, but his head and his heart were wholly focused on Eva. It broke Rhonda's heart to watch him.

"And we've got a victim down," Green told the lieutenant in charge. "GSW to the abdomen. Big bleed." He glanced over his shoulder at Mike, who looked lost and desperate.

"There's an ambulance on the way," the lieutenant said after double-checking with dispatch.

"Tell them to step on it," Green pleaded. "Tell 'em we've got a critical."

Rhonda felt as if another lifetime passed during the next several seconds, before the wail of another siren announced the rapid approach of the ambulance.

The restaurant, the terrified customers, and the rest of her team all faded away amid the eerie flash of red, white, and blue strobes that rolled against the walls and glinted off the broken glass.

Her gaze fell to Eva, who was now unconscious and who she feared was dying on the floor.

Fear for Eva, for Mike, for Taggart and Cooper pressed down on her shoulders as she watched the ambulance crew tend to Eva, load her up while the police provided cover, and finally race away to the hospital with Mike at her side.

Don't let her die. Please, don't let her die.

Several more police cars arrived in the meantime. As soon as the restaurant was secured, Green, Waldrop, and Santos took off to provide backup for Taggart and Cooper.

Rhonda and Stephanie stayed to supply information to the police. Sitting in the kitchen on a stack of boxes, Rhonda answered question after question . . . all the while thinking, pleading, and bargaining with the powers that be that no one else got shot.

6

Wrong! Everything had gone wrong!

Her hands shook with rage, making her fingers clumsy as she disassembled her rifle and rushed to pack it away.

She'd hit the woman, but it hadn't been a head shot like she'd planned. She must have estimated the thickness and the density of the plate-glass window incorrectly. The miscalculation had altered the trajectory of the bullet, deflecting her shot slightly off course.

Quickly setting the stage for her exit, she placed her props where they couldn't be missed and told herself it didn't matter that the shot hadn't been clean. The view through the rifle's scope had been clear. Judging from the blood and location of the wound, the bullet had riddled Eva Salinas Brown's gut. Chances of surviving an abdominal hit like that were minuscule. She'd have a massive bleed, most likely be dead before the paramedics even had a chance to take her vitals. One of the advantages of designing and packing her own bullets was knowing exactly what kind of damage they could do.

One last look around the nest told her that all was in place. She ran to the interior door, pulled out her handgun, and carefully checked the main hallway. Empty.

Then she heard the heavy steel door open from the inside stairway. Then footsteps on the concrete floors.

Shit. They'd found her hide.

Should she stay and pick them off like flies as they stormed the door to this room? Or cut her losses and retreat?

She fought the temptation to stay. She couldn't be certain but she had a good idea who was out there. She'd just killed their partner's wife, so it would be Taggart and Cooper to the rescue. As predictable as a fat man having a heart attack. God, she'd love to see their faces just before they died.

Yet if she stayed, she could end up dead. There'd be cops and feds all over this building in another few minutes.

Wisdom won out over excitement as she heard them out there, kicking in doors, searching for her.

When she'd arrived this morning, she'd rigged the hall door to her room in case anyone came snooping. She'd tucked a standard M67 hand grenade into a tin can, pulled the pin, then wedged the spoon inside the can so it couldn't release. Then she'd wired the can so when the door opened, it would pull away the can and arm the grenade. Her standard insurance against intruders; it worked every time. Whoever came through that door didn't stand a chance.

Carrying her rifle case, which resembled a valise, she slipped out a rear window that led to the exterior fire escape and raced down the stairs.

And all the while, she envisioned the investigators finding her hide and the bloody, mangled bodies of Taggart and Cooper. She could see the rest of their team finding her special "calling cards" and the wrong turns they would take before eventually realizing who had killed them.

Discovering that the woman they'd thought was dead had risen like a phoenix from the ashes of hell, to extract her long-awaited revenge.

"On my go," Coop said, his frosty breath clouding the air in the frigid hallway.

Taggart nodded. He was ready.

Coop sucked in a breath, gave a quick nod, then kicked in the door. He rushed into the room, Taggart diving low behind him.

The room was empty and deathly quiet.

Except for a soft hissing noise.

Coop instantly recognized the sound. "Grenade!"

He grabbed Taggart by his shirt and dragged him to his feet. Then they ran and dived across the empty room, as far away from the door as momentum would carry them.

● ● ●

She heard the explosion just as she hit the street.

She'd have to enjoy the satisfaction later. Right now, she needed to make tracks. Outside the building, there was nothing but litter and cracked asphalt and a little skiff of snow.

She calmly walked two blocks, looking like a businesswoman with an oversized valise hurrying to get to work. When she reached the Jeep she'd stolen in D.C. last night, she stowed her rifle on the floor in the backseat, then slid behind the wheel.

A healthy dose of fear raced with her along the backstreets behind her as the facts set in. She'd fucked it up. Had she lost her edge? Had the two-year hiatus, while she'd healed and mourned and plotted her revenge, taken her out of the game?

The Russians would not be happy. The entire team was supposed to be taken out or disabled. Brown, Taggart, and Cooper were supposed to be dead. Maybe Taggart and Cooper *had* died back there in the building, but maybe wasn't good enough. And for certain, Brown was still alive.

She glanced in her rearview mirror. Even though she'd changed the plates on the Jeep, she half-expected to see a squad car, lights and siren blazing, or a black sedan filled with hard-eyed, ruddy-faced Russians bearing down on her.

Regroup. Her mentor's voice echoed inside her head. *Regroup and redeem yourself.*

He was right. Of course he was right. This could still work out well. Her chest fluttered with excitement.

Now she'd have Brown and his team on the ropes. Have them on the defensive, hunting in the dark.

As for the Russians, maybe she could turn this to her advantage. Create another opportunity to squeeze them for more money. And enjoy more anticipation, knowing that whatever remained of Mike Brown's team would be running scared when they realized that a ghost could reach out and kill them at will.

It would take them a while to put the puzzle pieces together, but once they figured it out, they'd be looking over their shoulders for the rest of their very short lives.

Would she get them in bed, sleeping? In their car, stopped at a red light? One thing she knew for certain: there wouldn't be any more Monday breakfast meetings. No socializing, no lighthearted banter, no chance of anything being normal ever again.

That thought, coupled with what had happened to whoever had opened the door to her nest, finally made her smile.

"What did you say?" Coop poked a finger in his ear, then tried to shake away the incessant ringing.

Joe Green stood over him. "Can you walk back down the stairs on your own?"

"I can walk," Coop muttered. "What I *can't* freaking do is hear."

When the grenade had gone off, they were a good ten yards away from the rigged door, hugging the floor.

That's where Green, Santos, and Waldrop had found them. Then they'd dragged them down the stairs, where the ambulance Green had called—just in case—was waiting. Several police cars also filled the lot.

Now Taggart was at the hospital. The rest of them were back up on the sixth floor, studying the shooter's nest.

"What's the word on Taggart?" Coop asked Green.

"Concussion. Dislocated shoulder. Lots of bruises—he hit a radiator when he slid across the floor. He'll be fine. He's already awake and bitching to be released, but he'll be on the DL for a while."

Coop let out a huge breath of relief. Thank God. They'd been through the fire together more than once, and this had come too close to being the last time.

"Any sign of the shooter?" He wrapped the blanket the ambulance crew had given him tighter around his shoulders and winced. He'd taken some shrapnel in his left calf and low on his shoulder blade, and the local anesthetic the EMTs had used when they sewed him up had started to wear off.

He and Taggart were lucky to be alive. The grenade had exploded only partially inside the room; most of the damage had been done out in the hallway. The shooter had wanted to cover a partial breach in addition to a full one, which had saved them—though Coop was sure that hadn't been the intent.

He stared at the playing cards lined up like soldiers

on the dusty windowsill, where they were sure to be spotted. His gut knotted. The intent was now pretty darn clear.

A jack of hearts, burned around the edges, with "COOPER" printed precisely across the middle.

A jack of spades, with a slice through the center, had "TAGGART" written in the same bold, black ink.

Another jack of hearts, pierced with a bullet hole, had been labeled "BROWN."

And finally, a queen of hearts. The name "EVA" was clear beneath the black X that stretched from corner to corner.

One bullet had been carefully placed nose-up on top of each card. The four bullets were identical: .223 Remington cartridges that were almost exact matches to the bullets the U.S. military shot in the M16 rifle.

"What do you want to bet these cartridges will match the bullets we'll dig out of the wall in the restaurant?" Green said grimly.

Santos crouched down so he was at eye level with the shells and looked them over well. "These didn't come out of a box someone picked off the shelf. They're designer. Hand-loaded. Someone's very particular."

"Someone who's got it in for the One-Eyed Jacks." Waldrop frowned at Coop. "He even used ammo similar to ours. You thinking vendetta?"

Coop stared at the bullets and nodded. Someone was out to get them for a very specific reason.

"An Al-Qaeda cell bent on retribution?" Santos suggested.

Coop shook his head. "This is too staged. Too selective. Al-Qaeda or one of its splinter groups would have taken out the entire restaurant if killing us was their goal."

"Why Eva?" Waldrop speculated quietly, then glanced at Coop. "What does she have to do with the One-Eyed Jacks, other than being married to one?"

"She's the one who got the three of us back together." So that had pissed someone off? Or maybe they'd pissed someone off since they'd reconnected?

"Who knows that one-eyed jacks hold special meaning to you?" Green asked.

"Other than you guys?" Coop shook his head. "Family. Close friends."

"And apparently, someone with an ax to grind," Green added with a concerned frown. "We can talk more back at HQ. You've got to get out of the cold, brother."

"Fine," Coop said, unable to stall a bone-rattling shiver. "But no one else needs to know that I took a little shrapnel today, okay? No one." He would not be pulled off active duty for some BS minor medical incident. He needed to get to work and figure this out.

"And Mike doesn't need to know about any of this, either." He lifted a hand toward the playing cards and the bullet casings. "Not until . . ." His voice caught when he thought about Eva, fighting for her life. Possibly dying. "Not until Eva's out of the woods," he said, determined that she would make it. "He's got enough to deal with."

"He's going to be pissed if we keep him out of the loop on this," Santos pointed out.

Yeah, he'd be pissed, all right. "I'll take the heat," Coop said. "But I won't put any more on his shoulders. Not right now."

He glanced at the cards again. Specifically, the queen of hearts. "We need to get a protection detail at the hospital ASAP."

Green pulled out his phone and made it happen.

"Mike will realize they're guards, but he'll be okay with it. And for God's sake, everyone watch your back. This may be about the four of us, but you all may be considered targets by association." The blood oozing out of the bandage the EMTs had applied to Santos's arm was proof of that.

His shoulder hurt, and suddenly, he couldn't stop shivering. Whatever the shooter's reason was, one thing was clear: Anyone who would set up something this elaborate was on a mission.

Which meant he wasn't finished with them yet.

7

Rhonda hated hospitals. Fear, anger, despair, helplessness, loss—every desperate emotion possible funneled through her as she stood outside the entrance of Inova Fairfax Hospital. The antiseptic smell, the shush of soft-soled shoes on polished tile floors, the blips, beeps, and alarms of the monitors on the life-support machines in the ICU—just pulling up in front of the building brought back memories that made her lungs seize.

She stood outside, long after her red Mazda was driven away by a young man with a valet tag on his coat and a flirty grin on his face, totally impervious to her distress.

The bitter cold finally prompted her to move. She drew sharp, icy air into her lungs, watched her exhaled breath drift away in a white fog, then forced herself to walk through the lobby doors.

Only for Mike and Eva would she do this. And she *had* to do this.

She glanced around and spotted a volunteer at a desk several yards away. Her heels clicked on the tile as she headed for the desk, reminding herself how lucky they were that the only level one trauma center in northern Virginia was just ten minutes from where Eva had been shot. She wouldn't have made it this long otherwise.

After the police and all the alphabet agencies had finished questioning the team members who'd been at the restaurant, they'd all returned to work—except Taggart, who'd been treated and sent home to rest. Thank God he hadn't been hurt worse and that Cooper was in one piece, too.

At a quick team meeting, Cooper had given them all a rundown of what happened and what they had found at the shooter's hide: the exploding grenade, the four playing cards, the bullets. And he'd made them all swear not to reveal anything about the cards and bullets to Mike.

A personal vendetta, he'd said, looking grim. And the killer was still out there.

His words had chilled her more than the winter wind. She'd immediately started working up a profile on a possible killer. But like everyone on the team, she was distracted and on tenterhooks, waiting for news of Eva's condition, fearing the worst every time their operations manager, Peter Davis, appeared in their office doorway in his wheelchair or fired off an e-mail.

"She's hanging in there . . ."

"Unfortunately, there's been a setback. She was rushed back to surgery . . ."

"No, no word yet . . ."

"She made it through the last surgery, but let's not get our hopes up too high . . ."

Hour by hour, minute by minute, Rhonda attempted to work, but more often than not, she gravitated to the other team members, who wandered in and out of the break room, looking grim.

After she'd clocked out, Rhonda had driven straight to the hospital despite the demons that tried to best her. What if Eva died? She couldn't live with herself if she hadn't come. Though Eva had made it through the first ten hours, she still wasn't out of the woods.

"Hey, Rhonda."

She jumped and spun around.

Oh, God. Cooper was the last person she wanted to see.

"Hey," he said more gently, his brows furrowed as he searched her face. "You okay?"

He reached out and touched her arm, and for a moment, she wanted to lean into him. A weak, stupid moment. Why did he suddenly have to be Mr. Nice Guy, instead of the hotshot jerk who showed up every day at work?

She couldn't deal with him now. Not when it took every ounce of willpower to keep from leaving the hospital.

Without a word she continued toward the volunteer desk, determined to ignore him.

She knew he was following her, because his boot heels clicked half a beat behind hers. Black cowboy boots, the leather worn and formed to his feet, but always polished within an inch of its life.

An inch of its life.

An inch of her life.

An inch of Eva's life.

She shook off the scattered thoughts. She was *not* going down that road.

"Rhonda?" he said again. "Are you okay?"

"I'm fine. What are you doing here?" It came out like an accusation, when all she really wanted was for him to leave her alone.

"What do you think I'm doing here? I'm checking on Eva. Wait." He caught up to her, gripped her arm, and spun her around, fear in his eyes. "Has something happened?"

When she saw the tortured look on his face, she felt like an ass. She also felt herself soften. He cared deeply for Eva and Mike. And he'd risked his life today trying to hunt down the shooter. "No, no news. I just got here. I haven't heard anything more than Peter's last update."

"Still touch and go," Peter had said, after calling the team together just before they all left for the day. *"According to the surgeons, the next twenty-four hours will tell the tale."*

Cooper said nothing now, his hands stuffed back into the pockets of a black wool pea coat, the collar up against the cold outside, a gray cashmere scarf looped around his neck. With his hair mussed by the wind and his cheeks ruddy from the cold, he looked as if he'd walked off the deck of a whaling ship docked in some exotic port or onto a shadowy wharf and into a dark and foggy night filled with intrigue and danger. At the very least, he looked like a model or an actor promoting expensive whiskey or designer aftershave or—

"Rhonda?"

The unease in his voice jerked her back to reality again. She couldn't keep checking out like that. She had to face—

"Are you sure you're all right? You don't look so good."

"Wow." Her knee-jerk response was snark, because they both did it so well. And so often. And because she didn't know how else to cover her unsettling reaction to him and her discomfort at being inside a hospital after almost eight years. "I can see how you got your rep as a heartbreaker. You could charm a girl senseless."

"You know what I meant. You don't look like you feel well."

Her frayed emotions finally got the best of her. "My friend is fighting for her life. So no, I don't feel real good about that." The bite in her tone hung between them like the cheap shot that it was.

"She's my friend, too," he said quietly, and she felt as if she'd kicked a puppy.

She knew Cooper and Taggart thought Eva walked on water, and Cooper was like a protective big brother to her.

And as unsettled as she felt, this wasn't about her. It was about Eva.

"I'm . . . sorry." She touched a hand to her forehead, realized that she still wore her gloves, and slowly tugged them off. "I hate this. I hate that I'm here. That you're here. That we have a reason to be here."

"And you're scared."

"For Eva? Damn straight."

She stood there, drawing deep breaths to pull herself together, while he walked over to get the directions to Eva's room.

"Come on." He took her elbow gently. "Let's stop by the gift shop before we go up. Eva loves lilies."

The thought of the smell of flowers was the tipping point.

She looked around wildly for a restroom. One hand pressed to her abdomen, the other cupped over her mouth, she sprinted toward the door. She barely made it inside before violently throwing up.

A balloon bouquet in hand, Coop stood silently beside Rhonda as they rode the elevator to the third-floor ICU.

The Bombshell was a frazzled, emotional mess. She'd gained a little of her color back, but when she'd walked out of the restroom ten minutes ago, she'd been so pale he'd steered her unceremoniously to a bench and made her sit down.

She hadn't made any protest, but the look on her

face said "don't ask." So he hadn't. He'd just fished in
his pocket for the little pack of breath mints he always
carried and held it out to her.

Her hand had been shaky, so he'd tipped a mint
into his palm and held it out to her instead.

"Thanks." She'd popped it into her mouth, then
closed her eyes and leaned back against the wall.

It hadn't taken a psych degree to figure out that
she'd needed a little time. A little space.

A woman as strong as she was, a woman as strong-
willed as she was, would be horrified that she'd shown
such vulnerability. Especially to him. She always put
on a good show of being tough and not liking him
much, so breaking rule number one—never let 'em
see you sweat—had to be eating at her pretty hard
about now.

And while she'd clearly been embarrassed to lose
her cookies, it had made him respect her more. And
like her a little more, too—and damn, suddenly, he
was the one who needed space.

"Take some time," he'd said. "I'll be right back."

Then he'd gotten up and headed for the hospital
gift shop.

"No flowers," she'd managed to say, faintly but
with great conviction.

So . . . she had a bad thing for flowers? And she
clearly didn't like hospitals. Had she lost someone important to her? Someone she missed so much that she
erected walls to make sure she never got that close to
anyone again?

Oh, for God's sake. He was way overthinking this.

He glanced at her now in the elevator. He hoped she could keep it together when she saw Mike. He needed strength from his team right now, not weakness.

The doors opened, and he immediately spotted the two men Green had sent over. The guys were pros; they knew how to fade into the background, and to the untrained eye, they did just that. He was glad to see they were blending in and that Mike and Eva were being protected.

"You sure you can do this?" he asked Rhonda. "There's no shame in sitting this one out. You can wait over there." He nodded toward a small waiting room. "I'll get a full report from Mike and give it to you straight."

She breathed deeply, squared her shoulders, and walked toward the nurse's desk. "I'm fine now," she said, pulling herself together with guts and determination. "You don't have to worry that I'll upset Mike or Eva. I've got this."

And as she calmly told the desk nurse their names and asked about Eva, Coop knew that she did. The Bombshell was back, in charge, and bent on seeing this through.

But as they approached Eva's room and his chest tightened, he suspected that *she* was much more in control of her emotions now than he was.

8

If Rhonda hadn't double-checked the room number, she wouldn't have known it was Mike sitting behind the glass ICU wall.

She couldn't muffle an involuntary gasp. Beside her, Cooper reached for her hand, his own shaking as it grasped hers. She didn't even think about pulling away. Sometimes hanging on was the only thing that made sense.

Mike had pulled a straight-backed chair up to the hospital bed. He leaned forward, his eyes closed, his forehead pressed against the mattress, his hands clasped between his thighs. Haggard. Drawn. A man defeated.

Eva lay unconscious and unmoving, the pallor of her face little contrast to the white sheet covering her. Both arms were impaled by IV lines that administered medication and fluids and God knew what else. She'd been intubated; the ventilator sighed and wheezed, helping her breathe. Monitors over the bed tracked her heartbeat, blood pressure, respiration, and temperature, while the IVs beeped and the pumps sighed and clicked.

"Why is she restrained?" Cooper sounded horrified.

"For her protection." Rhonda pulled her hand away as old memories arose. "If she wakes up, she might be scared. They don't want her pulling at the vent tube or her IVs."

"Just give the door a light tap," a dark-haired nurse in pristine white said as she walked by, sensing their hesitation. "He's not asleep. You're on the visitors list, so I'm sure he'll be glad to see you."

When they continued to stand there, still in shock, the nurse tried again.

"I can take those for you, if you'd like," she added, with a nod toward the balloons that now seemed sadly frivolous. "They're not allowed in ICU, but I can have them taken to the children's wing. They'll love them."

Without looking away from Mike, Cooper handed the balloons over.

"Thank you," Rhonda whispered as the nurse walked away.

"I've never seen him like this," Cooper whispered when they were alone again. "Not even after Afghanistan. Not even after . . ." He let the words trail off, clearly shaken.

Since it was clear that Cooper couldn't do it, she lightly rapped on the glass with her knuckle. At first, she didn't think Mike had heard her. Then he slowly lifted his head, stared for a long, desperate moment at Eva's deathly still face, and finally turned toward them.

She knew what hell looked like. Knew what it felt like. And looking at Mike now, she understood exactly what he was going through.

Coop watched Mike slip out of Eva's room and quietly slide the glass door closed behind him.

One of the staff must have given him a scrub shirt, because that's what he was wearing along with the jeans he'd had on when Eva was shot. Dark blotches of blood stained the worn denim.

"You look like hell," Coop blurted out, because man, oh, man, he was suddenly as worried about Mike as he was about Eva. His eyes were bloodshot; the circles beneath them were big enough to use for target practice. "You need to get some rest, bud. And I'm betting you need food, too."

"I'm fine." Mike dragged both hands over his jaw and stifled a yawn that made him a liar.

"Like hell." Coop clapped a hand on his shoulder. "Let's go get you something to eat, at least."

When Mike only stared at Eva through the glass, Coop looked to Rhonda. She read his helpless expression and, bless her, took over the good fight.

"I can stay with her, Mike," she said gently. "Why don't you let Jamie take you to the cafeteria for a sandwich or some soup? A change of scenery might revive you a bit."

For the first time, Mike turned his attention away from Eva. He looked first at Coop and then at Rhonda. "I must look really bad, if the two of you agree on something."

"You aren't going to be any use to her if you keel over from exhaustion," Coop said firmly, though his heart felt as if it was being squeezed in a tight fist.

"I know you mean well, but back off on the double-teaming, okay? I'm not going anywhere. The staff brings me food. I'm getting by."

Coop bet that Mike barely touched the food. And "getting by" was a gross exaggeration.

"How's she doing?" Coop finally asked.

"There's been no change." Mike sounded as close to defeat as a man could possibly get. "She's not progressing, but she's not slipping back, either. Since they took her back in for a second surgery to stop that bleeder, she hasn't come around."

According to the report Peter had given them, they'd had to open her up from stem to stern in the initial surgery. They'd removed her spleen, sutured her liver, given her multiple units of blood, repaired other internal damage done by the bullet, and sewn her up.

They'd taken every safeguard possible to ward off infection and had thought she was making progress. Then her blood pressure plummeted without warning, and they'd realized she was bleeding internally. That's when they'd rushed her in for the second surgery.

Coop felt helpless and scared for both Eva and Mike. If . . . God, he didn't want to think about it, but if Mike lost Eva, he wasn't sure that Mike would recover. Or if he did, that he'd ever be the same again.

"Is that . . . normal? That she hasn't woken up?"

Mike cupped his nape with both hands, then stretched muscles stiff with inactivity and stress and waiting. "I don't know. I get a lot of double-talk. I don't think they know, either."

"Her body needs time to heal itself."

Coop turned his head toward Rhonda.

She looked pale but composed as she continued, her attention fixed on Eva. "Sleep's not a bad thing. As long as her vitals stay stable and they can stave off infection and keep her nourished and hydrated, sleep is her best friend. It helps her body heal."

The way she said it, as if she'd either heard it or said it many times before, had him studying her face sharply.

No emotion there. No way to guess what she was feeling.

When she realized he was watching her, she moved back just enough so Mike's shoulders blocked Coop's view of her.

"How about I go to the cafeteria, get us all something to eat, and bring it back here?" Rhonda suggested. "We can sit in the hall, there's a bench right over there, so you can see her, and she can see you if she wakes—"

Mike suddenly bolted toward Eva's door.

Coop raced into the room after him, his heart pounding. He sensed Rhonda moving up behind him as Mike's ragged whisper filled the hollow fear enveloping the small room.

"*Chica*. It's me. *Chica*," Mike repeated hoarsely, holding Eva's painfully limp hand in both of his. "You opened your eyes. I saw you. Please, *please*, open them again. For me, babe. Please open your eyes."

All three of them waited; Coop's breath caught.

Nothing. Nothing, nothing, and more nothing, until Coop was convinced that Mike's exhaustion and hope had played a cruel trick on him.

But then Eva's eyelids fluttered—so little movement at first that Coop thought he'd imagined it. Then they fluttered again and finally opened.

Mike lowered his lips to her hand. His throat convulsed. "About time you came around, Mrs. Brown."

Coop heard the tears in Mike's voice and felt some rise to his own eyes. Beside him, Rhonda squeezed her eyes shut tightly but not before Coop caught the misty gleam of moisture.

When Eva finally focused and painstakingly turned her head to meet Mike's eyes, Coop thought Mike would totally lose it.

"Hello, gorgeous," he said so gently, and with so much love, that Coop felt a staggering ache, deep and full of longing.

He wanted that. What they had together. And until this moment, when he saw Mike shower love and adoration and hope on his wife, he hadn't even known it was what he wanted.

Stunned, he watched as Mike touched a hand to Eva's hair, bent down, and tenderly pressed a kiss to her forehead.

Then he backed away, as did Rhonda, letting Mike and Eva experience this miracle in private. And this time, when Coop looked over at Rhonda, she was staring at him, instead of the other way around.

For a long moment, their eyes held, and damn if he didn't see the same thing in her expression that he felt. Mixed with her joy, he saw loneliness, emptiness, and longing—and he sensed it was as much of a surprise to her as it was to him.

Then she smiled—a tentative and achingly vulnerable smile—and nothing could have stopped him from reaching for her hand and pulling her into his arms.

He kissed her.

He hadn't meant to do it, but it happened. And it felt absolutely right.

Eva had almost died today. *They* could have died today. And by the time his common sense kicked in to remind him that his reaction was about life and death, not desire, it was too late.

Too much raw, exposed emotion was in play between them. And too much heat once she was in his arms and their mouths melded as if it was the most natural thing in the world to do. As if he'd done it a thousand times.

Her mouth opened beneath his, warm and welcoming, and he took the kiss all the way home. Damn if it didn't *feel* like coming home.

And then suddenly, she was gone.

Eyes wide, breathing hard, looking horrified, she pushed slowly away from him, clearly shaken.

So was he. He staggered back a step, then heard Mike say his name.

Mike. Shit. He'd forgotten about Mike, who, thank God, was still focused on his wife.

Coop ran an unsteady hand through his hair and backed another step away from Rhonda, needing the space as much as she did. "What do you need, bud?"

"Go let the nurses know that she's awake."

Without looking at Rhonda, he hotfooted it out of the room as if his tail was on fire.

Holy hell. What can of worms had he just opened?

9

Eva's room immediately became a beehive of activity. As staff rushed in and out, Rhonda eased into the hall to let them tend to business. Unfortunately, Cooper came with her.

She needed some distance—and chocolate—to help her figure out what had just happened.

"Smart. Really smart," she muttered under her breath.

"You say something?"

Her gaze shot to Cooper, who regarded her with uncertainty. As if he wasn't sure he wanted to hear what she said. As if he might need as much room from her as she needed from him.

"I said I'm going for chocolate. You want anything?"

"No. Thanks." He turned his attention back to Eva's room, where the staff made notes on charts and checked monitors.

She headed down the hall toward the waiting room, where she'd spotted a vending machine before.

What had happened back there?

A mistake—that's what happened.

"Hindsight," she muttered, feeding coins into the snack machine. "Where is it when you need it?"

She ripped the wrapping off the candy bar and bit into the chocolate. The first sweet bite didn't do much to calm her down.

All right, so they'd kissed. It was a human thing to do after the day's experiences. The uncertainty of life was never as obvious as it had been today. And yes, she'd had a physical reaction. He was hot, and she had a libido.

But overriding the chemistry had been her fear for Eva, intertwined with old but still-raw memories. Her relief at Eva's awakening had tipped her over the edge and into letting her guard down. So a celebratory hug was a reasonable reaction.

The kiss . . . not so much.

Their chemistry had been there since the first day she'd met him, which was why she generally refused to give him the time of day. Because that way lay trouble.

Even more trouble than she'd imagined, if she'd correctly read the look in his eyes after she'd pulled away. She'd seen the exact same things she'd been feeling.

Surprise. Interest. Heat.

Longing.

She'd felt way too comfortable in Cooper's embrace. Felt herself trusting the feeling a little too quickly. Responding to the warmth of his body, the scent of his skin, and kissing him back, though all she'd thought she needed was human contact.

Boy, had she been wrong.

"Crap, crap, *crap*." She tossed the half-eaten chocolate into the wastebasket and headed back to Eva's room.

When she reached the door and saw Mike's smile lighting up the room like floodlights, his happiness overshadowed every thought but the one that counted: Eva was going to be okay.

Cooper still stood out in the hall.

"How's she doing?" she asked without meeting his eyes.

"She's sleeping."

"I see they took the vent tube out." That was an even better sign.

"Yeah. She even managed to give Mike a little grief before all the activity wore her out, and she fell back to sleep."

For a long moment, they stood there, ignoring the elephant in the hall.

"Rhonda, look," Cooper said, then paused, and she got the very distinct feeling that he was wrestling with what he wanted to say to her. Which meant that she certainly wasn't going to want to hear it.

Thank God, Mike spotted her then and waved them in.

"Mike wants us." She shouldered around Cooper and into the room.

"Hey," Mike said softly, so as not to wake Eva. "Glad you're back. I wanted to tell you both what the doc said."

"Go for it," Cooper said.

"They were reluctant to take the tube out at first," Mike said. "Wanted her vital signs a little more stable and the sedation to wear off a little more, but she wanted it out. And she wanted the restraints off."

"That's our Eva," Cooper said, smiling.

"When she proved that she could breathe on her own, they agreed to pull it."

Rhonda knew that ventilators were invasive, and the goal was always to get them out as soon as possible. Sometimes a patient never got off the vent—another place she didn't want to go now.

"Her prognosis is still guarded," Mike said, "and she has a lot of healing to do and a long way to go, but he's highly optimistic that barring any unforeseen complications, she's going to be fine.

"She's not going to be well for a long time, though," he cautioned quickly, "and she'll be in here a long time. After that, extensive rehab. But she's going to make it!"

"Best news ever, man." Cooper wrapped Mike in a big bear hug, which Mike returned with the same gusto.

Rhonda's smile widened until her cheeks ached.

When Mike released Cooper and reached for her, she gave in to his infectious joy. She hugged him back as he swung her around in a circle before finally setting her down.

"Look who's awake." Cooper smiled gently at Eva, who was watching her husband.

"Wouldn't have . . . thought you'd have . . . the strength . . . to manhandle . . . another woman. And . . . in front of me . . . no less."

"That's my girl." Cooper leaned down and planted a tender kiss on Eva's forehead. "Give that man a ton of grief."

Mike nudged Cooper out of the way so he could get closer to Eva. "No. That's *my* girl. Awake, talking smack, and mean as a snake."

He leaned down and kissed her. The tenderness in his touch made Rhonda's eyes misty.

"And to think I was looking forward to hearing your voice again." He leaned in close. "If you ever scare me like this again, I swear I'll—"

"What?" Eva's barely audible whisper sent relief as loud as a brass band ringing into the room. "You'll . . . do . . . what?"

A tear trickled down Mike's cheek. "I'll lock you in our bedroom, where any good wife belongs."

When the corners of Eva's mouth turned up in the faintest of smiles, it felt as if the sun had come out.

"Yeah," she managed to rasp, "that'll . . . happen."

Rhonda suddenly felt like an intruder in the midst of the very deep, very fiery love her boss and his wife shared. "Maybe I'd better leave, before Mike ends up in more hot water."

"Good idea." Cooper leaned over again and pressed another kiss to Eva's forehead. "Feel better, darlin'. You give me a call if Mr. Personality here gives you any trouble, okay?"

He got a sweet, brief smile for his efforts.

"I'm so glad you're back with us." Rhonda squeezed Eva's hand. "A whole lot of people are going to be celebrating the good news when they hear it."

"Make him . . . get some . . . rest," Eva whispered, and closed her eyes again.

"You heard the woman," Cooper said pointedly.

"I'll walk you out." Mike followed them down the hall. When they were out of earshot of Eva's room, he got straight to the point. "Have you got any leads?"

Now that he felt confident that Eva would recover, he was all business. He wanted answers. He wanted his pound of flesh. And the longer they went without finding the shooter, the less chance there was that they ever would.

"Working on it." Rhonda stuck to the plan and kept her mouth shut about the calling cards the shooter had left behind. It went against the grain to withhold information from her boss, but she agreed that Mike didn't need any more weight on his shoulders right now.

"So are the FBI, the local PD, and DOD. DCIS, to be exact," Cooper added.

Rhonda was still learning the terminology and acronyms, but she knew that the DCIS was the Defense Criminal Investigative Service.

"Working on it *how*?" Mike demanded.

She'd want details, too, if she were in his position. "With very little to go on, I've had to work with generalities to start a rough profile of the shooter. To start, it clearly wasn't his first rodeo. He knew we'd be at the restaurant this morning. He knows how to shoot."

"And a shot at that distance," Cooper added, "says he has the goods. He had to have had a high-power scope. Long-range rifle. Skill."

"Right," Rhonda agreed. "And that said ex-military sniper to me. So I started running searches for any current or former military who might have a bone to pick with anyone on the teams."

It was a big field, considering she was searching through a million active- and inactive-duty names.

"I cross-referenced a variety of databases—the Army Military Occupational Specialty for enlisted snipers and the Marine, Air Force, and Navy counterparts—attempting to narrow down the list. Then I searched class rosters that list both the graduates and the washouts, men or women who may have learned enough to be snipers but didn't make it to graduation. Those same class rosters and military records should take care of ninety-nine percent of the possibles, including mercs, private contractors, and known assassins."

With no witnesses and no rifle, it made her search criteria pretty broad, as was her profile.

"While I'm not totally ruling out a woman, until I get more detailed intel, I'm playing the odds and looking for males thirty-five or younger, single, no kids, known loners, into weapons, with formal military training and experience. Specifically, military with urban combat and sniping experience or qualifying as expert with a rifle. It's the best I can do right now."

When Mike nodded his approval, she let out a relieved breath.

"In the meantime, while my systems continue to search, I 'borrowed' backdoor access to DCIS and FBI data banks. Local PD, too."

She half-expected a reprimand—hacking between government agencies was a big no-no—but a whisper of a smile tipped up a corner of Mike's mouth.

She continued, "They've compiled a list of all the patrons and employees who were in the restaurant this morning. So far, nothing suspicious has surfaced. No connections to organized crime, no arrest records, nothing that raised any red flags—but it's early yet.

"Oh," she said, remembering something else, "and I also reviewed DCIS's recorded interviews of everyone who was on site. If there was a gambler in deep with his bookie, a lover scorned, a gang feud that spilled over into suburbia, anything that might suggest someone other than Eva or the team was the target, nothing's popped up yet."

"Good work," Mike said. "Keep at it."

"Yes, sir."

Mike turned to Cooper. "Did you find the hide?"

Cooper shook his head, and Rhonda bit her lower lip as she listened to him lie. "Not yet, but we figure it was far enough away and high enough that both the sound of the shot and the muzzle flash would be negligible on the streets."

"Ballistics should give us a lead on the rifle. What's happening there?" Mike looked grim. Worry and exhaustion had carved lines in his face that Rhonda had never seen before.

Cooper was a bit slow to field this one. "The bullets they dug out of the wall and floor at the restaurant are at the lab."

"Whose lab?" Mike asked sharply, picking up on Cooper's hesitance.

Cooper breathed deep and braced. "The state's." That part was actually true.

Mike swore under his breath.

"It's been handled," Cooper assured him. "One of the cops on the scene dug the slugs out of the walls, bagged 'em, and, overzealous at working his first crime scene, labeled and sent them in to the state police lab. That was before DCIS took over.

"As long as they've got them, we're letting them have a crack at 'em." Cooper shoved his hands into his pockets. "Maybe they'll get lucky and find some rifling marks. Help us ID the type of gun."

"When are we getting them back? We need those bullets. A federal employee was targeted and shot."

Cooper glanced at Rhonda before shrugging. "We won't know for certain until we find the hide and ballistics gets a read on trajectory and angle, wind conditions—you know the drill."

"There were a lot of Black Ops people in the restaurant this morning," Mike said with a thoughtful nod. "Any one of us could have been the target. And that means someone knew where we were going to be and when we were going to be there."

Again, Cooper remained evasive. "So it would seem."

Jaw clenched, Mike looked away from Cooper and back into Eva's room. "I should be leading the investigation."

Cooper shook his head. "No way in hell would DOD let that happen. You know the protocol when a family member is involved."

"Besides, you need to be exactly where you are." Rhonda touched a hand to Mike's arm. "With her."

"And you will be," Cooper cut in. "Right after I take you home for a shower and a shave and a few hours of shut-eye."

"I'm not leaving her yet," Mike said. "You two get going. I'll talk to you tomorrow. In the meantime, Rhonda, would you call Peter so he can let everyone know Eva's going to be okay?"

"Absolutely." Rhonda dug into her bag for her phone. "I'll be happy to deliver the news."

10

She sat in the dark, smoke-stale room with the curtains pulled shut. A flashing motel vacancy sign bled through the thin drapes. The only other light in the room was a tiny red dot from the fire alarm mounted above the door.

A fire could only improve this dump, she thought darkly.

She longed for the luxury and comfort of Ray's Ontario penthouse. She longed for Ray.

She felt so very tired.

And so very defeated after this morning's debacle.

Her mole in the CIA had called three hours ago. Not only was Eva Salinas Brown alive, but Taggart and Cooper had escaped the booby trap with only minor injuries.

Fail, fail, fail.

She sat on a bed covered in a gaudy floral-print bedspread that smelled as if it hadn't been laundered in this decade. Her phone sat on the bedside table; it should ring again very soon. She was more than twelve hours overdue in making her after-action report to the Russians. But she'd needed time to think. To season the shooting debacle into something palatable that the Russians would swallow. Something she could turn to her advantage.

Repetition always helped her think, so she'd cleaned the Ruger while running damage-control scenarios through her mind. She disassembled, oiled, and reassembled it over and over again, until she was satisfied the gun was spotless—and she was content with the new version of her story.

I do so love that OCD quality of yours, my dear.

Ray's voice was as clear as if he were beside her, and a tear escaped and trickled down her face.

"Why did you have to leave me?" she asked the dark, empty room. "Why did you have to go? You were the only one to ever see me as a person. I need you to help me finish this."

You're very strong, dear heart. What you've suffered— at the hands of your parents, at the hands of others who should have protected you—has made you strong. You've always had to be. You can do this without me.

Another tear had her pressing the heels of her palms into her eyes. "I don't want to be strong anymore. I want to be with you."

The Ruger was loaded. She'd practiced placing the end of the barrel in her mouth to see if she could reach the trigger—and she could.

But Ray had stopped her. *Not yet, love. You have much work to do. You have debts to collect. And when this job is finished, not only will you have exacted our revenge, but you will also have the means to live like a queen for the rest of your life. I want that for you, darling. There's time enough to come to me. I'll always be waiting.*

She didn't want to wait. He'd been the only thing in her life worth living for. But she owed him to finish what he had started.

She startled when her phone rang, then settled herself with a deep breath.

"BLOCKED NUMBER" showed on the screen. The Russian. Again. She couldn't ignore his calls any longer.

She answered using the code name he would recognize. "Anya."

"Vadar. Where have you been?" he demanded in a high, nasal tone.

"Lying low," she said. "Getting as far away from the target as possible."

"Your report was due hours ago."

"As I said, I've been a little busy." He wouldn't like it, but what could he do about it?

"Report," he demanded after a pissed-off silence.

"The report is, there was a slight change of plans. A decision on my part that your employer will appreciate."

Another brief silence followed. She could feel the anger hum through the connection. "You will explain this decision; then my employer can make that determination himself."

"You're certain no one can intercept our call?"

She'd picked up the high-tech phone from a post office box in Toronto a month ago. The key to that box had been mailed to a post office box in New York City. The Russians loved their cloak-and-dagger, particularly former KGB and Spetsnaz, Soviet special forces agents who ran the mafia, while Putin and his minions turned a blind eye in exchange for a cut of the profits.

She, however, wasn't as confident of their technical ability as they were.

"The communication is secure. We have been over this before. Be careful what you say next, or I may think you are attempting to avoid this conversation. Now, did you or did you not eliminate the targets?"

"Better than that." Her voice expressed supreme confidence. "One is out of the picture. The other three—"

"Stop right there. You were not able to deliver?" His nasal tone escalated to high-pitched disapproval.

"It wasn't a question of inability. I made a strategic decision."

"You were not employed to strategize. You were employed to destroy that team." The venom in his voice sent a chill down her back, and her conviction wavered.

You can do this. Ray's voice rallied her strength.

"You're forgetting, Vadar. I handed your people this opportunity. If not for me, all of their plans would still be lost."

She let him think about that. Let him remember that because of her, they also had another shot at the Eagle Claw project.

Two years ago, when she'd escaped undetected from the Idaho compound after Brown and his team had blown it and Ray up, she'd made her way to Ray's secret residence in Ontario. There she'd slowly recovered. And grieved. Then, three months ago, while going through Ray's encrypted computer files, she'd discovered that his operation in Idaho had involved much more than gun running and drugs.

He'd had a deal in the works with the Russian mafia for the theft of revolutionary aviation technology the Americans were developing. A technology the Russians would have developed themselves, if not for Mike Brown and his team. Not only had they destroyed the Idaho compound that was to have been the Russians' staging area to breach the secret facility and steal back the Eagle Claw technology, but Brown's team had also recently facilitated the escape of the Russian scientist who'd created the technology. Dr. Adolph Corbet was now spearheading the Russians' project for the Americans.

The Russians wanted their scientist and their technology back. And because Mike Brown and his One-Eyed Jacks were a festering wound in their side, they wanted them eliminated. That's where she came in.

"Explain this new strategy."

"Oh, I will. But first, let me remind you of something else. I am the one who facilitated what you could not. I established contact with Dr. Corbet. I ensured that he was informed that the wife and children he thought were tucked safely away in Budapest were once again secured by Mother Russia's loving hand. I maintain communication with him and remind him that his family lives only if he continues to provide updates on the progress of Eagle Claw."

"Noted," Vadar said in a somewhat calmer but no less irritated voice.

"All right. I chose not to eliminate the entire One-Eyed Jacks team for one simple reason. The loss to the U.S. covert defense machine would be too massive if I'd taken them all out. A loss on that scale would engage the might of the Department of Defense. They'd consider it an act of war, perhaps the first of many acts to come. And they would put all of their resources on it—do you understand? They'd double and triple security on soft and hard targets here in the States, as well as abroad. And that includes the compound where Corbet, at this very moment, is working on the Eagle Claw technology."

When he said nothing, she knew she had him considering the wisdom of her "plan."

"It would take little time for the Department of Defense to put two and two together and point the finger of blame directly at your organization. Instead, with only one casualty, they are searching for a sniper acting alone, a gunman with an ax to grind, or a random act of violence."

After a long silence, he said, "Continue."

"They have circled the wagons, so to speak, intent on protecting their own and on finding the *person*—not the Russian mafia—who dared attack them. My decision has avoided an all-out nationwide state of readiness against an enemy attack.

"Because of my decision," she continued, "your team is now free to breach the air base and recover your Eagle Claw technology *and* your scientist. Occupied with searching for the lone gunman, they'll never see it coming."

And she was now free to pick off the One-Eyed Jacks at will. Free to savor the thrill of the hunter terrorizing the hunted.

"I will relay your report to my superiors," Vadar said at long last.

"You do that. And while you're at it, share this bit of information my source gave me today. If they want to breach that air base, they need to do it very soon."

Along with the disappointing news of Taggart and Cooper's survival, her mole had the one piece of good news that would turn the Russians' focus away from her.

"Dr. Corbet reported today that the technology is mere steps away from completion," she said. "He cannot stall or withhold the information from the U.S. government much longer. The window of opportunity has grown very short; the project will be complete within a matter of days."

"How many days?"

"If you don't strike within the next five days, the Eagle Claw technology will forever be out of Russia's reach."

Tuesday

The difficult we do at once, the impossible takes a little longer.

—U.S. Navy Seabees

11

Coop didn't like the role of temporary team leader. He was a doer, not a paper pusher. Give him some camo paint and his weapons, and drop him into the thick of a Taliban offensive—that was the work that mainlined adrenaline into his system and gave him purpose.

Since he and Taggart were both senior team members, either of them could have taken over in Mike's absence. But Taggart, who should have been in bed but had shown up sporting a black eye, wearing a sling, and struggling with a bitch of a headache, clearly wasn't up to it.

So as the men gathered in the briefing room the next morning, Coop ignored the burning ache in his shoulder and made additions to the notes about the shooting on the whiteboard that covered the top half of a sixteen-foot-long wall.

When the scent of Obsession drifted into the room, he didn't have to turn around to know who'd just walked in.

"She not only looks good enough to eat"—the scrape of a chair told Coop that Santos had risen—"but she also brings food to feed our hungry souls."

"I've never heard doughnuts referred to as soul food," Rhonda said with laugh, "but go right ahead."

Coop had known she'd be arriving soon. And he knew he had to handle it. He turned around and lifted a hand in greeting.

She nodded, barely met his eyes, and set the box of doughnuts in the middle of the conference table. Then she sat down and started fiddling with her tablet.

See? Two grown-ups. Team members. Acting as if nothing out of the ordinary had happened.

Had to kiss her, didn't you, dumbass? Had to smell that hair, feel those breasts pressed against you. Had to suddenly think about her as touchable . . . and vulnerable . . . and maybe open to the idea of the two of you together.

It was all well and good to fantasize about Bombshell Burns when he knew he didn't have an ice cube's chance on a BBQ grill of getting within ten feet of her. It was an entirely different story after he'd actually held her in his arms, tasted her lips, and felt her body yield against his. The reality was a huge game changer—one he wasn't ready for.

He'd stayed with Mike at the hospital for another

hour after Rhonda left last night, instead of following her out the door and dealing with "the kiss" right then.

Well, it didn't matter now. And the farther he got away from "it," the more he hoped they might just let "it" drift off into obscurity, and they'd never have to talk about "it."

But then he looked at her again. Tight, short, red skirt. White angora sweater. High navy-blue heels. He'd never look at the flag again without thinking of her.

He was so screwed.

"Guess we're taking a break," he said as Santos, Josh Waldrop, and Brett Carlyle helped themselves to the doughnuts.

"Sorry to sideline the meeting," Rhonda said with an apologetic look, "but I thought the good news about Eva deserved a little celebration."

"You thought right." Santos winked and shot her a wide smile. "Any with chocolate filling?"

Rhonda grinned at him. "This is me you're talking to. Would I forget something that important?"

"My bad." Santos made a sweeping, apologetic gesture with his hand, then grimaced.

"You hurting today?" Rhonda asked with concern. Beneath the sleeve of his T-shirt, his biceps were wrapped in a white dressing.

"I'm fine."

Santos had gotten by with a butterfly bandage on his upper arm.

"Don't be poking your grubby finger into every doughnut to find your precious chocolate," Carlyle grumbled, joining Santos at the conference table.

"Somebody pour me a cup?" Taggart asked.

Rhonda took one look at him and gasped. His left eye was red and purple and blue, heading toward black. The fingers of the hand that emerged from his sling were swollen and bruised. "You should be in bed."

"Been there. Didn't like it."

Coop totally got where Taggart was coming from. He wasn't nearly as bad off as Taggart, yet he felt as if he'd been run over by a tank. His leg didn't feel too bad, but his shoulder burned like fire where the stitches sank into his swollen flesh.

"Doesn't mean you shouldn't be there. Go home," Coop ordered.

"Bed rest is highly overrated," Taggart said. "Give me some grunt work; I'll be happy as hell. And you ain't the boss of me."

Well, he'd tried.

Coop surveyed the others. At least it was back to status quo for the rest of the team. Trash talk was a method of coping when one of their own was in danger, especially for Taggart. And Coop was getting to know what to expect from Santos, Waldrop, and Carlyle, too.

Mike had picked the three men for the ITAP team at Nate Black's recommendation. After working with them for the past year, Coop fully understood why.

Like him, Mike, and Taggart, all three were combat veterans of Iraq and Afghanistan, and they'd all done contract work with Nate's team. On a particularly nasty op in Sierra Leone, they'd all been injured. Carlyle had broken his ankle, and Waldrop had almost died. Santos had taken that bullet yesterday and hadn't even slowed down.

"Davis!" A unison greeting went up for Peter, the team's operations manager, when he rolled into the room in his wheelchair.

"Treats?" Davis's close-cropped hair was peppered with gray, though he was only in his mid-thirties.

"Help yourself." Rhonda walked to the coffeepot and filled her Betty Boop cup. "Oh, God." She gasped after taking her first sip. "I don't know how you guys drink this poison."

She walked out of the room, no doubt to dump the coffee and refill the mug from her personal coffeemaker.

"She's not *too* predictable." Davis laughed as he rolled over to the table and looked over the doughnuts.

Coop agreed with her: the coffee here sucked. He also kept a pot and his own fresh-ground beans — 100 percent Blue Mountain Jamaican and well worth the splurge — in his office.

Davis filled a mug, then returned to the table and found the doughnut he wanted. When he'd first arrived more than a year ago, he'd looked like a man on death row. But they took care of their own, and

Taggart even had him pumping iron for the last six months. He had an impressive set of guns on him now, and Coop could see how his self-confidence had grown.

Rhonda walked back into the room, met his eyes across the table, and *bam*. Coop flashed back to last night and that kiss and felt a full jolt of sexual electricity sear through him.

"Okay, people," he said abruptly, jerking himself back to business. "I know we're all in a celebratory mood, but we've got work to do if we want to find that shooter."

"Work that DCIS would knock our heads together for doing," Carlyle mumbled around a mouthful of doughnut.

Totally true. But they were used to calling their own shots, and screw any other dog that tried to take away their bones.

Coop razzed him. "Do you think you can eat and think at the same time?"

"Is that what they call multitasking?" Carlyle's grin split his face.

"For you? Probably."

The door opened on their laughter, and Nate Black walked in.

The room grew quiet as everyone stood to attention.

"For God's sake, you're not in the military now, boys. At fuckin' ease."

Nervous laughs skittered around the room as Black

joined Coop at the whiteboard and slowly looked it over.

They might thumb their noses at DCIS's "stand down" orders, but Nathan Black had teeth, authority, and, most important, their respect

A former captain in the U.S. Marine Corps, he'd been the commanding officer of all the men now serving on his Black Ops Inc. team. Tall, probably six foot three, he was big in all ways that counted. A veteran of any recent conflict you could name, as decorated as a May Pole on May Day, and a leader who led from the front, he was trusted, loved, and no one to mess around with.

So Coop held his breath as Black took his time reading the notes that made it clear what they were up to. If Black—the unofficial top dog on the Black Ops table of organization—told them to back off, there might well be resignations. And though it would be painful, Coop would be the first one to hand in his. He'd cover Mike and Eva's back no matter what it cost him.

"You know that DCIS and the FBI are all over this." Black looked Coop square in the eye. "They don't want you messing with their investigation."

"I know that, sir, yes."

Black considered him a few moments longer, then faced the rest of the team. Coop felt a sense of pride as they all showed no sign of backing down.

"Carry on, then," Black said, and a collective breath of relief moved through the room. "Just keep it on the down low."

"Yes, sir." Coop worked hard to contain his relief.

"One condition," Black added with a hard look. "Your other duties don't suffer. That goes for all of you."

"Count on it." Coop had gotten damn good at lying; he fully intended to give next week's security-check gig to Waldrop. That would get Burns out of his sight and off his mind and allow him to give all of his energy to this investigation.

"You need any of my team, say the word," Black added. "If they're available, they're yours."

"We can use all the help we can get. Thanks."

"And I'm sure you can use this information, too." He pulled a folded sheet of paper out of his chest pocket. "The ballistics reports just came in on the slugs they dug out of the walls in the restaurant and the four cartridges they found on the scene." He handed the information to Coop. "No prints on the playing cards, but we didn't think there would be. The guy is anything but sloppy. So far, no DNA, either."

Coop skimmed the report.

"What are we looking at?" Santos's expectant tone voiced the question that was on everyone's mind.

"As we figured, the slugs dug out of the wall match the cartridges the shooter left at the scene: .223-caliber, hand-loaded."

Carlyle gave a low whistle. "Anything special about the .223?"

"It's heavy," Black said. "Ninety grains."

Waldrop sat forward. "The military issue is sixty-two grains. So he's dead serious. A crack shooter behind the trigger can zap a target out to a thousand yards with that kind of load."

Coop let out a long breath. "Yeah. It's also too big to feed through an AR-15 or M16 unless you single-load it, which is a major pain in the ass."

"So you figure he was probably using a bolt-action?" Santos asked.

Coop nodded. "Yeah. Which means we're looking at someone who does both close and long-distance kills and knows what the hell he's doing."

"Contract hit?" Taggart asked.

All eyes turned to Nate Black, who said, "It's sure starting to look that way."

12

After Black left, everyone in the room relaxed, Rhonda included. He was an imposing man but clearly a fair one. And good to his word, it was only a few minutes before Gabe Jones and Johnny Reed from Black's team joined them. Which delayed the briefing again as the men exchanged a little trash talk, along with relief at the optimistic news about Eva.

While Reed and Jones got up to speed on the ballistics report, Rhonda scrolled through the data feeding into her tablet. Being the only estrogen-fueled person on the team, she'd felt pretty darned overwhelmed the first time she'd been in the same room with this much testosterone. Frankly, it had taken a while to get used to them.

To a man, these guys were alpha warriors. Intelligent, insightful, skilled, and deadly. Along with Black's team, they were the best of the best. She'd seen the proof when she'd been tasked to spend her first month reading after-action reports detailing their missions.

One in particular stood out in her mind. It involved an unsanctioned, off-the-books rescue of a U.S. soldier who had been presumed killed in action but who'd actually been held captive in Afghanistan for almost four years. They'd infiltrated a heavily infested Taliban stronghold in Kandahar Province, with nothing but very distant air support to back them up in case things got dicey.

Things had.

And speaking of dicey, she'd noticed how stiffly Cooper moved this morning, how he didn't raise his left hand and ducked his head to hide a wince. He was hurting, but he didn't want the team to see it. She probably wouldn't have noticed if she hadn't been so tuned in to his frequency because of that stupid kiss at the hospital last night.

Oh, who was she trying to kid? She'd been tuned in since the first time she'd set eyes on him. He moved with purpose, strength, and a fluidity that was as natural as it was sexy. So, yeah, as much as he irritated her, he commanded way too much of her attention. And it was very clear to her that he was in a world of hurt today.

"Okay," Cooper said. "Let's dial down the BS and get this briefing back on track."

She couldn't help but admire the way he sucked it up and took control of the team in Mike's absence. He must have been working all night, if the neatly compiled notes on the whiteboard were any indication.

She was also grateful that he hadn't attempted to corner her this morning to talk about what had happened at the hospital. He'd actually avoided even looking at her ever since she'd arrived.

So . . . that was probably good. It probably meant that he was as eager as she was to forget it ever happened.

She still couldn't believe she'd let him kiss her. Or that she'd kissed him back.

Or that she'd gotten lost in the feel and the heat and the scent of him, pressed against her.

She'd even dreamed about him last night. Woke up hot and bothered and . . .

"Rhonda?"

She jumped.

"Would you recap what you shared with Mike and me last night at the hospital?"

"Right. Sure." She concisely told them about her computer searches in progress, her loosey-goosey profile, and the information she'd gleaned from DCIS.

"DCIS granted you access to their interview info?" Gabe Jones sounded skeptical.

When Rhonda glanced at Cooper, he gave her a nod. "Let's just say, if they've logged the interviews on their computer system, I have access to it. And any other data pertinent to the shooting."

"So what you're *not* saying is that you've got crazy, badass hacker skills," Johnny Reed concluded with a "hell, yeah" grin.

Rhonda grinned back. "You think I was hired for my cooking skills?"

"Oh, no, darlin'. Your cooking skills never crossed my mind."

A cowboy and a comic, Reed never missed a chance to flirt. His wife, Crystal—Tinkerbell—couldn't care less. Everyone knew that Reed adored Tink—not to mention that the little redheaded firecracker wouldn't hesitate to separate him from his "package" if he even thought about cheating on her.

"Rhonda's locked into the McLean PD and FBI databases, too," Cooper added, quieting the room down again. "If they know it, we know it. What we need now," he went on, "is luck. Something to pop up that makes a connection to Eva. To the teams."

Then Coop said something that made Rhonda think he just might have that connection.

"Because there's a chance La Línea cartel could be behind this."

"Holy *frijoles*." Santos glanced up at Coop. "La Línea? You fingering those drug lords for Eva's shooting?"

Coop had been wide awake and restless most of last night. If it wasn't his shoulder and calf giving him fits, it was his constant concern for Eva, not to mention the questions about the shooter who was clearly taunting them. And in between, weaving in and out of every thought, he saw Rhonda. Felt Rhonda. Tasted Rhonda.

Finally, he'd thrown back the covers, made a pot of

coffee, and spent the wee hours working on theories to help narrow the search that Rhonda had so painstakingly started.

"It's a good possibility," Coop said now, answering Santos's question.

"Why La Línea?" Waldrop asked.

Coop glanced around the room. "For the new kids in class, two years ago, Eva and Mike infiltrated a geopolitical 'cult' called UWD, United We Denounce."

"As in denounce the U.S. government?" Waldrop asked.

Coop nodded. "Exactly. Their main compound was in Squaw Valley, Idaho, run by an anarchist type, Joseph Lawson. Lawson was taking his orders from a guy by the name of Brewster, a former Army general. Both are now deceased, thanks to Mike, Eva, Taggart, and yours truly. Mike and Eva went in posing as UWD devotees, hoping to find information to clear the three of us from false court-martial charges that dated back eight years—and involved Brewster."

He noticed that Rhonda was paying very close attention.

"Once Mike and Eva got in and started gathering intel, they found that not only was Lawson linked to the false court-martial, too, but he was also planning an offensive against several government offices. And most pressingly, he was funding the operation by selling guns and ammo to La Línea."

"Nice company," Waldrop said with a grunt.

"Nate Black's boys"—he nodded toward Reed and

Jones—"located Taggart and me, and we joined Mike and Eva on the undercover sting. We destroyed their operation and exposed and took out the UWD top dogs, along with several high-ranking soldiers in La Línea's organization."

"There's your vendetta," Santos said. "La Línea's been biding their time, waiting for an opportunity to take the four of you out. Payback for their lost guns-and-ammo pipeline."

"*If* it was them," Carlyle pointed out.

Coop conceded the point. "Rhonda, did you see anything in DCIS's data banks that indicate they're looking in La Línea's direction?"

She shook her head. "No, but I haven't been back on their servers since the middle of the night. Hold that thought."

While she pecked around on the tablet, Coop walked over to the coffeepot and forced himself to pour a cup of sludge.

"Here it is." Rhonda sounded excited. "Looks like DCIS has interfaced with DEA, DHS, CIA, FBI, Interpol, and . . . even the Mexican National Security and Investigation Center. So I'd say yes, they are definitely on it."

"Then let's let them run with it. Another possibility," Coop continued, "is that there may be some disgruntled UWD disciples upset that we destroyed their stronghold, took out their leaders, and sent the majority of the fold to prison. It's a good bet there could be an ex-military sniper in their ranks."

He returned to the podium and, gritting through the pain that stabbed into his shoulder, dug into the folder of information he'd compiled last night. He found the profile he wanted and held it up. "This one in particular."

"Looks like a real thinker," Waldrop said, as he checked out the photo of the man with Charles Manson eyes, a bushy beard, and unkempt graying hair.

"Barry Hill," Coop said as Waldrop passed the photo on. "Hill was Joseph Lawson's number one disciple. A real fanatic. Former Army."

Jones checked out the picture, then passed it on. "Hill's not in prison?"

"He was," Coop said. "He was released a couple of months ago on a technicality. I checked with a friend at DHS last night, and the word is that Hill continues to spout UWD rhetoric, labels Lawson's death an unjustified execution, and has made promises on a UWD underground Web site to do something to make the 'bastards' responsible pay."

"So we definitely have another horse in the race," Reed said.

"Something we haven't talked about," Santos said, sounding reluctant. "Whether it was personal or not, hired or not, these kinds of birds who kill professionally are rare, and they don't hang around waiting to be discovered."

Santos was right. The shooter could have gone so far to ground and so deep in the shadows that there was a huge possibility they'd never find him.

"An organization like La Línea might bring in a professional long-distance killer, but considering that snipers are specialized and expensive to keep around, they might have attempted the hit by themselves instead. They also like to do their dirty work up close and personal." Coop took a sip of coffee, then shuddered at the horrible taste. "Same for Hill. He sees himself as quite the killing machine."

The room fell silent as the teams considered Coop's theories.

"Opinions? Anyone?" he asked after several moments.

"Yeah." Taggart looked thoughtful. "Some of those women at the UWD camp were pretty screwed up. Brainwashed, browbeaten, and force-fed propaganda that Lawson was the equivalent of the Messiah. Could this be a 'stand by your man' type of vendetta?" He shrugged a shoulder. "Nothing says revenge like a crazy woman with a cross to bear."

He had a good point. They shouldn't overlook the mind-set of women who'd been coerced into a dark, subservient lifestyle. Stockholm syndrome could come into play.

"So the cartel, Hill, and maybe some brainwashed UWD followers have incentive," Rhonda said. "All are very familiar with you, Taggart, and Mike and Eva's connection."

"Just want to point out that leaving the playing cards and the cartridges behind smacks of a cartel calling card," Reed said. "Both a promise and a threat."

"True," Coop said with a thoughtful nod.

Jones zeroed back in on Hill. "Does Hill have the chops to pull off something like this?"

"He *looks* stupid," Coop agreed, "but he's crazy stupid. The kind of stupid who would stage an elaborate 'scene of the crime' just for shits and grins."

The room grew silent again while they all chewed on their thoughts.

"ICE just made that bust on Ibarra last month," Jones said after a long moment. "My money's on any drug- or mob-related players, including La Línea, to lie low for a while." He frowned as he talked through his thoughts. "While it fits that they'd want their pound of flesh, I don't think they'd have waited this long. And I don't think they'd draw attention to themselves on the heels of the Ibarra arrest. It's too risky."

Coop was inclined to agree. "Hill, on the other hand, needed time to regroup and recruit reinforcements." He looked out over the room. "We want to toss our marbles into that game?"

Slow, thoughtful head nods indicated agreement.

"All right, then. We go with Hill and let the alphabet boys look deeper into La Línea. Let's track him down, see what he has to say about his whereabouts yesterday morning. And while you're at it, see if you can get any leads on the women who were at the camp. Let's not leave any stone unturned."

"Hold on." Rhonda's voice rose over the sound of chairs scraping on the floor as they got up to leave. "This just came across from DCIS, and it's something you all need to know," she said, holding a hand in the air to keep their attention.

"They checked every security and traffic camera in a five-block radius of the shooter's nest, and every single one of them had been disabled in the two hours before the shooting."

"You're shitting me." Reed looked incredulous. "That takes connections. Just like it took connections to find out we were going to be at Brewed Awakenings yesterday morning at that time."

"Which means your phones might be compromised. You're all going to need new units." Over their groans, Rhonda said, "You know where to turn the old ones in, and the sooner the better, so we can start mining the SIM cards for possible data."

"Quick question," Santos said. "I get why the shooter left the playing cards. He wanted to make certain you knew this was personal. Same with the four cartridges. It leaves no doubt they were the same as the ones that hit Eva and me and who the next targets are. But why leave bullets that might be traced?"

Coop shook his head. "I wish I knew. But I have a feeling that when we figure out that piece, we'll know for certain who's out to get us. Until then, the best bet we've got is finding Hill."

13

Coop stood alone in his office after the team had gone to work digging up leads on Hill. They'd root him out, he had no doubt. UWD followers weren't necessarily the sharpest knives in the drawer. They liked to bitch and brag. The boys would find some-one who knew someone who knew Hill and knew where he was.

He only hoped they were looking in the right place. Did Hill have the means to pull off the shoot? Would La Línea be a more likely suspect? Or was he looking in the wrong direction altogether? That thought chilled him to the bone.

Rhonda knew she was going to regret this—in fact, she already did. But she knocked on Cooper's office door anyway and, on a bracing breath, opened it before he had a chance to say "come," "go," or "leave me the hell alone."

He looked up from the papers spread across his desk and scowled when he saw it was her.

"I'm just as surprised as you are," she said, reacting to the look on his face. "Don't worry. This won't take long."

She closed the door behind her, walked to his desk, and laid out the medical supplies she'd gotten from the infirmary.

He looked from them to her. "What won't take long?"

"You took shrapnel in your shoulder and in your leg yesterday."

"The EMTs took care of it."

"Yeah, and I'm betting they told you to follow up with a doctor today."

"And?"

"Did you make an appointment?"

He grabbed a fistful of papers. "I'm busy. And I'm fine."

Exactly what she'd figured. "Take your shirt off."

He blinked, clearly taken aback by her sharp order. But he quickly recovered and made a show of looking shocked. "Why, Miss Burns. You just sent my heart all aflutter."

She'd been hoping she wouldn't have to deal with his nonsense, but she'd come prepared for it. "You know what your problem is?" she asked, holding his arrogant gaze. "You don't know when to stop being a jerk. Apparently, you don't know how to take care of yourself, either."

"So you've taken it upon yourself to take care of me?" The sexy glimmer in his eye almost had her walking back out the door. But that was what he wanted. To goad her into leaving, so she wouldn't see that maybe the big bad warrior was feeling a little exposed right now.

"If you don't get those bandages changed, you're going to get an infection," she said. All this macho posturing really made her wonder if that was what he was trying to hide.

He worked his jaw, then turned his attention back to his papers. "I appreciate the concern, but—"

"For God's sake, Cooper," she interrupted him. "What good are you going to be to Eva or the investigation if you end up in the hospital? Quit being such a Rambo and let me redress those wounds. Or would you rather I tell Mike that you were hit and have him put you on the disabled list?"

That got his full attention. And his anger. "You'd do that?"

"You don't want to test me." She held his stormy glare for a long moment.

Then, muttering under his breath, he stood and started tugging his black T-shirt out of the waist of his pants.

She gave him some time, but when he struggled to get the shirt off, she couldn't stand there anymore and do nothing. "Oh, the hell with it. Let me help. How did you even get this on?" she sputtered, working the soft cotton over his head. Then, careful of his left shoulder, she peeled it down his arm. "You can't even move your arm."

"It's stiffened up a little, that's all," he admitted grudgingly.

"It's also bleeding." She showed him his shirt.

The large circle of blood that had seeped through his bandage was barely visible on the dark knit.

"Good thing you wore black, or the guys might have actually seen that you're not invincible. Hope you've got a change of clothes."

"In the top drawer of the file cabinet," he said grumpily.

"You want to do this standing up or sitting down?" she asked, going for all-business but working like hell to keep from looking at all that sculpted bare skin.

With no luck at all.

He rose from his chair and hitched a hip up on the corner of his desk, supporting his weight on his right leg.

And she simply couldn't stop herself. His skin was the color of buttered caramel. His chest was free of hair, and she wondered if he was that smooth and his muscles that taut all over.

The rumble-strip abs, the biceps he'd call guns, the sculpted chest and shoulders pretty much said that it was. And that mouth—

"Rhonda?"

"What?" She startled when he barked her name.

"Are you going to do this or what?"

She *was* going to do this. As soon as her heart started pumping blood back to her brain.

Then she looked at him and, because they were

now at eye level, ended up staring straight into his eyes—where she saw way more than dark chocolate irises framed by absurdly thick lashes. That alone was enough to make her breath catch. But the rest—the physical pain she saw there, the impatience, and a sexual awareness that rivaled what she was feeling— sent her heart racing.

She felt the moment his thoughts drifted back to last night, when they'd kissed in celebration of the life they'd almost lost.

His gaze shifted to her lips. Lingered there.

He leaned toward her, and she *so* wanted to meet him halfway. To see if that kiss was as amazing as she remembered. To see if they could repeat the sensation.

The sound of footsteps passing by his closed door broke through the cocoon of sexual longing and snapped her back to her senses. She pulled back.

Reluctantly, so did he. His eyes were sober now, and the silence that filled the office weighed down on her like all the bad decisions she'd ever made in her life.

"Let's get that bandage off and see what's going on under there," she said, working hard to keep her voice steady. But her hands trembled as she started to carefully peel the gauze away. "This is going to hurt, I'm afraid. The blood is dried in places, so it's going to stick to the wound."

"Just rip it off," he said, his jaw tightening in anticipation.

"Not a good idea. It might cause more bleeding."

"And you got your nursing degree when?"

Last night. Thank you, Google. "I know enough to change this dressing. Hang in there."

In the end, she had to use alcohol to loosen the gauze. It amounted to a lot of touching, a lot of heat, and a lot of remembering what a bad idea he was.

A fine sheen of perspiration broke out across his brow and dampened his shoulders as the alcohol bit into his raw flesh. His jaw bunched tightly, and he gripped the edge of his desk as she worked to get the bandage free.

He didn't make a sound during what had to be an excruciating experience. But the curses flew out of his mouth like beer at a bar brawl after she'd finally peeled the matted gauze completely off.

One look at the depth and severity of the wounds, and she felt light-headed.

"Breathe deep," he said when she swayed.

His hand gripped her arm, her hip touched his thigh. Heat melting into heat. For a moment, it didn't seem so wrong.

Then she looked at his shoulder again. "Cooper. It's horrible."

"Looks worse than it is."

She hoped so, because between the stitches and the torn skin, it looked as if he'd been run through a meat grinder.

"You sure you're up to finishing this?" he asked.

"Absolutely not." She forced a tight smile. "But

one way or the other, it's going to get done. Let me know if I hurt you."

He grunted. "That ship has already sailed."

Because there was a hint of a smile in his voice, she relaxed a little, swallowed back her queasiness, and went to work.

Another heavy silence settled between them. The longer it stretched, the more difficult it was to break it, and the more aware she became of the intimacy and all the tactile sensations.

Did he feel them, too? Did he feel the way his skin heated everywhere she touched him? The slight tremble when his heat tingled though her fingertips? The rise and fall of their breath that inexplicably matched in rhythm?

She was very close to him now. And very glad she was behind him, so he couldn't see her staring. Couldn't see her gaze fix on the strong column of his neck, the softness of his hair, which was a little too long to be neat but fell perfectly against that tender skin behind his ear.

He sucked in a sharp breath, and she realized she must have hurt him.

"Sorry."

He looked over his shoulder at her. "You're doing fine."

She quickly pulled her gaze away from those intense brown eyes and concentrated on her work again.

After carefully cleaning the wounds, she covered

the area with a large gauze pad, then secured it with surgical tape. Finished.

Except for his leg.

Just wanting to be done and out of here, she dropped down onto her knees in front of him.

"Seriously?"

His exasperated tone brought her head up, right in line with the V of his crotch.

Oh. That was why there was gravel in his voice.

She was a smart woman, so why wasn't she using her head? Why hadn't she thought about the sexual undertones of kneeling directly in front of him?

Because she'd been too busy thinking about sex with him.

"Um . . . maybe you could—"

"Redress the leg myself," he interrupted firmly. "Get off your knees, Buttercup." He held out his right hand and helped her to her feet. "Never thought I'd say that to a woman."

Upright again, she straightened her skirt, searching for something to say, something that didn't make her look like a bigger fool.

"You want to grab a shirt for me?" he asked quietly.

"Sure." Glad to put distance between them, she practically sprinted to the file cabinet, opened it, and pulled out another black T-shirt.

He held out a hand, but she hung on to the shirt. Back under control now, she meant to show him that she wasn't a blushing schoolgirl falling prey to hormones.

"Let's not do that whole 'I don't need help' thing, okay?"

That actually got a sheepish grin out of him. And made her breathe a little easier. And made her knees a little weaker when he said, "Let's do this."

He lifted his right arm so she could slide the sleeve over it. But when his hand popped through the shirt sleeve, it connected firmly with her left breast.

They both pulled back as if they'd been zapped by an electric fence.

"Sorry," he said. The wild look in his eyes told her he really was. It had been an accident.

"My fault," she said, trying to act as if his touch hadn't affected her. But her suddenly taut nipples said she lied. "Let's just get this over your head, and I'll get out of your hair." And back to a place called sanity.

Somehow, they got him into the shirt without further mishap. Then she hurriedly gathered up the leftover supplies and headed for the door.

"Why'd you do this?" he asked, stopping her from leaving.

"Because I knew you wouldn't take care of it," she said evasively.

"You could have sent someone else."

"Yup. But then I wouldn't have gotten to see you sweat."

She had to get away from him before she blurted out something stupid, like *I did it because I was concerned about you. I did it because yesterday made me realize that you're not the Neanderthal creep I want you to be. I did it because I couldn't not do it.*

She had her hand on the doorknob and was about to swing it open, when he said her name.

His soft, tentative tone stopped her cold. And the look on his face when she looked over her shoulder at him almost melted her.

"Thank you."

He actually looked humble and sincere, and she wondered if she was getting her first glimpse of the real Jamie Cooper.

"You're welcome," she said shakily, and let herself out the door, not liking what she was thinking.

Why did you do this?

Because maybe she felt something for this man that she hadn't let herself feel in a very long time.

And that scared her half to death.

"What? Wait. No . . . no. That was scheduled for *next* week." Coop tried to contain his annoyance when Nate called him into his office later that day. He hadn't yet recovered from the Bombshell's "house call," where the scent of her perfume and her hands on his bare skin had made him crazy. And now Nate dropped this bomb.

"The time table's been stepped up. NSA picked up some cyber-chatter this afternoon. It could be nothing, it could be something, but we need to make sure these particular bases are air-tight secure."

With his jaw clenched to keep from saying something he'd regret, Coop picked up the file folder Nate slid across his desk. He flipped it open and scanned the operation orders for routine security checks in Colorado and Utah, then tossed it back onto the desk. "I'm ass-deep in the investigation. You don't need me for this. Any one of the guys—"

"Could do it," Nate agreed, cutting him off. "But any one of the guys' names didn't come up on the rotation. Isn't that how you all decided to resolve undesirable assignments? Your name comes up, you go. No substitutions. No bitching."

He was right—but damn. "Nate. Come on. You *know* I need to be working the investigation."

"Look, I know what's on the line here. And I know where your heart is. I'm sorry, Coop, it's out of my hands. But I'll personally handle things in your absence. You shouldn't be on the road more than three days—four, tops, if you find problems."

Not seeing any way out, he walked stiffly toward the door, cursing his bad luck.

"Remember, you're to take Burns with you."

He spun around in panic. *No. Please, God, no.*

"How about I take B.J. instead?" He tried to sound as if his sanity didn't depend on getting Burns off the detail. After that little Florence Nightingale session an hour ago, he knew he'd end up over his head if he was alone with her. "She's always done the cyber-threat analysis part of the check."

"B.J. needs a break from the travel. Besides, it's time Burns completes her first field assignment."

"If I've got to do this now, I'd really prefer to take B.J.," he tried again.

Nate sat back in his chair, regarding him thoughtfully. "Is there a problem with you and Burns that I need to know about?"

Shit. If he told Nate there was a problem, he'd assume that Coop didn't think Rhonda was up to the task, which was not the case and wouldn't be fair to her. She'd aced every assignment she'd been given.

"No," he lied. "There's no problem."

"Okay, then. Go let her know. Wheels up at five a.m."

It took a conscious effort to keep from slamming the door behind him.

He thought about her hands on his back today. About how gentle and careful she'd been, trying not to hurt him. About how freaking bad he'd wanted to kiss her. Again.

Things had gotten way too complicated between them.

By the time he reached her office door, his mood was as black as tar.

Wednesday

There is a difference between giving up and knowing when you've had enough.

—Unknown

14

"So unbelievably awkward," Rhonda muttered, tossing her suitcase onto the bed.

Cooper had turned into a first-class asshat the moment he'd shown up in her office with Nate Black's orders. That was late yesterday afternoon, and he hadn't taken the damn hat off since. She did *not* need the drama. Now she wished she'd never gone to his office and changed his bandage. His shoulder could fall off, for all she cared.

She dug into her purse for her cosmetics bag and went into the bathroom to freshen up her makeup. She'd looked forward to her first field assignment so eagerly. It was a rite of passage, a vote of confidence. It meant that when her probation period ended next month, she'd be a full-fledged member of the team.

And Cooper was single-handedly wringing all the joy and sense of accomplishment out of the experience.

She knew he was worried about Eva and that he was upset about being pulled off the investigation. But it was pretty clear that there was more to it than that. He was upset about being paired up with her. She knew it had nothing to do with her abilities; she did good work. So that meant this was about that stupid kiss. She had hoped he'd be able to put it behind him and move on.

Even though *she* hadn't been able to, either.

She braced her palms on the bathroom counter and glared at her reflection. Even surly, rock-jawed, and silent, Jamie Cooper was impossibly gorgeous. Sitting beside him on the cramped commercial flight this morning, she'd felt the undercurrent of his sexuality radiate from his body, which did things to *her* body, regardless of how hard she tried to ignore him.

She'd even dreamed about him last night, even though she knew she'd never get involved with him. The vibes he'd been giving off, however, suggested that he might think she should.

Not happening. She dug a hair pick out of her bag and went to work. She wasn't opposed to good, healthy sex, although you'd never know it from her recent dating history. Or her not-so-recent history, for that matter. Sex was one thing; a conquest was another, and that's what a man like Cooper would consider it.

That might be a little harsh, but she told herself it was the truth. She had never been and would never be some man's spoils of war, even if it was simply a war of the sexes.

But oh, she did wonder what a night in a bed with him would be like.

She tossed the pick down in disgust. She was as guilty as he was.

But she had no desire to let someone like Cooper interfere in her life. Or get too close. Which was why it bothered her that she kept thinking about what he'd said at the briefing yesterday: "Mike and Eva went in posing as UWD devotees, hoping to find information to clear the three of us from false court-martial charges."

How horrible it must have been for them. If he'd been halfway communicative on the flight this morning, she'd have asked him about the charges. But her sympathy had disappeared when he'd gone Surly Sam on her.

They would need to have that talk after all, she decided. She had to cowgirl up and let him know he was wasting his time and hers.

A sharp knock drew her out of the bathroom and to the door. It must be Cooper, but she looked through the peephole to confirm it. Then she stepped back and swung the door open to reveal Asshat Man in all his pissed-off glory.

Arms folded belligerently over his chest, fingers tucked under his armpits, feet planted wide apart, he looked as gorgeous as ever and as combative as a submachine gun.

Oh, brother.

When he saw her, his expression of grim resolution slowly turned to disgust, and her plan to have that "talk" collapsed like a pup tent in a strong wind. She wasn't up to dealing with his hostility right now.

Irked with him for being such a dick, and with herself for not making him own up to it, she turned away. "Let me grab my coat, then I'm ready."

"For what? Speed dating?"

His clipped, judgmental words had her turning back to him with narrowed eyes. "What exactly does that mean?"

"We're going to a military facility, for God's sake, not a photo shoot. Must you *always* be camera-ready?"

Rhonda knew she sometimes pushed the acceptable limits of professional attire. It was who she was, and she didn't intend to change for anyone. She'd worn the black sweater, black skirt, and black heels because she'd needed to feel powerful enough to match whatever crap Cooper sent her way.

Apparently, he planned on sending plenty, and she was now officially pissed. "What are you, the fashion police?"

He gave her another contemptuous once-over. "Forget it. I want to get to the base and get a few hours under my belt today. Let's just go."

"You know what? I'm not going anywhere." Mimicking his stance, she crossed her arms beneath her breasts and stood her ground. "Not until you tell me who shoved that stick up your ass."

• • •

Damn stubborn, bullheaded woman. Short of dragging her out of the hotel room and shoving her into the elevator, it looked as if they were going to have that talk he'd hoped to avoid for, oh, the next decade or so.

"Look. I don't want to be here, okay?" Not lying but not exactly telling the whole truth.

She snorted. "Alert the media. I never would have guessed."

He walked over to the window and glared out at the parking lot. "I need to be back at Langley, working on the investigation."

"That much I figured out," she said from behind him.

Which was a good thing, because she looked so damn hot all he could think about was the fact that they were alone together in a hotel room. With a bed.

"I want to be back there helping out, too," she continued. "But there's more going on with you than that."

Oh, hell, yeah.

"You think I'm not up to the assignment? Is that what this pigheaded silence is all about?"

He shifted his attention to a jet trail in the clear blue sky. "I don't think that, no. I think you'll do fine."

"Then that only leaves one thing."

When she left it at that, he finally turned around. She looked like a runway version of an Amazon priestess. Expression hard and unbending, body lush and curvy, legs long and . . . man, oh, man, he wanted them wrapped around his waist.

"*You* kissed *me*," she said, cutting right to the heart of the matter. "If you're having trouble with that, then it's on your head, not mine. So if you want to be ticked off at someone, go look in the mirror, and quit taking it out on me."

She was right. His foul mood *was* about the kiss, and he *was* taking it out on her.

But she wasn't finished clearing that up for him. "And grow up, while you're at it. We were happy for Eva and Mike. We were relieved she was alive. We were relieved *we* were alive. It was instinctual. It didn't mean anything."

He stared at her, wanting to agree with everything she said. But he couldn't. Because looking at her in all her magnificent glory, he was hit by a blinding rush of awareness.

She was dead wrong.

That kiss *had* meant something. It had meant a helluva lot of something, which scared him stupid. And *that* was why he was angry. He dragged a hand through his hair, stunned speechless.

Then he met her eyes and, with a single beat of his heart, shot from bewilderment to total clarity. She was just as afraid as he was. That was why she'd lied and said it meant nothing. That was why she'd come to him yesterday full of concern about his shrapnel wounds.

Well, he'd never run away from fear in his life before, and he wasn't going to start now.

She wanted to be pissed? Maybe he'd give her a reason.

He stalked toward her. "So that kiss didn't mean anything? Then this won't, either."

Ignoring the pain in his shoulder, he banded one arm around her waist, gripped the back of her head with the other, and pulled her flush against him.

"What the hell do you think you're doing?"

"I think I'm about to ruin your lipstick. But don't worry, it doesn't mean anything."

Then he covered her mouth with his . . . and dived into a hundred fathoms of ocean.

And kept diving deeper.

She melted against him like hot wax, meeting the heat and intensity of his kiss with all the fury that had prompted him to go caveman and drag her into his arms.

Another first. Women pursued him; he didn't go after them. And now he knew why.

Because they weren't her.

Because she wasn't just another woman.

Terrified by the track his thoughts had taken, he abruptly broke the kiss and set her away from him.

She looked dazed and unsteady, and he wasn't so damn solid on his own feet, either.

He cupped her shoulders in his hands and walked her backward the two steps to the bed. When the backs of her knees hit the mattress, she sank right down.

"I'm sorry I've been such a jerk. You didn't deserve

it," he said, meaning it. "And I'm sorry about what I just did. I was way out of line."

She had yet to speak. It was the most unhinged he'd ever seen her.

It was the most unhinged he'd ever felt.

Before he could stop himself, he reached out and brushed the pad of his thumb over her lower lip. "Better touch up that lipstick."

She blinked, a "what the hell just happened?" blink that had him backing toward the door.

"I'll meet you in the lobby in ten." Then he sped out of her room, feeling as if he was swimming for his life in shark-infested waters.

15

Peterson Air Force Base was located on the east side of Colorado Springs. The Air Force shared its runways with the local municipal airport, but the sharing pretty much ended there.

R&D laboratories made this air base a top security facility, which was the reason Rhonda and Cooper had been dispatched to fly out here. It was also the reason they'd flown commercial. Had they arrived via Air Force transport, they'd have been tagged as DOD watchdogs before the plane ever hit the ground, and there went the surprise element of the audit.

And speaking of surprises, Cooper was full of them.

"You all set?" he asked as they drove up to the security checkpoint in their rented Jeep Cherokee.

"I'm good." She didn't meet his eyes, because she still hadn't figured out what to say to him.

After he'd left her sitting on the bed, her hair a mess, her lipstick smeared, her equilibrium shredded, she'd walked shakily to the bathroom.

And gasped when she'd seen her reflection.

She'd looked as if she'd just had sex. As if Cooper had taken her for the ride of her life—and in some ways, he had. Except that she was still all achy and hot and restless, and, dear God, her hands were still shaking half an hour later.

This was *so* unprofessional.

And Cooper, well . . . she didn't know what to think.

But one thing she was sure of: she had a job to do. And right now, the only way she could do it was to focus on the work and nothing but the work, so help her God.

She'd been prepared to deliver a little speech on decorum and professionalism when she met Cooper in the lobby, but he'd outmaneuvered her again.

He'd met her with coffee and croissants to go. And his gaze had never strayed below her face. "Figured you could use an afternoon pick-me-up." He'd looked ridiculously unsettled when he handed her the Styrofoam cup. "You like it black, right?"

"Um, yeah."

"Took a chance on the croissants, but I figured I couldn't be too far off with that sweet tooth of yours."

She hadn't known which had been more disconcerting, his polite, careful smile or the fact that he knew she had a sweet tooth. And liked her coffee black.

"The valet already brought the Jeep around. You're going to want your sunglasses," he'd added before she could open her mouth, and, lightly gripping her elbow, he'd ushered her outside. "Nice to get away from the deep freeze, right? There must be a forty-degree difference in temp from Virginia to here. Freaky weather, huh?"

He'd closed the car door behind her, walked around to the other side, and slipped in behind the wheel. Thirty minutes later, here they were. Stopped at the U.S. air base's security gate, flashing their credentials.

She hadn't said a word during the drive, but he'd talked constantly. Talk about mercurial mood shifts. He'd talked about the weather, asked if she needed more heat, remarked on the beauty of Pikes Peak. Asked her if the altitude affected her at all.

She'd shaken her head no, but they *were* six thousand feet above sea level. Maybe that was why she felt short of breath and her heartbeat revved up every time she glanced sideways at his perfect warrior-poet profile, or every time she focused on those soft lips and the steely strength of his arms, or when she thought about all that hard, toned muscle beneath his shirt.

Something was definitely wrong with her. Because she'd let him kiss her senseless, and, worse, she'd participated. Enthusiastically. Who knew how far she'd have let things go if he hadn't suddenly pulled away, a deer-in-the-headlights look in his eyes?

She'd felt him rock-hard and ready against her—all male, all the time. And yesterday in his office, when she'd dressed his wound, she'd felt his sexual arousal as powerfully as if he'd stripped her naked and taken her right there on his desk.

Yet now he acted as if nothing had ever happened. As if the earth hadn't tilted, and the stars hadn't come out, and . . .

Okay. Stop.

She should be grateful. He'd apologized. He'd admitted to being out of line.

But now she knew the truth. Only one thing was going to settle things between them. Whatever this was, it wasn't going to end until they both got it out of their systems.

Coop had made a decision. Silent and surly, which he'd thought was a surefire way to keep distance between them, hadn't worked out so well. In fact, it hadn't worked at all, except possibly to make her think he was psychotic.

Hell, *he* was starting to think he was psychotic. He'd worked with her for more than six months and kept his shit together. Yet in the past twenty-four hours, she'd shoved him so far out of his element he didn't know up from down. Pain he was used to. He rolled his sore shoulder. Pain he could handle. But this constant state of "what the hell?" was going to be his undoing.

It could not go on.

So he was backing away from the Bombshell. From this point on, she was as dangerous as a minefield, a grenade without a pin, a block of C-4 with a live blasting cap.

And how did you treat explosives? With great concentration and care.

It was all polite, inane conversation and business from now on—and it would have been in the first place, if he hadn't gotten his shorts in a twist and decided to prove a point.

Didn't mean anything? Well, I'll show her.

That strategy had backfired big-time.

Uh-uh. Not going there. He was horny; she was hot. But sex was not happening. Case closed.

They were on assignment. This was business. It was also Rhonda's first field assignment, and success was critical to her. Hell, it was critical to him; he didn't take his job lightly.

The faster they got their work done, the faster he'd get back to Langley.

So his head was firmly on straight again when they entered the base and were greeted by the commander of the unit. He turned them over to Master Sgt. Lowden, their contact with the staff in charge of the computer center.

Lowden walked them to the top secret command center. He seemed like a decent guy, but if Coop was in his boots, he'd have a significant problem with letting an outsider in.

Well, he amended, with a reluctant glance toward Rhonda. He'd have a problem letting *him* in. The Bombshell was a welcome addition anywhere the testosterone level hit the top of the charts, and despite the female techs, this place was full of it.

So far, the physical security on the base looked good, as it should. Once they were past multiple security checkpoints, Lowden led them through a maze of corridors to the main computer operations center. The large, windowless room was dimly lit; the walls were covered in monitors showing maps, graphs, and other data. Dozens of airmen, dressed in camouflage air-battle uniforms and flight suits, hunched over banks of computer terminals. Lowered voices and air-conditioning fans made the room buzz in a low hum.

As in most operations centers he'd ever been in, and the reason Coop could never do Rhonda's job, the air was tasteless from being processed to death. Give him a dusty desert or a steamy, smelly jungle any day.

"Tight ship," Coop said with a nod to Lowden. "Well done. If the rest of the base meets your standards, we'll be out of everyone's hair in short order."

"Thank you, sir."

"It's all yours, Burns," he said. "I'll meet you outside the building at six p.m."

She was already across the room, gathering the technicians, explaining why she was here, and attempting to make them feel comfortable, as he walked out the door to wreak some havoc back at the security gate over a couple of practices he'd seen and hadn't been particularly impressed with.

He was already dreading six p.m., when he'd meet up with the blond bomber again. He hoped to hell she had her pins underneath her by then, because a confused and vulnerable Rhonda Burns was a damn difficult sight to resist.

One thing he knew for certain. There'd be a few technicians who'd still be picking their jaws up off the floor by the time she left them. Poor suckers. They had no idea what kind of hell she could put a man through, and that was before she even started her testing.

As for her reaction to him, he was thankful she'd pretended indifference again. That worked for him.

Rhonda was in her element. Once Cooper left, it felt as if a cloud had lifted. This was what she was paid to do, and she did it well.

"I'm not here," she told the room in general, and got a ripple of nervous laughter. "Just go on about your business."

Then she started the first phase of her penetration testing—or pentesting—electronically attempting to breach the IT systems. She'd work on phases two and three tomorrow. For the first time today, she smiled. None of them knew what tortures she had planned, but they all appeared eager to give their best effort.

Her first attack on the base cyber-security was simple but brutal. The "distributed denial of service" bombarded the network with thousands of attacks per second, basically body-slamming the network in an attempt to overwhelm it. If security was lax, that would cause the system to crash, leaving it wide open.

As the attack ramped up, she watched how everyone reacted, noting that they appeared calm and worked together as they assessed the threat and methodically dealt with it over the next hour.

Well done, people, but I'm not through with you yet.

She typed another command into her computer and smiled. They'd be sweating and shouting at each other before the day was over.

16

The sun had started to sink behind the Rockies when Rhonda walked out of the computer complex four hours later. Cooper was waiting for her, sunglasses covering his eyes as he leaned against the rental Jeep, arms folded over his chest, one ankle crossed over the other. His benign expression almost hid the fact that he was as dangerous as a rattlesnake. The light breeze ruffling his hair added to the illusion that he was harmless.

Only his edgy bearing suggested that he might be one of the most lethal weapons in the Department of Defense's arsenal.

He was dangerous, all right, in more ways than one. Yet even knowing he represented the worst kind of trouble, she got that sizzling ache low in her belly when he tugged off his shades and those dark eyes met hers.

I kissed you, and you liked it.

Nothing about his expression said that, but she read the words into it anyway. Because she *had* liked it.

He pushed away from the Jeep and opened the door for her. "How'd it go?"

She slipped into the passenger seat. "Okay."

With her focused one hundred percent on her testing, the four hours had flown by, and she hadn't once—okay, maybe once, or twice—thought about him. Now she had a splitting headache and flat out didn't have the mental or physical acuity even to talk to him, let alone try to figure out what his game was.

"You?" she asked, going for distant politeness.

He shifted into gear. "Good. These guys are on their game."

A good ten minutes of silence followed, and she resisted the urge to ask him how his shoulder felt. Because she didn't care.

She stared straight ahead.

He drummed his fingers on the steering wheel, then finally turned to her. "I don't want to belabor this, and I'm sure you don't, either, but I really am sorry I've been such a jerk." He actually sounded repentant.

It threw her enough that she fired before she aimed. "Amazing how you arrived at past tense so quickly."

He wrinkled his brow. "There's a past tense for *sorry*?"

She pressed her fingers to her temples and rubbed.

"Oh . . . I'm sorry I *am* a jerk, not that I've *been* a jerk. That the past tense you were going for?"

She wanted two extra-strength Tylenols, room

service, and bed. Alone. "Something like that." She closed her eyes and let her head fall against the headrest, feeling his gaze on her. "Watch the road."

"You feel okay?"

"I will. As soon as I get back to the hotel and take something for this headache."

"Tension headache?"

"Now, why would I be tense?" She pushed each word through clenched teeth.

"Damn. I really have upset you."

She wouldn't give him the satisfaction of knowing he'd affected her way beyond a headache. "The testing was intense, okay? That's all it is."

"Look, Rhonda. Before you say anything else . . . what happened in your room was a new low for me. I've been dishing out grief with a shovel ever since you signed on, and you haven't deserved any of it."

Rhonda stared at him. *Now* what was he up to?

Coop glanced over to see those amazing blue eyes narrowed in suspicion. He couldn't blame her. He'd been Mr. Multiple Personality for too long now. And while he was determined to be completely professional from now on, he knew they had to clear the air.

"Let's get this out in the open so we can put it behind us," he said firmly. "We got off on the wrong foot, and I want to make that right. So for the record, you've done a great job on the team since you started. I have complete confidence in your work. You deserve respect—and my mother would stand me in a corner for the way I've behaved."

Her attention was now riveted on the windshield.

Somehow they had to get past this. Then he could get the hell on with his life, without thinking about how badly he wanted to—

Nope. Not going back there.

"You think we could we start over?" he asked.

Still nothing.

He started to sweat.

Then she surprised him.

"I haven't exactly been Miss Congeniality," she admitted after a long moment, and Coop felt a knot the size of a football ease inside his chest.

She made an effort to smile at him then—and man, oh, man, if it wasn't the weight of the world that lifted from his chest, it was at least the weight of the moon.

"Damn." He heaved a huge breath. "I'm glad we got that out in the open."

She nodded. "Me, too."

"Bygones and all that?"

She thought about it for a while and finally said, "Sure. Why not?"

"Great. Now that we've got the air cleared, I can do something about that headache."

"He said, wiggling his brows lasciviously."

"No, seriously."

"Right. Silly me. You'd never do anything out of line."

"Point for you. But I'm driving, which makes me

harmless. And as you know, I'm injured, which makes me a wimp. Give me your hand."

She pushed out a weak laugh. "Yeah—no. That's not happening."

"Come on, Burns. I thought we'd established that you can trust me now. You have my permission to knock me senseless if I step out of line."

"Whose line?"

He grinned. "Yours. Now, give it."

Rhonda considered. They were in a car, driving down a major highway. What could he possibly do? Besides, he'd badger her to death until she finally gave in. And she really wanted to establish a new normal for them, one that wasn't fraught with sexual awareness or tension-filled hostility.

She finally extended her left hand.

The instant the rough heat of his fingers touched her skin, electricity zinged from her fingertips to that part of her that hadn't been zinged in a very, very long time. She tried to jerk her hand away, but he'd latched on and held tight.

"Relax."

Then he pinched the fleshy part of her hand between her thumb and index finger and applied pressure. And oh, her headache eased, ever so slightly.

"Wow. How'd you do that?"

"I know a few reflexology techniques. This," he said, pinching a little harder, "is a trigger point for tension headaches."

Maybe it was, because her headache had started to ease. Or maybe it was that she was tired of being bitchy, or maybe she just had a weak moment. Whatever the reason, she didn't pull her hand away.

"Better?"

She nodded. "Yes. It is." She finally relaxed then, lulled by the rhythm of the road and the firm, gentle pressure of his strong fingers manipulating her headache away.

"That should tide you over until you can get to your Tylenol." He slowly pulled his hand back to the steering wheel.

She didn't want to, but she felt oddly bereft. Just as she had when he'd pulled away from her in her hotel room.

Altitude, she assured herself. It had to be the altitude.

There were high-stress jobs, and then there were *high-stress* jobs.

Working with Rhonda "Could Have Been Eve in the Garden" Burns had shot Coop way past stress and straight to SRS—sperm retention syndrome.

Man, he was such a dick.

Act like a jerk.

Take her to bed.

Be cordial and polite.

Take her to bed!

Maintain a working relationship only.

Take her the hell to bed!

His plan and his mental state bounced around like water drops in a hot frying pan. Whom exactly was he trying to kid? He didn't even recognize himself anymore.

Had to touch her again, didn't you? Just had to do it.

Well, no more. Not even for headache control.

Despite all his good intentions, touching the Bombshell had shot him straight into a sexual fantasy that made his head reel.

Apparently, he'd triggered a similar reaction in her, because the minute he pulled up in front of the hotel, she'd scrambled out of the Jeep and into the lobby as if it was pouring rain out. Coop hadn't asked about her plans for the night; she hadn't asked about his. She seemed as determined to stay away from him off duty as he was determined to avoid her.

Once in his room, he took a quick shower, shaved, and put on a pair of clean jeans and the black cashmere sweater his mom had given him for Christmas. Then he checked in with Taggart, who proclaimed that he was "fit and fine," doubtless an exaggerated self-diagnosis. Next he called Mike and felt a huge rush of relief to hear that Eva continued to improve. His last call was to Nate Black.

"Working every angle," Nate assured him. "We haven't found Barry Hill yet, but the boys have some solid leads and expect to turn over the right rock and find him under it momentarily. How's Burns doing?"

"Seems to have things well in hand. We should be out of here day after tomorrow and heading for Utah.

What I've seen so far tells me I'll have a fairly clean report. She says it's looking good on her end, too."

After hanging up, he went down to the hotel dining room. If Rhonda decided to eat there instead of ordering room service, he figured he'd be finished before she reapplied her makeup, touched up her hair, and whatever else she did to make herself look like the perfect vision she always was.

Wrong. Story of his life lately.

She was seated at a small table in the corner of the large restaurant that was occupied by only three other sets of diners.

"Will anyone be joining you tonight, sir?" The host approached him with large leather-bound menus in hand.

Unfortunately, he glanced at her at exactly the same time she looked up and saw him. He felt about as exposed as a sniper in a floodlight.

"Sir?"

"Sorry. No. It's just me." He deserved a halo and wings for his determination to leave her in peace—and *maybe* keep some peace of mind of his own.

"Very good, sir. If you'll follow me, then."

Twenty empty tables in the room—and the host led him to a table directly across from hers.

Perfect.

17

He'd never seen her with her hair up. She'd pulled it into a loose, sexy knot on top of her head, and golden strands trailed perfectly down her neck. Her neck was elegant, her shoulders delicate. She wore a butter-yellow sweater with a deep, round neckline. Soft, fuzzy angora again—how many of these seductions did she own?

And she was wearing jeans instead of a short, tight skirt. Deep blue denim that disappeared into knee-high black leather boots and made her legs look as if they went on forever.

Something else was different. Her makeup. Her eyes weren't as heavily defined. Not that she had a heavy hand to begin with, but the effect of the lighter touch lent a softness and vulnerability to her face that made him wonder if it hadn't always been there. If maybe he had simply chosen not to see it.

Someone cleared her throat, and he looked up from his menu.

It was Rhonda. And she was smiling. "This is a little silly, don't you think?"

Not silly—imperative. He could *not* be near this woman on their downtime. Only work had made it possible for him to keep his distance earlier today.

"I didn't want to intrude," he said. "Thought maybe you'd had your fill of me today."

He felt her gaze on him as he tried to concentrate on the menu. It could have been written in Mandarin, for all he knew. The letters all sort of bled together, as he did his damnedest not to look up at her. He felt ridiculously self-conscious. Him! Mr. Sydney, Australia, Model of the Year 2010!

Before he could come up with a semi-intelligent thought, she broke the awkward silence.

"You're bleeding."

Damn. He touched a fingertip to his jaw. He'd nicked himself shaving but thought he'd taken care of it.

"No . . . here." She pointed to a spot on her own neck, just below her ear.

He moved his finger to his neck, checking for blood.

She shook her head, stood, and walked to his table. Then she used her napkin to dab at his neck.

He stopped breathing, a moment too late to avoid the sensual scent of her signature perfume. Too late for a lot of things.

Heat radiated from her body like a furnace.

He closed his eyes, made himself breathe, then opened them again. Her breasts were at a level with his nose, and the low-cut sweater showed a generous glimpse of the heaven a man would find if he buried his face there.

"That took care of it," she said, straightening up.

Too late to squelch the vivid image of his face pillowed against those amazing breasts, his mouth finding a hard nipple and playing with it with lips and tongue until she arched against him, begging for more as he kissed his way down her body and found the heat and the heart of her sexuality.

Oh, God. Stick a fork in him—he was so far past done he was charred.

"You're seriously going to sit over there?" she asked, seated back at her table.

When he could draw a breath that wasn't shaky, he made himself speak. "Actually, I thought I might order dinner to go, then head back to my room. Got some reports to do tonight . . . you know the drill."

She didn't respond for a while, and when she did, he had to school his gaze back to the menu to keep from looking at her, um, sweater.

"You feel okay?" she asked.

He almost laughed, because boy, did he have an answer for her. *Actually, I'm hard as an armor-plated missile, and it hurts like hell. Want to help a guy out?*

"It hurts" might have worked in the backseat of a car when he was seventeen, and the sweet, naive girl with him fell for the pity ploy, but it wasn't going to work on Rhonda.

"I'm fine," he said. "The shoulder feels much better today, too—thanks."

"Then don't be ridiculous." She pushed out a chair with her foot.

If he refused, he'd look like a coward.

Using the menu to conceal his raging erection, he stood, walked to her table, and sat down.

Apparently, she lacked the good sense to be wary of him.

"How's the head?" he asked.

"Better."

"Good. That's . . . good."

The waiter came then, thank God, because he'd been reduced to one-syllable words. She explained about the switch in tables and ordered the salmon.

"Steak," he said, not even looking. "Rare."

They both passed on drinking anything stronger than soda, since they were on the job. Which was just as well, Coop thought. He wasn't feeling all that strong and as full of conviction as when he'd walked into the restaurant, because nothing had changed about the way she looked and how much she turned him on.

He was committed, however, to keeping everything platonic between them.

"I talked to Taggart." There was some safe ground.

"How's he doing?" She sounded anxious.

"Typical Boom Boom. Acts like all he's got is a hangnail."

She smiled, then asked, "Did you check with Mike?"

"Eva's in a lot of pain, but she's strong, and she's determined to get back on her feet."

"I feel so bad for both of them." She shook her

head, sending a tendril of hair spilling out of its loose knot.

He quickly looked away and dug his fingers into his thigh to keep from reaching out and tucking it behind her ear, just so he could feel the silk of it.

"What about the investigation?" she continued. "Any breaks in the case?"

"Nate says they've got some leads on Hill but nothing solid yet. It's frustrating." And he wished with everything in him that he was back there in the trenches, fighting for his friend.

"I know you really wanted to be in the front lines on this."

He shrugged. "Yeah, well, when duty calls . . . Speaking of which, how did your first day go?"

"It went very well. I really put them through their paces on phase one of the pentest, and they handled it like pros."

"What exactly is a pentest?"

"You really want to know?"

"I want to not sound stupid if the term comes up again. But use English, not cyber-geek-speak, please."

"Electronic penetration test—hence pentest. It's an electronic attempt to breach Internet technology systems from the outside. It tests both the system and the people running it."

"And how do you do that?"

She hesitated, clearly not certain if he seriously wanted to know. "Here's an example. Tomorrow I'll leave a USB thumb drive somewhere near the computer-room door or on the floor in the main room. If some idiot picks it up and plugs it into their computer to see who owns it—very much like you'd check the ID in a wallet if you found it—they're going to get a hard lesson. Because if a certain setting on that person's computer isn't shut off, the program on the thumb drive will breach the network. Then whoever planted the thumb drive owns the system—that would be me. The problem is, it could have been a spy."

"Sneaky." He grinned. "I wouldn't want to be the person who picks it up."

She gave a little shrug. "I think this group is on top of their game. But I don't want you nodding off over your salad. How about you? How'd things go?"

"Oh, I was the most popular guy on the base wherever I showed up. So far, I haven't found any notable problems. They can make some improvements in their best practices and security procedures. They're a little lax on their entrance-and-exit logs, and a few security cameras could have better placement. I'll dig deeper tomorrow, but I don't anticipate I'll find too much to write up."

The rest of the meal was all shoptalk. It was kind of nice. And besides being sexy as hell, she was pleasant when she wasn't feeling defensive, which was how he'd made her feel since the day she'd joined the team.

For a supposedly smart man, he'd been doing some damn stupid things.

18

Rhonda stood in her doorway, watching Cooper walk down the hall, not believing what had just happened.

After a perfectly congenial dinner, he'd walked her to her door, shaken her hand, and told her he'd see her at 6:00 a.m.

If he was playing a game, he was damn good at it. If he was actually sorry about all the crap he'd pulled, he was damn good at apologizing, too.

She closed the door behind her, flipped the safety bolt, then walked slowly to the bed.

She didn't know whether to be relieved or disappointed.

Of *course*, she was relieved. This was exactly what she wanted—for him to stop acting like a teenager, one minute hating girls, the next minute trying to back them up against a wall and cop a feel.

She took a quick shower, slipped on her short nightgown, and went to bed with her tablet to finish up reports from today and tweak the testing she had set up for tomorrow.

For a while, she half-expected a knock on the door, Cooper wanting to know if his apology and good behavior had earned him enough points to have a fun little romp in her bed, the leopard showing his true spots.

She glanced toward the door, wondering what she'd do if he did show up. All sleepy bedroom eyes and mussed hair, barefoot, shirtless . . .

There went that "girl parts" zing again.

She looked away from the door. She liked this new Jamie Cooper. *If* that was really him, a little voice warned. Could he be a nice guy after all? Or had an alien invaded his body? Was he really repentant, or was this just another way of angling to get into her bed? And if it wasn't, was she relieved or disappointed?

Or had *she* been invaded by an alien and . . .

Crap.

Her head started to pound again, and her brain was clearly running low on functioning cells.

Disgusted, she scrolled through the documents on her tablet, found the one she was looking for, and got back to work.

She looked at her door three more times before she finally shut down her tablet in frustration and turned off the light. At nine freaking thirty.

She was still awake an hour later. And an hour after that.

Frustrated, she tossed back the covers, turned on the bedside light, and searched for the TV remote. Maybe an old movie would put her to sleep.

She stopped searching when she landed on a rerun of *True Blood*, mesmerized as a very naked and aroused Sookie got it on with a very naked and very, very buff Alcide, the werewolf. His dark, smoldering eyes and thick black hair made her think of the man just down the hall, and instead of Sookie and Alcide naked and wrapped around each other in sweaty, sensual knots, she saw herself and Cooper.

She quickly punched the off button, headed straight for the bathroom, and turned on the tap. The water was lukewarm. She needed something cold to drink, and the minibar was off limits; it would only make things worse.

After grabbing the ice bucket and her key card, she undid the dead bolt, opened the door, and peeked outside. The hall was empty. Counting on everyone being asleep, she quietly shut the door and made a beeline for the ice machine just down the hall.

She didn't even look as she hotfooted it by Cooper's room. She got her ice, stepped back into the hall—and ran straight into the solid wall of his bare chest.

"Sorry," he said, then stopped dead when he realized it was her.

He, too, carried an ice bucket.

He, however, had had the good sense to get dressed. Sort of. He was barefoot and shirtless, in his jeans. And just as she'd imagined, his hair was bedmussed and beautiful.

Long moments passed as he stared at her, his gaze

slowly sweeping from her own bed-mussed hair, to her bare shoulders, to the thin strap of her pale pink nightie that had slipped down one arm . . . then to her nipples, which had stood at full attention the moment she'd laid eyes on his bare, muscled chest. And finally, down to her legs, bare from mid-thigh down to her feet. There was a lot of bare going on here.

Oh, God.

"Couldn't sleep?" His voice sounded like it scraped across gravel.

"Um." She reached up to tuck a strand of hair out of her eyes and behind her ear. "Guess that would make two of us?"

His gaze was now riveted on her lips. "Yeah. Guess so."

"Well." She curved her shoulders in so her nightgown didn't showcase her ridiculously erect nipples. "Good luck with that."

Then she all but ran back to her room.

She was breathing hard when she leaned against her closed door, clutching the ice bucket. And she almost dropped it when she heard his door slam across the hall.

Yikes. Couldn't mistake the anger in *that* sound.

When his door slammed again only a few seconds later, followed by the solid rap of a knuckle on her own door, she jumped.

"Open the door, Rhonda."

She closed her eyes and leaned her head back, considering ignoring him.

"You want me to wake up the entire floor?"

When her heart had settled back down, she opened the door a crack and peeked outside.

There he stood. Still barefoot. Still shirtless. As tempting as an apple in Eden.

"I want to come in." The smoky darkness in his voice and eyes left no doubt about what he planned to do once he got there. The packet of condoms in his fist cinched it.

An electric bolt sizzled through her body, yet she tried. "I don't think this is a good idea."

"That's not what your nipples said."

She almost laughed. Yes, the thought of him in her bed made her that stupid.

"I was cold," she lied, so weakly that even she didn't buy it.

"You were hot." The sensual grit in his voice rivaled the heat in his eyes. "You *are* hot."

She pressed her forehead against the door frame, wanting to give in, knowing she'd be sorry if she did, sorry if she didn't.

"We've tried, Rhonda." His voice softened. No less sexual. No less frustrated. "We've both tried damn hard. We've sniped, we've made nice, we've tried to ignore it. But it's not working."

No, it wasn't.

"If you tell me to go back to my room, I'm gone. But ask yourself this question first. Do you really want to keep fighting this?"

She *should* fight it.

She didn't *want* to.

She *should* be smart enough and strong enough.

She didn't *want* to be either right now.

So when she finally raised her head and saw the hot desire in his eyes, saw all that glorious golden skin covering solid muscle, she knew the fight was over.

19

When she unhooked the chain and then stepped back, Coop was the one who hesitated.

In this moment, he wanted her more than he'd ever wanted anything in his life. More than he'd wanted his name cleared after Operation Slam Dunk. More than he wanted his next breath.

This could be life-altering, and he didn't want to screw it up. So he stood there, his fist wrapped tight around the condoms, his gaze riveted on her eyes—eyes that spoke of desire and surrender and that irresistible vulnerability.

"Now?" She backed into the room, a look of utter confusion on her face. "After all that door slamming and demanding that I let you in, *now* you're going to stand out there and give me a chance to regret my decision?"

Hell, no.

He stepped inside and, never taking his eyes off hers, shut the door and turned the lock. In the dimness, the bedside lamp made her thin nightgown translucent, leaving very little to the imagination.

In two steps, he had her in his arms. Two more, and he'd backed her against the foot of the bed. Two deep breaths, and his heart slammed against hers, his bare chest pressed against the fullness of her breasts and the erect wonder of her nipples.

Then two words stopped him cold.

"Ground rules." She pressed her palm against his lips just as he went to kiss her.

"*What?*"

If she wanted him on his knees, it was a pretty sure bet it would happen. Very little blood remained in his head; most had gone south, where it pulsed and demanded relief.

"We need to establish ground rules." She sounded as aroused as he felt.

"Okay. Fine. Pick a safe word." He groaned, pressing his erection against her taut, concave belly. He wasn't into kinky sex, but if she —

"That's not what I meant." She pushed him inches away.

He felt like weeping. "Then what? *Please.* Just tell me what you want."

He drew her back against him. Filled his palms with the sweet, fleshy roundness of her ass and ground her hard against the aching length of him. He knew what *he* wanted. He wanted that filmy pink silk on the floor, her legs wrapped around his waist, and his mind blown like a fried circuit as he buried himself deep inside her.

"We keep this real, okay?"

He arched his hips against hers again, bent his head, and nuzzled the soft spot beneath her ear. "This is as real as it gets."

"This . . . tonight," she said, sounding breathless but committed as he nipped her earlobe, tugged, then nipped again. "It's just about sex. All right? That's all."

Her words registered in his brain, but his body was in charge. And his body was about to go up in flames.

"Just sex. Whatever you want."

She gripped his face in her hands, pulled his head up, and made him look at her. "No commitments. No looking back when it's over. We're just scratching an itch here."

The intense emotion in her eyes told him she wasn't fooling around. This was important to her.

And while something about her fiery insistence didn't feel right, in this moment, whatever she wanted was fine with him. He wasn't looking for long-term, either.

"Whatever you want," he repeated. "Can we please quit talking now? I promise I'll make it worthwhile."

Apparently, she'd reached her limit, too, because when he lifted his hands, wrapped them around hers, and guided them down to touch him, to show her what she'd done to him, her eyelids fluttered shut, and her entire body trembled. Her sharp intake of breath told him she was done talking, all right. And after the initial hesitance of her fingers on his hard flesh, she enclosed him, stroked him, then rose to her tiptoes to slip her tongue into his mouth, confirming that she wasn't turning back now.

On a groan born of six long months of frustration, he wrapped one arm around the backs of her thighs, the other around her shoulders, and lifted her off her feet.

Digging one knee into the bed, he lowered her onto her back. Resisting the raging need to shuck his pants and pound into her until they were both seeing stars, he leaned back and looked his fill of the woman who had tied him up like a dozen sailor's knots.

"Take it off." His throat muscles were so tight the words barely came out as a whisper. "I want *you* to take it off."

Her muscles tensed all over, like a silky, sexy cat anticipating that she was about to be petted and rubbed in all the ways she liked best.

He felt the anticipation as keenly as she must have when she gripped the hem of her gown and worked it up over her hips, then sat up. Crossing her arms in front of her, she pulled the pink silk over her head.

He barely managed to stay still, not entirely believing that the reality exceeded his very vivid imagination.

She was so stunningly beautiful that for a moment, he lost his breath.

He'd been with a lot of women, a lot of them models with beautiful faces and bodies. But none of them had ever made him feel what he felt when he looked at her.

Her blue eyes were full of yearning. Her hair trailed down one shoulder, over skin that was as pale and creamy as porcelain. And her lush breasts, round and firm, were topped with the prettiest pale pink nipples. Knowing he was finally going to touch them and taste them sent a fire shooting through his groin and dropped him to his knees on the floor.

He wanted them in his mouth. He wanted all of her in his mouth.

He leaned forward and drew her to the foot of the bed, where he buried his face between her breasts. Silken hair fell over his shoulders; impatient hands caressed his head as he nuzzled her.

She gasped as he nipped her with his teeth, then soothed the velvet tip with his tongue before sucking her deeper into his mouth. He pressed her breasts together against his face, drowning him in tactile pleasure.

She arched her back when he sucked her harder, and she spread her legs until the damp crotch of her black lace panties pulsed against his throat. He could smell her arousal and her impatience.

His lips felt swollen as he reluctantly pulled away. Her nipples were engorged from his sucking, the tender flesh around them reddened by his stubble.

"Lie back," he whispered, gently guiding her down on the bed.

Still on his knees, he locked his eyes on hers and slowly peeled the black lace down her legs.

She'd hiked herself up on her elbows and looked

down her body at him. For as long as he lived, he'd remember that sight. Her hair trailing down to the bed, her pink nipples pointed upward, her flat abdomen rising and falling with her shallow breaths.

He leaned forward and worked his tongue over her belly, a promise of what was in store.

She dropped back onto the bed and groaned. "Hurry."

That wasn't happening. Not when he finally had her where he wanted her and how he wanted her. Kissing his way down her stomach, he lifted her thighs and draped them over his shoulders. Only then did he raise his head and look at the heart of her.

She was as open and vulnerable as a woman could be, soft and pink and bare there. He lowered his head and kissed her, once, twice. Then, as her fingers clutched the sheets, he slipped his tongue into her secret folds.

Her sharp intake of breath was all he needed to delve deeper into her sweet, slick core. And as kitten-soft noises transitioned to sounds of aching pleasure and finally to desperate demands, she fueled his own desperation.

"*Pleeease . . .*"

The scent and taste of her, the delicious wild sounds she couldn't hold back, triggered the loss of his own control.

He cupped her hips in his hands, tipped her toward his mouth, and annihilated them both.

20

Gasping for breath, Coop landed spread-eagle on his back, which was exactly where she wanted him—and wanted him *now*—if the force with which she'd bucked him off and shoved him to the bed was an indication.

Only moments ago, she'd melted into a sweet, boneless puddle after she'd come in his mouth. Then she'd lain there, wet and satisfied, while he'd kissed his way slowly up her body, finally joining her on the bed. He'd coaxed her mouth open, stroking and exploring inside. He'd have to remember that thing he'd done with his tongue, because when he'd touched the roof of her mouth just so, she'd shifted from sleepy kitten to hungry tiger.

Her hands tangled in his hair now, pressing her mouth harder onto his, as her fingers raced across his chest and she scraped her nails across his skin, arching her hips against him. She was smokin' hot, all fierce passion, with zero inhibitions.

A woman like her didn't hide behind smoke

screens and mirrors. She delivered what she promised in the way she dressed, the way she smelled, the way she oozed sexuality like a candle did fragrance.

Then she knelt over him, her lips and nipples rosy pink and swollen from his kisses, her hair falling in a golden mess across his bare chest. Watching his face, she opened a condom packet with her long nails, then slowly rolled it over his engorged flesh. He had to clench every muscle in his body to keep from coming right then. Perspiration dampened his skin as she took him in her hands and eased him inside of her. Then, her eyes still on his, she lifted her hair away from her neck with both hands and took her sweet, torturous time impaling herself to the hilt.

Only when she was good and fully seated did he breathe. Only then *could* he breathe, as she tightened around him, gloving him in exquisite heat.

"Be still," she whispered when he closed his eyes and arched up into her. "Just be."

He opened his eyes then, and man, oh, man. Her eyes were closed; her lower lip was caught between her teeth. Her head tilted to the side, and her expression—intent on feeling their union in the purest, most sensual way—stopped his breath again.

He ran his hands from her knees to her hips and held her there against him, savoring the way she indulged herself, then groaned low in his throat when she met his gaze and started moving.

Slowly at first. A little rocking motion of her hips. Back and forth. Then side to side, then up and down.

Higher. Harder. Wilder, until the sensations inside him blasted past finesse and control and rocked them to the hot, explosive edge.

He came on a strangled groan, arching into her one last time as she tensed and clenched and then, on a gasp that was part sigh, part cry, and all release, collapsed across his chest.

For long, long moments, his climax stretched and intensified, then slowly mellowed to a stunning simmer before finally dying. An amazingly sensual death.

Yeah. She'd definitely killed him.

When Cooper rolled onto his stomach, exhausted and spent, Rhonda had plenty of time to stare at the bandages on his back and calf.

She'd been aware of his wounds, old and new, when they'd made love. How could she not? There wasn't an inch of her body he hadn't stroked, kissed, or finessed. So yeah, she'd reciprocated. And yes, she'd been very aware . . . but unable to process anything but what he was doing to her. He'd been thorough. And oh, my, he'd been good.

Now, though, in the aftermath of the storm of sensation and pleasure he'd brewed up and demanded she give in to, she had to know.

"You're lucky you weren't killed Monday."

He yawned sleepily and then, with effort, turned onto his back to look at her. "As I recall, you were also in the line of fire. And speaking of fire . . ."

She looked away when a warm flush spread

through her body at the memory of how bold she'd been with him. How uninhibited. He'd made it easy. He'd made it incredible.

"Hey." He reached across the pillow and smoothed the hair away from her face. "Don't be embarrassed. You were amazing."

"I could have hurt you."

He chuckled, pushing up on an elbow. "You can hurt me anytime you want."

She didn't want to go all serious and concerned on him, but seeing those wounds made her realize things about him—and about herself. "I was scared to death."

The amusement in his eyes faded to understanding as he realized she was referring to the sniper attack. "You think I wasn't?"

She searched his eyes and, because she couldn't help herself, searched his beautiful, sculpted face. Thought of the perfect union of his muscle and sinew and bone. Of the silky dark hair that fell over his forehead as he regarded her in a way that made her feel like they'd just shared a whole lot more than casual sex.

"You do, don't you? You think that getting shot at doesn't scare me spitless."

He was trying to make her feel better. "I didn't see any fear. Not from you. Not from any of the team members."

"Hell, no. You saw us react like we've been trained to. But if you'd felt my heartbeat, you'd have known just how scared I was. Just like the rest of the team." He reached out and, with a gentleness that unnerved her, brushed his thumb across her cheek. "It's our job not to show fear. It's our job to handle threats."

She looked away, just now realizing that she might be way out of her element. "I was pretty much useless. I couldn't help Eva. I couldn't help anyone."

He nestled down into the covers and drew her into his arms. His body was big and hard and as warm as a furnace as he curled himself around her. "You're not a trained soldier. And you did exactly what we needed you to do. You kept calm. You kept Mike calm. You didn't make yourself a target that would have endangered all of us. And you've done the job that *you've* been trained to do ever since. You have nothing to regret."

Oh, she had plenty of regrets. She already knew that tonight would be one of them, but she didn't want to give in to that reality yet.

She shifted to her side so she could see his face. Before Monday's shooting, she'd thought she knew who he was. Turned out she hadn't had a clue. She still didn't.

"How do you do it?"

His eyes slowly came open.

"How do you face gunfire and secret operations and flying black into terrorist strongholds? How do you deal with the threats? Over and over and—"

He sighed, pressing his fingertips to her lips. "Somebody's been reading too many after-action reports about old missions." He smiled, then kissed her temple. "That's old news."

Maybe it was. But still, she wondered. Every man on the team was an adrenaline junkie. But adrenaline wasn't all that drove them. They were patriots. Some of them had lost someone—in Iraq, in Afghanistan, when the Twin Towers went down. All of them wanted to right wrongs. She got that. But what was it about these men, about this man in particular, that compelled him to willingly face his own death just by doing his job? "*Why* do you do it?"

He made an annoyed sound and snuggled deeper into the covers and into her. "Do what?"

She should let him sleep. Actually, she should kick him out of her room and go to sleep herself. It had been a difficult three days, and they'd just done their best to wear each other out. A sizzle fired through her when she thought of one particularly athletic move she'd never even heard of.

She'd just decided that he was asleep and their conversation was over when he wearily pushed himself up on an elbow. Sleepy dark eyes regarded her from beneath dark hair and ridiculously thick lashes. His lips were as soft as pillows and as skilled as an artist's brush. The beginning of a five-o'clock shadow darkened his cheeks and jaw.

"Why do I do what?" he repeated.

"The job," she said, before she lost her nerve or got distracted by the possibility of messing his hair up even more.

He flopped onto his back and crossed his arms behind his head. "The same reason anyone does their job."

Not even close. "Does it have something to do with those one-eyed jacks you guys always carry? Something to do with your tour in Afghanistan? The trumped-up court-martial charges?" She couldn't stop wondering what had happened. Wondering how those events had shaped him into the man he was today.

He turned his head and looked at her. "Why do you want to know?"

Okay, it *was* a very personal question. One that a woman who cared about a man might ask.

"Because the ITAP team was built around you, Mike, and Taggart. I'm part of the team now. I feel like . . . I should know what drives you."

God, she hoped that sounded plausible. Because this was *not* personal. She couldn't let it be. This was about work.

But she shouldn't even have asked. Should have left it at sex. That's all this was supposed to be about, and that's probably why he'd suddenly become so tense. He didn't like this up-close-and-personal stuff, either.

"Tell you what." His mood was much more somber than it had been moments ago. "You answer a question for me, and I'll answer one for you."

The dark edge in his tone made it very clear that she wasn't going to like his question, and she had no one to blame but herself.

Before she could tell him to forget it, he asked, "What's the deal with you and hospitals? And flowers?"

Her heart jumped.

She was *so* not going there with him.

"Look. Let's just drop it. You'd better go back to your room. We both need to get some sleep. Big day tomorrow." She rolled over on her side, her back to him.

"Oh, no. I'm not letting you off that easy. But just to show you what a sport I am, I'll retract that question and start with an easier one."

He sounded very much awake now and very determined.

"Where do you get those sweaters?"

Sweaters? Wary, she looked over her bare shoulder at him. "What?"

"Your sweaters. Where do you get them? And how many do you have, for God's sake?"

She rolled onto her back and frowned at him. "You don't like my sweaters?"

"I *love* your sweaters. They make me think of old movies with Jayne Mansfield or Marilyn Monroe or Brigitte Bardot."

So, he was an old movie buff, and he noticed things. Since this was relatively safe, she answered, "That's because they're vintage. I love the old angora wool and the dyes they used back then. So I haunt vintage shops and buy them when I find them."

"Me and the guys thank you for that."

He was smiling again, which made her smile. "You and the guys, huh?"

"Yeah. Every day, there's a pool on what color you're going to wear."

She laughed, because it really was silly. And silly

was a good thing now, after her stupid idea of trying to find out what made him tick.

"Okay, Miss Burns. Your turn. A simple question this time."

Relieved, she asked, "Why do they call you Hondo?"

He groaned and covered his eyes with a forearm.

"These are your rules, not mine," she reminded him.

He heaved a resigned breath. "Okay. I'm an old movie buff, right?"

"Marilyn Monroe, Jayne Mansfield."

"And westerns. John Wayne, especially. He was in a movie based on an old Louis L'Amour book that I'd read over and over again. Anyway, there was this scene in the book and the movie where John Wayne—Hondo—wanders onto a ranch with nothing but a saddle and a rifle."

"No horse?"

"No horse. So he jumps onto this wild bronc no one's been able to break and rides it, bucking and rearing all over the place until he finally tames it, all while managing to look like a manly man and never even losing his hat."

"And?" she prompted after he stopped talking.

"And," he said, clearly reluctant to go on, "I was stupid enough to retell the story to the guys when we were deployed."

"And . . . they call you Hondo because you were a fan of this book and movie? There's got to be more."

He groaned, then gave up the rest. "We had this

mission in Afghanistan. In the mountains. The only way to get to our target was on horseback."

She tried not to smile. "I think I see where this is going."

"Let's just say I lost more than my hat and my pride. It wasn't pretty, and I sure as hell wasn't John Wayne. They've called me Hondo ever since."

She didn't laugh, but she couldn't help the smile.

Until he turned to her. "Okay—my turn."

She braced, afraid he'd circle back to his original question.

"What did you want to be when you grew up?"

Relief filled her. This she could handle. This she *wanted* to handle. Lying here with him, so aware of everything male and stunning and sexual about him, she was ready for a diversion. Especially when he traced one finger slowly down her arm, then moved to her breast and circled her nipple, reawakening all of her erogenous zones.

She tossed back the covers and climbed on top of him, straddling his lap and seating herself deep. As she'd expected, he instantly grew hard.

"Well, it's funny that you mentioned horses . . . because I always wanted to be a cowgirl."

He gripped her hips and arched against her. "A cowgirl, huh?"

"Yup. Think you've got a little buck left in you, pardner?"

He laughed and pulled her down to kiss him. "That would be a big yee-haw!"

Thursday

If you find yourself in a fair fight, you didn't plan your mission properly.

—David Hackworth

21

Depravity pulsed with the deep, pounding rhythm of the rock music blaring from dozens of speakers hidden in dark corners of the dance floor. Smoke permeated the packed space as midnight-blue strobes swept over damp, sweating bodies writhing to the primal beat, rubbing and sliding against each other, simulating sex and sin and desperation.

She'd selected this bar not only for its reputation of uninhibited decadence but also for its clientele. Gay, straight, bi, transgender, androgynous—it was open invitation. And open season for a predator.

A girl squeezed in so tightly beside her at the crowded bar that her flesh burned and her scent enticed.

"Flippin' fake ID." The bartender tossed the ID back at the girl. "Get lost."

She gave him the finger and spun around, hiking her elbows on the bar which was sticky with spilled booze. There she stayed, pouting, glaring through her heavily made-up eyes.

"Asshole," she muttered loudly enough for anyone within earshot to hear. "Like this place gives two flying figs about the law."

She was a pretty little thing—in a streetwise, chip-on-her-shoulder, hungry-for-attention sort of way. Her hair was hacked short in the back, shaved over her left ear, long over her right eye, and streaked with red, purple, and blue dye. Her very scant white halter top was nearly transparent and hugged full, high breasts. Young breasts. Soft and supple and probably tasting as good as they looked. A ring in her left nipple poked against the thin fabric, announcing to the world that she was a sexual creature. The glimpse of metal that pierced her tongue solidified the message.

Maybe it was hunting season after all. Maybe a taste of this sweet young thing would make her forget about Ray for a little while. Or maybe it would bring him nearer. He'd not only loved making love to her, he'd also loved watching her with other women.

"Buy you a drink?"

The girl turned her head, looked interested, then wary. "What do I have to do for it?"

She smiled, looked from those pretty pouty lips to the nipple ring. "Nothing you don't want to do."

The girl glanced at her bald head. "You sick or something?"

She laughed and ran a hand over her recently shaved head. "A new look for me. Like it?"

The girl shrugged. "Doesn't matter what I like. I'll have a tequila and lime."

An hour and four tequila shots later, they left the bar together and walked the short distance to the "no-tell motel," where a room was waiting.

The girl was asleep in the middle of the ruined bed when she walked into the bathroom in the middle of the night. She'd hoped that a purely sexual, animal release would fill the hollow cause by Ray's absence. And the girl had been good. Energetic. Adventurous. But nothing erased the truth.

Fail.

The word echoed, haunting and harsh.

Fail.

She'd spun her story ten different ways to satisfy the Russians, and Vadar had actually bought it.

Only it would never be acceptable to *her*.

Only twice in a fifteen-year career had she failed. Both times had involved Eva Salinas and Mike Brown.

It stuck in her craw like a fish bone that Eva still lived. But the woman was not invincible. And there was time to finish what she'd started.

Meanwhile, it was amusing to think about all the others scrambling in the dark, searching desperately to find the person who would dare attack one of their own.

A bunch of bumbling, muscled-headed fools. They weren't patriots, as they no doubt thought of themselves. They were murderers. They had murdered the one person who had ever meant anything to her. The one person who had cared for and loved her.

A warm body pressed full breasts against her back. Small hands wandered over her nipples, then lower, coaxing. "Come back to bed."

She met the girl's brown eyes in the mirror. All that need. All that energy. And suddenly, she was angry. "Get dressed, and get out."

The girl looked shocked, then hurt. "It's the middle of the night."

"Your point?"

That hurt look again. "Did I . . . did I do something wrong?"

"I'm done, that's all. Don't attach anything more to it. Now, go. There's money on the side table."

Tears pooled in the girl's eyes, then spilled over. "I . . . I don't have anyplace to go."

She laughed. "You say that like you think I'd give a shit. Life's a bitch."

"But—"

"Go!"

The girl backed away as if she'd been hit, eyes wide and scared.

"Now you've got the picture. I'm not a nice person."

The girl scrambled for her clothes and jerked them on. "Asshole."

"You got that right. Go home to Mommy and Daddy. You're never going to survive on these streets."

Long after the girl was gone and forgotten, she lay in bed, the light on beside her, one of her specially loaded cartridges in her hand. Absently studying it. Pleased by its perfection.

The plan had been perfect, yet it had failed.

It could be perfect again, Ray whispered.

He was right. After all, the bastards didn't even know what was happening. Didn't know why they were targets, let alone who was targeting them.

And while she was lying here, an idea took shape. An idea that grew in appeal.

Perhaps the failed attempt to kill Eva Salinas Brown *could* actually bring a better outcome, as she'd told Vadar. Better for them to wonder who was going to kill them. To wonder if dear Eva was safe or if she must always be kept under lock and key.

The thought brought a tight smile. Perhaps she should up the game. Tempt them with a little clue, then watch them stumble all over themselves trying to solve the puzzle.

That would make the outcome even sweeter. Embarrass the "elite" warriors by making even bigger fools of them, dangling an unmistakable clue in front of their bumbling noses, then laughing at *their* failure.

After all, where was the challenge in total anonymity? Where was the sense of satisfaction in knowing the enemy was at a disadvantage, operating with two hands tied behind their back?

She warmed to the idea. Maybe, in the interest of

fair play, they should be allowed another small clue. Give them the opportunity to try to figure out who was after them, so they would know who the *true* elite warrior was—just before they died.

The idea held much appeal. They'd see who was the failure then.

It was time to fuck with their minds. If nothing else, it would be amusing.

Oh, to be a fly on the wall when they opened up the special-delivery package she'd mail first thing in the morning.

And oh, to have a bird's-eye view when Vadar and his team attacked the Air Force compound. She'd told them that the weekend would be the best time to strike, and it was already Thursday. Which meant Vadar had to act soon—or the window of opportunity would slam shut.

22

Mike glared at his team as they arrived in the ITAP briefing room. They clearly hadn't expected that he'd be waiting for them at 6:45 a.m. Or that he would have already studied the notes on the whiteboard.

"Playing cards? Designer bullets?"

Waldrop dropped his pen and disappeared under the table to retrieve it. Santos was suddenly preoccupied with his belt buckle. Carlyle appeared mesmerized by his mug of coffee.

Only Taggart met his eyes, no doubt figuring he'd get a pass because of his injuries.

When no one responded, Mike jabbed a finger at the whiteboard, where Coop had diagrammed each step of the case as it had developed.

"Three one-eyed jack playing cards, clearly marked with our names." Now even Taggart wouldn't look at him. Maybe because he was nearly yelling. "One queen of hearts with Eva's name crossed out. Four matching designer bullets. And no one thought this information would be of interest to me?"

Taggart finally stepped up to the plate. "The general consensus was that you had enough to deal with and didn't need the burden of this additional information. How's Eva doing, by the way?" Taggart asked in an obvious attempt to sidetrack him. "And why aren't you at the hospital?"

"Eva is holding her own," Mike said stiffly. "And I'm not at the hospital because I'm here, where I clearly wasn't expected."

If someone lit a match, the room would explode in a powder keg of tension. He dragged a hand over his jaw and settled himself down.

"Coop made the call, right?"

Everyone avoided his eyes again, a sure sign that he was correct. No one was going to rat on Coop.

And Mike got why Coop had decided to withhold the information. He'd correctly assumed that if Mike had known that this psychopath had targeted the three of them and Eva, it wouldn't have been productive. But he was still pissed.

That was his *wife* who'd almost died. That was his *wife* suffering in that hospital bed and facing a long and difficult rehab. And that was his *life* the sick sonofabitch had tried to take away from him.

"Do not ever withhold information from me again." He narrowed his gaze around the room, pausing at each man until he was certain his message was received loud and clear.

Then he moved on; there was no value in beating a dead horse. "Tell me where you're going with this,

and make it clear and fast. I've got to get back to the hospital."

Five minutes later, he was up to speed. They'd ruled out any of the restaurant employees and customers as having any involvement, directly or indirectly. All the alphabet agencies, including Interpol, had turned their energy toward terrorist links, including the La Línea cartel. The team had a solid lead on Barry Hill and were hoping to haul him in for questioning within twenty-four hours.

Still, Mike had questions. "How'd he find us? How'd he know we were going to be there Monday morning?"

"We're stumped on that one." Carlyle looked embattled with frustration. "We're the only ones who know about those breakfast meetings. The commo stays between us. B.J. mined all the SIM cards on our old phones—nothing."

"What about the traffic cams? How did he manage to shut them all off simultaneously?"

Santos said, "By paying off a city employee named Maxwell Robbins, as far as we can figure."

"So we've got a possible witness? Someone who could ID our shooter?" For the first time, Mike felt a glimmer of excitement.

"Unfortunately, no. Robbins hadn't shown up for work since Monday. One of his coworkers stopped by to check on him yesterday and found him dead. Apparent overdose."

"Apparent?"

Santos leaned back in his chair. "One of the de-

tectives working the sniper case just happened to get called in on the Robbins case. He put it together that Robbins worked in the traffic division—specifically, traffic cams. So now the ME's looking at the death as a possible homicide."

"We need to talk to Robbins's coworkers," Mike said. "Find out if he has a girlfriend."

"Already on it, boss." Waldrop rose to fill his coffee cup. "No one who worked with him saw anything amiss. No significant other. Parents live on the West Coast. Dead end there, too."

"So what you're saying is, we're running blind," Mike concluded.

The killer shared a history with them. It was someone they'd hurt financially, in global status, or personally—because those cards and the bullets seemed damn personal to him.

"We're missing something. Something obvious," he said, more to himself than to his men.

He turned back and studied the board. Studied the reports on the designer bullets. "Who's checking the database on known pros?"

"I am," Carlyle said. "Haven't found a known assassin with an MO that uses these particular loads."

"Keep looking," Mike said, then headed out the door.

It wasn't until he got to the hospital and found his brother Ty and Ty's wife, Jess, in Eva's room that his dark mood lifted.

"Look what the wind blew in." Eva, looking pale and exhausted, smiled from the bed.

Mike walked to Eva's side, leaned down, and kissed her good morning. After he assured himself that she was okay, he turned to his kid brother. "Damn, if you aren't a sight for sore eyes." He'd told Ty that he didn't have to come, that Eva was doing well. But man, was he glad to see him.

Ty grinned at him. "Coldest winter in Minnesota's history. We're more than happy to get away for a while. Although it's none too toasty here, either."

Mike wrapped Ty in a big bear hug, not knowing until he held the solid bulk of his brother in his arms how much he'd needed someone to hold on to. He hadn't let down his guard for one second during Eva's life-and-death battle, and suddenly, he felt the weight of her suffering, of almost losing her, like a cargo plane on his shoulders. "Glad you're here, bro," he whispered, and damn, he had to fight tears.

Ty hugged him harder. "Try to keep me away."

Mike pulled himself together and pulled back from Ty, who also knew about the fear of losing the woman he loved. And who also knew about fighting for the people he loved.

"You okay?" Ty asked softly.

"I am now." Mike turned to Jess. "You get prettier every time I see you."

"And you're just as big a flirt as you ever were." She grinned and returned Mike's embrace.

"Thanks for coming, sis. Who's watching the store?"

"Don't worry, it's covered. Kabetogama isn't exactly a hotbed of activity this time of year."

Jess had taken over running her parents' general store at the northern Minnesota lake several years ago. Now that she and Ty were married, Ty spent his time between Minnesota and Florida, where his air-cargo business was located.

"The folks are on their way," Ty said.

"They don't have to do that," Mike protested, but he was grateful they were coming to shore him up and lighten his load. "How long are you here?" he asked when Eva had closed her eyes and slipped back to sleep.

"As long as you need us, bud. As long as you need us," Ty repeated in a tone that said he understood what Mike had been going through.

Mike looked into eyes that were the same color as his, into a face that, but for the age difference, could have been his. And the dam that he'd piled all of his fears, anger, and frustration behind finally broke. Overcome with relief that he no longer had to do this alone, he let the tears fall.

23

"So we're on the same page about last night, right?"

Coop scowled at Rhonda as he drove toward the Air Force base the next morning. "Right. Same page. No *problemo*."

At least, there shouldn't be. But once again, this woman had messed with his head to the point where he wasn't exactly sure what was up, down, good, bad, or verging on insanity.

He'd awakened in her room bright and early, as erect as the Washington Monument. Problem was, she wasn't lying naked beside him to appreciate his very impressive good-morning salute.

But water had been running in the shower, and he'd totally been up for that.

So he'd rolled out of bed and ambled over to the bathroom. The door was locked. *What the—* He gave it a rap. "Need your back washed?"

Seconds later, she'd turned the shower off.

A few seconds after that, the door had opened. She

was wrapped in a towel, with another one around her hair.

She'd just looked at him. "You should go back to your room. We need to get ready to head out to the air base."

He'd glanced at the bedside alarm clock, then planted a hand on the top of the door frame, blocking the doorway. "We've got plenty of time for what I have in mind."

Then he'd reached for her—and come up with a handful of empty towel.

She'd snatched it away from him, ducked under his arm, and quickly wrapped herself up again in a clear "hands off" signal.

"Um . . . did I miss a memo or something?" he'd asked, watching her rummage around in her luggage.

Her shoulders had stiffened. She'd straightened slowly, then turned to him, a pair of pink lace panties and matching bra clutched in her hand, and damn, if his mouth didn't go dry.

"Look. Cooper—"

He'd cut her off with a hand in the air. "Don't you think maybe it would make more sense if you called me Jamie now?"

"Cooper," she'd begun again after a deliberate hesitation, "I never intended for you to stay the night."

Ahh. Then he'd gotten it. She was dealing with a bad case of morning-after regrets. In deference to

her discomfort, he'd found his jeans on the floor and tugged them on. Zipping them closed, however, had been out of the question.

"Sorry about that. I guess I fell asleep."

"Yeah. Well, it happens. Let's just move on."

"Move on?"

"That was the deal, right?"

Another light bulb had finally flickered on as he mined the rubble from the explosion the Bombshell had set off last night. He'd made promises.

We keep this real . . . It's just about tonight . . . Just about sex . . . No hanging on or looking back when it's over.

Yeah, he'd agreed to all that. In the midst of getting naked for wild monkey sex, he'd have agreed to anything. He'd even been impressed that she wasn't clingy.

But this morning, being the one invited to leave, he wasn't so sure he liked those damn rules. He'd sure as hell had more than one night in mind when he'd made that promise. He'd figured they could at least continue until the end of this assignment, before they went back to the "real" world.

"Isn't this our turn?" she asked now.

Yeah, it was, and he'd been so caught up in replaying the morning conversation that he'd almost missed it.

He flicked on the turn signal and exited toward the air base, then glanced at her again. She was reviewing notes on her tablet, cucumber-cool. The earth had moved several times last night, and she'd filed it away as a one-night stand.

He drummed his fingers on the steering wheel. Hokay. That's what she wanted? That's what she was going to get.

"So what have you got in store for the poor, unknowing masses with your testing today?" he asked as they approached the security gate.

She looked up from her tablet and smiled. "They're going to be screaming for their mommies by the time I'm through with them."

He almost felt sorry for them.

At lunch, Coop grabbed a sandwich and a soda from the base commissary, headed outside, and found a spot directly in the sun and sheltered from the wind. Then he made a call that he'd put off too long.

"Hi, Mom. It's Jamie."

"Jamie who?" Rossella Cooper asked in a pouty voice. "I had a son by that name. But he must be dead, because he has not called his mother in months."

"I love you, too," Coop said with a grin as he envisioned his mother's fiery black eyes snapping with injured rage while her voice gave away her pleasure at hearing from him. "And it hasn't been months. It's been one month. Maybe a little less."

"You may be able to split hairs with your gullible women, but you can't mollify your mother as easily."

Thirty-five years ago, his Colombian-born mother had been a soap opera star in her native country.

Lawrence Cooper, an American businessman, had met her at a cast party while there on a business trip. They'd fallen in love—a storybook love at first sight—and gotten married. It had taken some convincing on his dad's part, or so his mother said, but she'd given up her career and followed him back to San Diego, where Lawrence's business was based.

She may have given up her career to marry Coop's dad and then raise Coop, but she'd never lost her flair for theatrics. And while she hadn't been a "stage mom," she'd tried her best to establish a career for him in TV or film. If Coop's heart had been in it, maybe he might have had some success. Modeling gigs were the most he'd ever gotten, but they'd been lucrative and plentiful and had kept him in cars and women until he'd enlisted when he was twenty-one.

"I'm sorry," he said, giving his mother her due. Ever since he'd come back from Australia, where he'd distanced himself from even his family for many years, he'd tried not to give her reason to worry that he'd dropped out again. "I should have called before now. So how are you and Dad doing?"

"We're fine. I'm busy volunteering at the local theater company. Your father should retire, but that business . . . Don't get me started."

Coop grinned again. This was a long-running disagreement between his parents. They were still very much in love, but she wanted to travel more, and his dad still felt the need to micromanage his exotic-wood import business.

"Where are you, Jamie?"

"You know I can't tell you that."

"Can you at least tell me if you're in danger?"

"No danger, Mom. Pretty tame assignment."

She gave up the pretense of anger and started quizzing him as only a mother could. Was he eating right? Did he get enough sleep? Was there a woman in his life?

"Yes, yes, and no." An image of Rhonda, blond hair falling across her face, blue eyes heavy-lidded with desire, flashed through his mind.

"No woman?" she asked again.

He swallowed hard. "No. No woman." *Liar, liar, pants on fire.*

"That's because you don't look for the nice girls. You always want the bad, pretty ones."

"Hey." He laughed, feeling as amused as he did defensive. "What if Dad had looked for a nice girl? What if he hadn't gone for the pretty one?"

She had no comeback for that.

He chuckled, then checked his watch. "Look, Mom. I've got to go. Duty calls and all that. I just wanted to check in."

"Promise me again that you're not in danger."

"I promise."

"And call your father," she added. "He also worries."

"I'll call him. Love you, Mom. Take care of yourself, okay?"

"I love you. Stay safe."

He thought about his parents and their relationship on and off the rest of the afternoon. By the time he wrapped up, he was feeling a little melancholy. And maybe a little cheated. He'd never wanted to be tied down in a long-term relationship. Couldn't see the value of it.

And yet—how much more could a man want out of life than what his father had with his mother? Or what Mike had with Eva . . .

24

By the time Coop had finished putting security through their paces later that day, the wind had picked up and the temperature had dropped by fifteen degrees. It was nippy, to say the least, and heading for sundown, when it would get even colder.

Rhonda was waiting for him beside the rental Jeep when he walked across the parking lot a little after 6:00 p.m., their agreed-upon meet time.

"Sorry." He quickly unlocked the vehicle. "Hope you haven't been waiting long."

"Just got here." The fact that she'd flipped the collar of her coat up around her ears and wrapped it tightly around her said she lied. Her nose was red with cold, and she didn't waste a second scrambling into the passenger seat.

"Should have some heat soon." He shifted into gear and started across the lot to the exit point.

She buried her nose deeper into her coat and shivered, and he found himself wishing he could pull over, drag her into his arms, and kiss her until her internal furnace cranked up enough to make them both hot.

But Bombshell Burns had made it very clear this morning that she would not appreciate that kind of gesture.

"I'm ready to wrap things up here," he said. "How about you?"

"Yeah. Me, too. I'm satisfied this crew is top-notch. I've got a few more tests I could run if I had to, but it would be redundant. They're in great shape."

"Except for a few minor tweaks that they've already put in place, same goes for the physical security. So are we agreed that we can move on to Utah in the morning?" That was the last stop of this trip.

"Fine by me."

Several minutes of silence passed as they headed toward the hotel.

And another night.

Which would *not* be a repeat of last night, because that's the way she wanted it.

Feeling restless and a bit out of sorts, he drummed his fingers on the steering wheel.

"You do that a lot," she said.

He glanced her way. "I do what a lot?"

"Tap your fingers on the wheel. Like you've got a song playing in your head."

"Just eager to get this next assessment in the bag and head back to Langley."

Where they hadn't come up with anything solid on the case. Where, according to the phone call from

Mike, Coop was due for extra grunt duty for withholding the information about the playing cards and designer bullets.

He didn't care. He knew Mike would cool off.

What he cared about was nailing the bastard who'd shot Eva.

She could have died. Her life over, just like that. Sudden death wasn't new to him; men had died beside him in battle. He'd had five very near misses himself and probably more that he didn't know about.

Which was something he generally worked hard not to think about. The uncertainty of life. The inevitability of death. It made him think about things he wished he'd done but had never gotten around to.

He glanced at Rhonda and, for some inexplicable reason, decided there was *one* thing he was going to do right now.

"The One-Eyed Jacks was a joint task force."

She turned her head toward him, surprise brightening her eyes.

"As you already figured out, we got our name because every guy in the unit carried a jack of hearts or a jack of spades, one-eyed jacks. The cards were symbols of solidarity, I guess. That, and we spent a lot of time playing cards between ops.

"Anyway, our unit was an experiment set up by the Joint Special Operations Command. They recruited us from three Spec Ops branches: Rangers, Special Forces, and Delta Force from the Army, Navy SEALs, and Force Recon Marines."

"You were a Marine? Force Recon?" she asked hesitantly.

If she knew about Force Recon, she knew what he'd gone through to make the grade. Everyone heard about the grueling regimen that Navy SEALs went through to make it. Force Recon was just as horrific.

"Yeah. I was. Anyway, Mike, Taggart, a select handful of other good men, and I were put together as a unit and shipped off to Afghanistan."

"Isn't that unusual? I know they perform joint missions, but an actual mixed unit?"

"It's unusual, but it had been done once before. Look up Captain Nathan Louis Black sometime."

He saw the moment it registered. "You mean Nate? Our Nate?"

"He was the CO of the first experimental unit ever, during and after Desert Storm. Jones, Green, Reed, and several more—all of the Black team were part of Task Force Mercy."

"Like you, Mike, and Taggart were the One-Eyed Jacks."

He still didn't know why he was telling her this. He'd never told any other woman. But he liked knowing that she was interested. And he liked knowing that someone other than the team and his parents knew about what happened. About what they'd all gone through.

"We're what's left of the One-Eyed Jacks."

The rest spilled out like a lava flow from a volcano.

"We'd been kicking ass all over Kandahar Province, messing with the Taliban's supply routes, destroying their ammo dumps, generally playing havoc with their entire operation." He paused as he thought back to that one brutal and deadly night.

"What happened?" She was hesitant; he could see it in her eyes. She wanted to know, and yet she didn't.

"Operation Slam Dunk happened. The brass sent us out to find out if the Taliban was still giving a local village trouble. A recon mission, nothing more. But it didn't quite go down like that.

"It was night. Mike had set the Black Hawk down like a baby in a cradle in a wide spot in the mountains. Webber—" He stopped and swallowed, thinking of his dead teammate. "Webber flew copilot. Taggart was on the mini-gun, ready to fire if we had unexpected visitors. I was running commo. The rest of the team had offloaded as soon as Mike set the bird down, heading for the village that was just over a ridge.

"We were getting worried, because they'd been gone too long. They finally radioed in to report that Taliban fighters were randomly killing the villagers, and they requested permission to engage. I got hold of our command post, and Mike relayed the urgency of the situation. They denied us permission to intervene."

"What . . . why?" The bewilderment in her tone was eclipsed only by outrage.

"The answer to that comes later. Mike tried to call the guys back to the chopper, but he couldn't raise them. We knew then that they were in trouble. Mike and Webber had to stay with the bird, so Taggart and I went out to scout."

He stopped again, his throat suddenly thick. "The Taliban had them. And we were way outnumbered. We hightailed it back to the bird, relayed the info to Mike, and he radioed command, again requesting permission to engage. They told him to stand down and wait for airship support."

"So you waited?"

"Hell, no. Mike lifted off, and we headed for the village. And all we found were bodies. All of our guys dead, along with the villagers."

He had a vague recollection of Taggart screaming at the top of his lungs, leaning on the mini-gun, and scattering Taliban in every direction.

"I don't remember a lot after that. We took a direct hit and went down. Webber was dead on impact. I was unconscious. Taggart had a broken leg. Mike had a dislocated shoulder and some pretty bad burns. Somehow, he managed to drag us both out of the bird and behind cover before the chopper exploded. Next thing I remember, I was in a military hospital. And I'd been charged with negligence in the line of duty, willfully disobeying orders, dereliction of duty, and being responsible for the deaths of my team members and innocent civilians."

"How could they *do* that to you?"

"Not just me. Mike and Taggart, too. Our court-martial was scheduled. Then, suddenly, it wasn't.

Mike had cut a deal. We ended up with less than honorable discharges, and they let us go."

"But you didn't do anything wrong! Why would Mike settle for that? Why not fight it in court?"

"That was my question. Taggart's, too. It was tough to swallow, but it looked like Mike had betrayed us. Cut himself a deal and dragged us down in the dirt with him. At least, that's what we thought at the time."

"What was his explanation?"

"He didn't stick around long enough to give us one. We wouldn't have listened anyway. *Hate* isn't a strong enough word for what I felt for him back then. Anyway, Mike dropped off the grid, ended up down in Peru, drinking his way through several years before he finally got sober. I didn't know that until later, because I dropped out, too. I found out later that Taggart had signed up with the first military contractor who would take him and ended up back in Afghanistan fighting the Taliban again."

"Where did you go?"

"I couldn't face my family. I wasn't guilty of anything, but I felt like I was. I didn't want to hear their sympathy or see the questions in their eyes that they were afraid to ask. So I split for Australia. Did a lot of surfing, some modeling, and generally tuned out. Then Eva Salinas came along."

"Eva? How does she possibly tie in?"

He dragged a hand through his hair. "It's complicated. Her husband was killed in Operation Slam Dunk."

"Oh. My God."

"She'd been told he'd died in a training accident. Then, eight years later, the file on OSD mysteriously found its way into her hands. It laid the blame squarely on Mike's shoulders, and she made it her mission to find him and make him own up to what he'd done."

"Only he hadn't done anything wrong."

"That's what she finally figured out. She and Mike also figured out that our commanding officer in Afghanistan, a man we all idolized, had set us up. He had a lucrative side business with the Taliban, cashing in on the opium trade. We'd been too effective rooting them out, and Brewster—our CO—needed to put us out of commission."

"So you weren't expected to come back from the mission that night?"

Pure rage burned in his belly. "None of us was supposed to walk away alive. The three of us ended up as pesky loose ends. He hadn't counted on us living, just like he hadn't counted on Mike making a deal that broke our spirits but saved our lives."

"So Mike didn't sell you out. He saved you."

"Yeah. Too bad it took eight years to get it sorted out and to take down the man who set us up to die."

25

_____

Rhonda ate dinner alone in the hotel restaurant that night, hoping Cooper would make an appearance, railing at herself for the all-time-stupid move of leading with her libido last night. And with her heart this afternoon.

When it became clear he wasn't going to show up, she finished her meal and headed back to her room.

Damn him, she thought, as she walked past his door. Why did he have to turn out to be a nice guy? Why had she asked him about the One-Eyed Jacks last night—and, worse, why did he have to decide to tell her about them and about what had happened in Afghanistan?

She didn't *want* to know this much about him. They were only supposed to share a few laughs and hot sex. Now she had way more insight into who he was and what made him tick than she wanted.

His story had forced her to look beyond his blatant sex appeal to the man who'd been through hell and back. He'd suffered, cut himself off from his family, his life, his friends. Even from his own country for eight long years.

She slipped her key card into the lock, then went inside and closed the door. Thank God Eva had brought the truth to light and the three men had re-united and been cleared.

It made her feel small for not sharing her own truths with him. And made her realize something that she tended to overlook: she wasn't the only person who'd experienced catastrophic loss.

She tossed the card onto the credenza, and as she walked past the bed, she remembered him there, golden and gorgeous, smiling and sexy.

And why did he have to be so generous in bed? So thorough and selfless. So sweet. And funny. He hadn't been afraid to make fun of himself; his story about Hondo had amused her . . . and softened her.

And what had she contributed? Her passion for vintage angora and a playful lie about wanting to be a cowgirl. Nothing that made her feel vulnerable. The way he must have felt this afternoon.

The way he must feel tonight.

Or maybe he actually felt liberated, as he'd said when they'd pulled up to the hotel.

"I've never told that to anyone before." He'd sounded self-conscious yet a little relieved. As if a heavy weight had been lifted from his shoulders. "Bet you're sorry you ever asked about the One-Eyed Jacks."

She was sorry, all right; she didn't want to know him that well. But she did now, whether she wanted to or not.

Thoughtful, she undressed and headed for the shower.

What would it be like, she wondered as she adjusted the water temperature, to share something that personal and that painful with him? Telling Cooper about Dan . . . wow, it hurt even to think his name . . . Would it make her feel even more vulnerable than she felt now? Or would it be liberating, as Cooper had claimed?

She'd never know. Never know what it felt like to have a man understand why she was like she was. Never experience what it felt like to have a man look at her with empathy and understanding and see more than what she'd chosen to show the world, a ball-busting flirt in a skintight sweater.

She knew she hid behind her looks—which made her no different from Jamie Cooper.

She gave the faucet a hard twist and reached for her towel. *Double damn him.*

The only thing she knew for certain was that she'd been smart to lay the ground rules last night and put a stop to their "fling" this morning.

They'd agreed that anything more than a fling would jeopardize their professional code. On top of that, it was becoming increasingly clear that if she didn't end things swiftly and cleanly, she'd have a hard time ending them at all.

Long-term was not on her agenda, and it wasn't on Jamie's, either.

She smoothed on body lotion, then slipped into a fresh blue nightie and dried her hair. Yup. She was right to have put a stop to things this morning.

So she really had no answer for why she lifted her key card from the credenza, tiptoed across the hall, and rapped softly on his door.

She had him on his back again, panting and destroyed. She'd knocked on his door, taken advantage of his complete surprise, backed him up to the bed, and annihilated him. It had taken all of five minutes—that's how quickly she'd taken him to heaven.

He swore he'd heard angel harps.

Or maybe that was his ears ringing.

Still gasping for breath, he knotted a handful of her hair in his fist and tipped her face up to his. "It . . . would seem . . . that I'm not on the same page as you . . . after all. I could have sworn this wasn't supposed to happen again."

"Are you saying you want me to leave?"

"Hell, no! Just . . . let me catch my breath . . . while I wait for the blood to get back up to my brain, so I can figure this out."

"Fine. I'll leave."

He laughed and pulled her back down. "Don't make me wrestle you. The shape I'm in now . . . you'd win. My fragile ego couldn't take it."

She rolled her eyes but relaxed and settled back against him. One long, silky leg draped over his . . . lap. Her head nestled on his shoulder. A perfect breast smooshed against his chest. His hand felt like lead when he lifted it, then slowly ran it down her back, dipping low over the delicious curve of her ass. She felt like heaven. She smelled like sin.

And he was as confused as hell.

"What changed your mind?"

She inhaled deeply, and there was no missing the self-rebuke in that breath. "It wasn't my mind that compelled me to come to your room."

"Hmm. I know *men* do a lot of thinking with their di—"

"Shut up, Cooper."

He chuckled. "Damn chemistry. Always causing trouble."

He felt her lips curve up against his collarbone. "You really *do* want me to go, don't you?"

He shifted to his side, reached between them, then touched her in that place that made her moan. "No," he whispered as his fingers finessed her tender flesh, massaging, dipping inside, until she was wet and swollen and he was hard as stone again. "What I really, *really* want is for you to come."

Much later—Coop had taken his sweet time with her—he lay in the dark, listening to her breathe as she slept beside him.

So, he thought, slowly sifting her hair through his

fingers. Her showing up was prompted only by an itch she needed scratched. At least, that's what she'd said.

But actions speak louder than words.

And she'd touched him differently from last night. With more tenderness, more . . . he wasn't sure what.

He was probably just loopy from the great sex, reading something into her touches, her kisses, her eyes when he'd risen above her. He'd never seen her so . . . open. Attentive, even caring, surprisingly vulnerable.

A rush of tenderness swept through him, along with an odd longing. What if they could take this further?

And that *was* loopy. This little interlude was as temporary as those bubbles he used to play with when he was a kid. Bright and beautiful, then gone with a small gust of wind.

They had an agreement, and he was okay with that. He had to be, since they worked together. Problem was, the more time he spent with this spectacular, free-spirited, and damn fun-to-be-around woman, the more he questioned the rules.

And more and more, he found himself thinking, the hell with rules.

He was deeper into her than he'd ever been into a woman, but last night, she'd made it crystal-clear that she'd boot him out of her bed if he started making "commitment" noises. And it was way too soon to be thinking in those terms, anyway.

She'd come here because she had an itch he could scratch.

Fact was, he wasn't sure he even cared what had brought her here. He was just damn glad she'd come.

Several times.

He grinned, kissed the top of her head, and settled in to sleep.

Friday

The easy way is always mined.

— Edward A. Murphy

26

4:14 a.m., Colorado Springs, Colorado

It took Rhonda a while to push through the heavy cobwebs of sleep and realize that a phone was ringing.

Suddenly wide awake, she sat up in bed and looked around the room, lit only by a tiny slice of light from under the bathroom door.

A hotel-room bathroom door. And not *her* hotel room.

A strong arm reached out and wrapped around her waist, pulling her back down beside him.

"Wake up—your phone's ringing," she said. When he cinched his arm tighter, she rolled away from him and out of bed. "Get the phone," she repeated.

"Time is it?" he mumbled into his pillow.

She glanced at the bedside alarm. "Four fifteen."

He rolled onto his back, then dragged his hands roughly over his face. "This can't be good."

He reached for his phone and, after some fumbling, turned on the bedside lamp. "'Lo," he said softly as she scooped her nightgown off the floor and headed for the bathroom.

Once inside, she dragged on her shift, then stared at herself in the mirror.

Her hair was a mess. She still felt a little boneless. And she had . . . She squinted and leaned closer to the mirror to get a better look.

"Oh. My. God."

A hickey on her left breast peeked above the top of her nightie. Heat flooded her face, and she closed her eyes. Unfortunately, she remembered asking him to give her one. Asking him to mark her in the heat of a very rowdy and arousing act that had apparently made her crazy.

"Rhonda." His voice carried loud and clear through the bathroom door, and he sounded wide awake now. When she stepped out into the bedroom, he was already out of bed and stepping into his boxers. "You need to get dressed. Get your things together. We're moving out."

"What's going on? Oh, God, did something happen with Eva?"

"No." He glanced over his shoulder, then crossed the room to her. "This has nothing to do with what's going on back at Langley." He pulled her into his arms and lowered his cheek to the top of her head. "Eva's fine. We've had a change in orders."

"What kind of change?"

He stepped back and cupped her shoulders in his hands. "All I know is that we're no longer going to Utah."

"Where are we going?"

"I don't know. I'll tell you everything Nate told me on the way to the airport; right now, we need to boogie. We're going wheels up at five fifteen."

Then he kissed her. "Meet me here in half an hour."

A U.S. Air Force pilot stood beside the open air door of a small business jet that was revved up and waiting for them. The pilot appeared to be in his early fifties, and, as expected from the Air Force, he was fit and trim in his flight suit.

"Captain Ramsey." Coop extended a hand after reading the pilot's nameplate on his breast pocket. He had to shout to be heard above the jet engine's roar. "Cooper and Burns, reporting as instructed."

"'Morning, sir, ma'am." Ramsey returned Coop's handshake, then shook Rhonda's hand. "I'll need to see some ID, please. Then we can get airborne."

Coop dug into his hip pocket for his wallet and credentials, while Rhonda produced hers from her purse.

Ramsey looked them over, handed them back with a nod, and lifted his hand, inviting them to board. "I'll take care of that luggage, sir, ma'am."

They'd both traveled light, with only one bag apiece plus Rhonda's tablet and purse, which had made for quick packing.

"I didn't know that the Air Force flies private jets these days," Coop said, fishing for information as Ramsey closed the air stairs behind them, shutting out the bulk of the engine noise.

"Some days we do, sir," Ramsey replied without any inflection that might reveal if this was par for the course or as out of sync as it felt to Coop.

"First Lieutenant Baxter," Ramsey said with a nod toward the cockpit, where the copilot sat.

Baxter was younger but no less professional than Ramsey, although he did execute a classic double take when he got an eyeful of the Bombshell. "Welcome aboard," he said, then turned back to the instrument panel and his preflight checklist.

"If you'd be kind enough to buckle up," Ramsey instructed, "we'll get you to your destination."

"And where exactly would that be?" Coop asked.

Ramsey slipped into the cockpit as if he hadn't heard him and shut the door.

"The plot thickens," Rhonda said dryly. "Did you notice the windows?"

Yeah. He had. They'd all been painted black— on the outside, to make certain no one inside could scrape it off. "I think this is what you call running blind," he said.

"Ya think?" Her eyes were wide and more than a little nervous. "What's going on?"

Coop lifted a shoulder as the Gulfstream eased forward and started taxiing down the runway. "Blackout measures are generally reserved for night ops, so the bad guys can't see you coming. And Air Force personnel flying a civilian jet? I've got no explanation for that."

"Does this happen often? Last-minute schedule changes, all this cloak-and-dagger?"

Thoughtful, he shook his head. "While it's unusual to go into a job without being prepped, it isn't unheard of. And the hush-hush nature of this reassignment tells me it's something big."

"What exactly did Nate say when he called?"

"Just that there'd been a change of plans. Something with higher priority had come up, and Utah was off the agenda. He said that at this point, information would be available on a need-to-know basis. Guess he feels we don't need to know yet."

He felt the g-force as the jet reached liftoff speed, and then they were airborne.

He glanced at Rhonda, who was gnawing on her lower lip but looking a little badass in spite of it. For a change, she actually looked the part of a commando. Well, sort of. She'd topped black boots and pants with a black sweater—another vintage angora—and a black wool scarf that she'd tucked into a black leather jacket. She could almost be his clone—except her sweater had much nicer bumps than his black T-shirt.

He *had* to quit thinking about how hot she was and about the ride she'd taken him on last night.

He got his head back in the game. "Look, Nate's not sending you on any mission you're not qualified to handle. We're not going to be in any danger."

"I hadn't even thought of that," she said. "I just don't like going into an assignment unprepared. What if this is some kind of, I don't know, baptism by fire? What if he's setting me up to fail?"

"You've got a bit of a problem with paranoia, you know that?"

"Just exploring all the possibilities."

"In the first place, Nate doesn't operate that way. In the second, you're an ace at what you do. This is no baptism by fire. This is not about you. So relax."

"Right. I'll just sit here and stare at the black window and think happy thoughts."

He grinned. "Might be a better use of your time if you'd try to catch a few winks. We didn't exactly sleep much last night."

Her gaze shot to the cockpit door before she glared at him.

"They can't hear us." He grinned again.

"They can if the cabin's bugged."

"P. A. R. A. N. O.—"

"Stop it. I'm cautious. And I don't like being kept in the dark. Surely you've got *some* idea about what's going on."

He shrugged. "If I were to hazard a guess, somebody—NSA, Homeland Security, whoever—picked up something out of the ordinary that concerns security at one of our top secret bases. So we've been rerouted to check it out."

She mulled that over. "Okay. I can see that."

"That's just a best guess; I may be way off. So we should try to get some sleep."

Then he closed his eyes and hoped she'd do the same.

Rhonda couldn't sleep; she was too wired. When they touched down less than two hours later, she was the first one out of the jet. Cooper followed right behind her.

The sun burned bright, and a cold wind stung her face as she took in their surroundings. She'd never been to the proverbial middle of nowhere before, but this just might be it. The airstrip appeared to be at the bottom of a shallow crater or an empty lake bed.

She bundled her jacket tighter around her and squinted at the cold, barren landscape resembling the moon's surface.

A handful of armed guards were positioned around the landing strip, and as she looked farther out, she spotted more uniformed men standing guard above them on the lip of the crater—or whatever it was they were in. Floodlights and air horns hung suspended from tall poles. And everywhere she looked, they were surrounded by tall, heavy-gauge chain-link and barbed-wire fencing.

"Holy crap," Cooper muttered. "No wonder Nate wanted this hush-hush."

She spun to face him. "You know where we are?"

"Indeed I do." He turned in a slow circle, taking everything in. "It's frickin' Area Fifty-One."

She stared at him for a long, doubtful moment before realizing that he was dead serious. "Area Fifty-One? As in flying saucers? Aliens? Roswell?"

"Add supersecret weapons and an aircraft research and testing facility, and you've got yourself a bingo."

"Holy crap is right."

While legends abounded regarding the alleged flying-saucer crash here in 1947 and the highly speculative government cover-up of the incident, the Area 51 military and research facility in Nevada was very real. Few people, however, ever got to see it up close and personal.

"Tell me what you think you know about the Groom Lake facility," Cooper said.

It took her several moments to collect herself, then sift through the stockpile of intelligence she'd gathered during her years at the NSA. "It's covered by approximately fifty square miles of restricted airspace, for starters. Originally, it was an extension of Edwards Air Force Base, and it shares a border with the Yucca Flat region of the Nevada Nuclear Test Site."

"And," he prompted.

"Well, it's a salt flat that's been used for runways for the Nellis Bombing Range Test Site. It was also a CIA test facility for several unsuccessful projects, and the government didn't admit it even existed until the last decade. Supposedly, they only 'fessed up then because any top secret operation or developmental projects had been shut down. Oh, and when aircraft talk to the tower at the air base, the controllers ID themselves only as Dreamland. And once upon a time, the base housed the Air Force's super-top-secret aeronautical facility," she finished. "They invented much of our new avionics technology here."

"Yup. There's all kinds of technology that our enemies would kill to get their hands on."

"*If* it were still developed here," she said.

The look he gave her sent a chill down her spine. "Tell me something," he said thoughtfully. "Where's the best place to hide something?"

She immediately saw where he was going. "In plain sight."

He nodded again.

"So . . . no matter what Uncle tells the world, you're thinking . . ."

"Exactly what you're thinking. That the basic mission here is still to support the development, testing, and training phases for new aircraft weapons systems or research projects, after they've been approved by the Pentagon."

"But if that's the case, why are *we* here? Why would they risk anyone outside their tightly vetted teams finding out that the facility is still in operation?"

His eyes met hers, leaving no doubt in her mind that he thought he had the answer.

Before he could share his thoughts, Ramsey joined them and handed them their luggage. Then he reached into a pocket in his flight suit, produced a small sealed envelope, and handed it to Cooper. "You'll find your answers inside. Good luck." Without another word of explanation, he climbed back up the air stairs and pulled them closed behind him.

"Why do I get the feeling something big is about to happen?" Rhonda asked as they watched the jet streak down the runway, then lift off.

Coop opened the envelope, then tipped it upside down. A zip drive fell into his cupped palm, followed by a sealed envelope addressed to the head of security.

And as a Humvee raced down the tarmac toward them, Rhonda said, "I'm starting to feel like I'm in a Tom Clancy novel."

27

A somber young MP with the lean, carved look of a hardened military cop pulled up beside Coop, stepped out of the vehicle, and asked to see their credentials. Coop gave him credit; the guy managed to check his double take when he saw the Bombshell. She had that effect on men even when she wasn't decked out in heels and a short, tight skirt.

When the MP was satisfied that they were legit, he loaded their bags into the shotgun seat, and indicated that they should sit in the rear. Without another word, he climbed behind the wheel, shifted into gear, and gunned the motor.

"Mr. Personality he's not," Coop whispered close to Rhonda's ear, hoping to ease some of her tension as they raced down the tarmac.

Apparently, Rhonda was too cold to appreciate his efforts. The side curtains were up in deference to the winter weather, but at six thousand feet, the air was brittle. And considering the light skiff of white on the runway, a snowfall wasn't out of the question, either.

Beside him, she huddled inside her jacket as the Humvee roared up out of the lake bed and onto a well-traveled road. Dead ahead, a large, low structure sat alone, like a big solitary rock in the middle of a sand beach.

Though it looked like a run-of-the-mill warehouse, Coop knew better.

Beneath that tin roof was a fortress. The exterior security reinforced that conclusion. No-fly zone. Both marked and unmarked security teams. Barbed-wire fencing, air horns, floodlights—and he'd spotted a couple of discreetly placed surveillance cameras. He wouldn't be a bit surprised if they had parabolic microphones hidden in the scant foliage on the desert floor.

So much for Groom Lake being decommissioned as a top secret R&D facility.

More proof that he was right came when the MP pulled up in front of the building and didn't have to announce their arrival. A heavy metal door instantly opened, and another MP stepped outside.

He also asked to see their creds and handed them back when he was satisfied.

Overkill. More confirmation that something hinky was going on.

He said, "Follow me, please."

"Wait." Rhonda looped the strap of her purse over her shoulder. "What about our bags?"

"You'll find them in your quarters."

"Our quarters?" Rhonda mouthed to Coop, looking wary.

That they were expected to stay here was a surprise to him, too. He gave her a subtle head shake as they followed the MP inside.

The first level of interior security was what Coop expected in a high-value target facility, more corroboration that more was going on here than the world had been led to believe by Uncle Sam.

Access was via a two-factor authentication. They were asked to press their index fingers against a biometric reader mounted on the wall, and then a middle-aged woman, as drab and austere as the gray-on-gray interior, took their photos and walked back behind her desk.

"Spooky," Rhonda said. Even though she was no stranger to covert security measures and knowing that arrangements had to have been made in advance for their fingerprints to be available to the biometric reader, it was clear she was still rattled.

"That's spooks for ya," Coop said, and actually got a little smile.

He handed the sealed envelope to the clerk. "This is for your security chief."

She took it, looked it over, and noting the DOD seal on the corner of the envelope, disappeared through a door at the rear of her small cubicle.

"Another friendly soul," Rhonda whispered with an eye roll.

Less than five minutes later, the clerk returned. "Lieutenant Dodd will be with you in a moment."

She didn't invite them to sit. Coffee from the pot on a small utility cart beside her desk wasn't offered, either.

Coop was about to ask for a cup when the cubicle door opened.

A tall, slim man with laser-sharp eyes and an Air Force uniform, so crisply pressed you could have cut paper on the crease, honed in on Coop, then on Rhonda. He didn't say a word to either of them.

"Full-access cards," he told the clerk. He handed the letter back to Coop with a look that smacked of disdain and then disappeared through the door.

Rhonda looked at him questioningly.

"Later," he mouthed, and they waited for the clerk to do her thing.

Several minutes later, they both had personal photo ID badges and total-access key cards, making them officially legit. In addition, they each had an orientation packet that was no doubt standard operating procedure for anyone visiting the facility.

"Thank you, Helen," Coop said politely, after reading the badge clipped to the breast pocket of her navy-blue uniform shirt.

Helen grunted and returned to work on her computer.

The MP materialized again out of nowhere. "This way, please."

They followed him down a short, brightly lit gunmetal-gray hallway, the same gray as on the concrete floors and ceiling. At the end of the hall, a thick, heavy door was flanked by twin cameras suspended from the ceiling.

"Fingerprint and key card, please."

Though it might seem like overkill, since they'd already been admitted inside the building, this additional measure was a fail-safe to ensure that both the outside access door and the interior access doors couldn't be opened at the same time.

They followed the MP's actions, standing in front of yet another camera for what Coop knew was a photo comparison. This final measure ensured that only the people who were supposed to be inside got inside, for the length of time they were supposed to be inside, based on what their business was. If a janitor showed up in a server farm or a secretary made an appearance in the logistics room, where neither would have any business being, you could bet that alarm bells would blast your eardrums, and the security guards would have the place locked down within seconds.

What Coop had seen so far was exactly the way he'd have set up this place. It made him itch to see the rest of the facility.

The MP opened a door to a small, sterile room, then stood back and waited for them to step inside. "This room has been made available to you for the duration of your stay. Should you need additional resources, make your needs known at the admissions desk. The commissary is on level five, as are your temporary living quarters." Then he left and closed the door behind him.

"Suppose he's got a lot of friends on Facebook?" Coop mulled as he walked over to the closed door and tested it, half-expecting it to be locked.

"Like *you've* got friends on Facebook?"

"I don't need Facebook." He grinned at her. "I've got charm."

"Just hand me that zip drive."

She'd sat down on one of two metal folding chairs at a bare-bones gray table, on which sat a state-of-the-art computer and a printer.

"Sure you want to end the suspense?"

She snorted and held out her hand. When he handed over the drive, she plugged it into a port. "So what's the deal with all the hostility?" she asked while she waited for it to open up.

"Could have something to do with this letter." He held out the letter that had been returned to him by the lieutenant.

"Just nutshell it for me," she said.

"It's from the secretary of defense. Sec Def issued the lieutenant orders to give us unrestricted access to his security plan, the facility, computers, network, and anything else we need."

"Doesn't explain why he's so hostile."

"Do you like someone checking on your work?"

She thought about that. "Not so much, no."

"Well, there you go."

When the file finally opened, Rhonda said, "It's a Word document, encrypted with ITAP code."

"Sweet. A letter from home." And it was exactly that.

The letter was from Nate Black. After they read it, Cooper sat back and assessed her reaction.

Rhonda was pretty sure that she saw shock.

"So. We're here to complete a level ten security analysis," he said.

She blinked at him. "And according to Nate's letter, we can't know what, specifically, we're to ensure is adequately secured or why there's a reason for concern about security. Nothing like working with a blindfold and handcuffs."

"Nicely put." He sounded equally amused and frustrated.

"Is this kind of secrecy typical on a field test?"

"Yeah, if we're tasked with poking holes in the security of a project that's so hush-hush that only the president, key members at the Pentagon, the secretary of defense, and those directly involved with the development, testing, and delivery of the project are in the know."

Unbelievable. "And this happens often?"

"You're familiar with the phrase 'once in a blue moon'?"

She had to let that settle. And gather herself. "So it's never happened before?"

"Nope."

She was as puzzled as she was shocked. "Why detour *us* here to do a security analysis for a project that's cloaked in this much secrecy and not let us know what we're supposed to protect? And why now?"

She must have sounded a little hysterical, because Cooper looked at her with a hint of a grin.

"This is not funny," she said.

"It is if you're expecting answers. I'm as much in the dark as you are."

"But you've got some ideas. I know you do."

Oh, yeah. And as he sat there, his brows pinched in thought, she knew he had a really good idea.

"Tell me," she said.

"Just speculation, okay? But here's what I think. The whole place is infested with private and military security, right? Some to verify IDs and others to look menacing. But since we were allowed to land, that means we'd already been cleared to be here. So why all the extra precautions?"

She didn't like where this was going.

"Let's say," he continued, "that they've got this supersecret project in the works. Maybe they've just started it and want to get ahead of the game, security-wise, and they want a thorough analysis from someone outside the loop."

"Is that what you think?"

He scrubbed a hand over his jaw. "I don't know."

"Give me another scenario."

It didn't take him long to come up with one. "Okay . . . maybe this 'project' is well into the completion phase, and they're getting jumpy and want to make sure that there's no possibility of a security breach."

"Or maybe there's been a leak," she said, feeling sick to her stomach. She'd played this spy game before, when she was at the NSA. "Maybe they're afraid the bad guys are on to their top secret project. Or maybe the bad guys *are* on to it, and NSA picked up some cyber-chatter about an attack plan and labeled it an imminent threat."

He was quiet for a long moment, long enough that

she became aware of the constant flow of stale air moving through the small room. "You may be on to something there," he finally said. "Apparently, this security check was scheduled for next week. But Nate's letter said DOD stepped it up a week because they'd picked up some chatter that concerned them."

When she managed to speak, she sounded much calmer than she felt. "He couldn't have told us this before?"

"That's how we operate. Apparently, there was no need to know until this morning."

This bit of team protocol failed to settle her down, and Cooper seemed to notice.

"Look, there's a huge difference between concern, a credible threat, and an imminent threat. There's no 'imminent' in this letter. ITAP is the top dog when it comes to security threat analysis, but Nate would warn us if he thought we were biting off more than we could chew. He'd never put any of our team in that position. And the Pentagon wouldn't put a sensitive project in that position."

"I realize ITAP's status, but I'm a rookie. Why not call in B.J. or Steph to analyze cyber-threats? Why not the entire ITAP and Black team?"

He leaned back and crossed his arms over his chest. "You don't think you can handle it?"

"Of course, I can handle it." Once again, he'd gotten her to rise to his bait, damn it.

"Well, then, there's your answer. Nate clearly thinks so, too. And so do I."

28

"As the first order of business"—Coop clipped his access key card to his jacket—"let's take the grand tour."

The extensive briefing package from Helen contained a lot of useless information. How many bathrooms, how many meals served a day, blah, blah, blah. But one piece was actually useful: a fairly detailed and comprehensive map of each floor that ID'd everything from elevators and emergency stairwells to each floor's function.

While Coop knew Rhonda was still uneasy, he also knew she'd cowgirl up and do her job. There was no bigger turn-on than a woman who felt vulnerable but refused to give in to it.

And there was no bigger fool than a man who let a distraction—no matter how demanding—interfere with his job.

So he was all business as they walked back down the hallway.

"According to this site map, besides monitoring

new arrivals, the security station on this level monitors all five levels for unauthorized persons and facility breaches. Isn't that right, Helen?" Coop asked as they reached her desk.

Still as prickly as a cactus, Helen gave him a crisp nod in reply.

"Are there surveillance cameras capable of monitoring every area of the building?" Rhonda asked.

"Not all areas. Some projects are too top secret. They don't want cameras on them."

Coop laid the map on Helen's desk. "Point out for me exactly where those particular areas are."

"Here," she said reluctantly. "Level four."

"You're too good to me, Helen. Thanks again."

After going through the access protocol to gain admittance to another hallway, they found the bank of elevators they needed. Before going to level four, though, they made a stop on level two, the first subterranean level of the building.

"According to the map," Rhonda said, "this level contains more administrative offices."

"We all know how the government runs on paperwork."

"And the computers on this level support the equipment for running the physical plant—electrical, cooling and heating, plumbing, communication. Looks like it also connects with surveillance aboveground."

The second level was a clone of level one, as Coop suspected all of the subterranean floors would be. The construction was poured concrete, more government-gray walls, and highly polished floors. The minuscule attempts at circumventing the unrelenting drabness amounted to a few neutral paintings and the occasional motivational poster.

The ceilings were covered with pipes and wire runs. Cameras blinked at every corner and doorway. He noted the emergency lighting system, the periodic fire extinguishers and water sprinklers.

At the back of level two was a stairway that he suspected connected every floor, no doubt used for emergency evacuation. He made a note to check to make certain that once someone vacated the building via the emergency door, it shut behind them and couldn't be opened from the outside. So the only way to get back into the building was through the front entry door.

Next to the emergency exit was a freight elevator large enough to move a variety of equipment.

"This is what I want to see," Rhonda said as they stepped out of the elevator on the third level. Level three was a server farm containing computers housed in multiple layers of racks. "Amazing," she said, sounding awed.

Besides the racks of computers, Coop recognized servers and supercomputers. "Overkill?" he suggested, tongue in cheek, as they walked through the floor.

"Oh, no. You've got to have a lot of computational power to design and do virtual testing of complex prototypes. And these bad boys are also tied into everything from the surveillance cameras, to the commissary inventory, to the power grid. They've got fail-safes in place, as each floor has its own network. But it's all wired through this farm, with override capabilities built in."

"Do you ever think they're going to take over the world?"

He'd hoped she'd grin, and she did.

"Level four," Coop announced once they were back on the elevator. "The labs where the brains design their supersecret toys and a major-league testing area with simulators to test them. Hence the camera-shy supersecret rooms."

"Do you suppose some of these sections are off limits even to us?" Rhonda asked as they did a quick walk-through.

Coop paused at a door marked "No Admittance." "Not according to these badges."

She tried her pass key and was denied access. "Try yours."

He was watching the red light that had blinked on above the door after Rhonda inserted her key. "It's not going to work. But I'm pretty sure it launched—"

Two security guards materialized from around a corner and raced toward them, M16s shouldered.

"—a code red," Coop finished, obeying their shouted orders by lifting his hands in the air and pressing his face against the wall.

It took a few minutes to sort things out with the guards, who finally left them with a caution.

"Do not to attempt to access *any* area marked 'No Admittance,' because it means exactly what it says."

"We were granted total access," Coop pointed out.

"If the president himself showed up with his Secret Service agents, *he* wouldn't be allowed inside, either."

Rhonda's lips had paled nearly as light as her skin as she watched the security unit leave. Her hand shook as she raked it unsteadily through her hair.

"First pat-down at gunpoint?" Coop asked cheerfully.

She glared at him. "Are you serious?"

"Actually, it was supposed to be funny."

"What *is* it with you?" she asked grumpily. "Why aren't you rattled? How can you always make jokes in bad situations?"

"Because that's how I get through the rough parts," he said, serious now. "You'll figure out your own way of coping."

"The hell I will. I don't *do* guns and bullets. I do algorithms and encrypted code and pentesting."

He didn't point out that for someone who preferred a mother board to a water board, she'd been in some pretty dicey situations lately. The fact was, for her sake, he didn't like the danger factor, either. Which was why he wanted to get this gig done and get out of here yesterday.

"What do you think's in there?" she asked, making a credible effort to pull herself together.

"Well, it wouldn't be practical to house an underground wind tunnel, especially when there's most likely one on the AFB, so we can rule that out. Same thing for building the really big stuff; you need to get materials in and out, power the machine tools, et cetera. You don't want to build an airplane down here, then have to knock out the walls to get it out."

"So?"

"So I'm betting it's a bunker, housing a major-league testing area."

"For whatever supersecret project we were sent here to protect but that we can't know about," she surmised.

"Yup. For something like that." He stared at the sealed door. "We need to get in there."

She cut him a horrified look. "No, we don't. In the first place, I don't want to know what's behind those doors. Someone might have to kill me if I found out. Second, if we were meant to be in there, we'd have been given access."

"You think anyone trying to steal it is going to give two figs about access?"

She had nothing to say about that.

"Come on," he said. "Let's go to level five and check out our temporary housing."

"I don't want to stay here. I want a hotel. Preferably in the next state." There was the pouty look that he'd come to know and enjoy.

"I'm hungry, and I think better on a full stomach," he coaxed. "Come on. We've got to work out a plan of action, then do our job and get the heck back to Langley."

• • •

Besides the cafeteria lined with long rows of tables, a complete kitchen, and vending machines, level five appeared to be where back files, old equipment, and miscellaneous furniture went to collect dust. It also provided housing for the building's environmental systems—heating, cooling, and water purification.

The living quarters were furnished with typical government-issue surplus. From the single bunks to the communal showers, a Hilton it wasn't.

But the food was surprisingly good.

"You'd better eat that." He nodded toward her lunch tray. She'd selected soup and a sandwich and coffee, but the only thing she'd touched was the coffee. "It might be a while before we eat again. You need your strength." He was starting to get a bad feeling about this assignment. Starting? Hell, he'd had a bad feeling ever since he'd talked to Nate this morning.

"How many people do you suppose staff this building?" she asked, instead of eating.

"Tell you what, you eat your lunch, then I'll let you plop yourself down at that computer, and you can hack into the system and find that information for us."

"What makes you think I can hack into the system?"

He leaned across the table to whisper, "The same thing that makes me think you had your first screaming orgasm last night."

He loved shocking her. He might have overdone it this time, though. Fire shot from her eyes, and her face flamed. He was pretty sure that if there hadn't been staff in the cafeteria, she'd have laid into him.

"Sorry," he said, not sorry at all. "It just came out."

Her hand shook with rage when she brushed her hair back from her face. "We could be bugged."

He reached inside his jacket pocket and pulled out a pen that wasn't a pen. "This little gizmo would have told me if there was a bug within ten yards of us."

"That doesn't excuse you."

"True," he agreed. "But it did accomplish what I wanted."

"To piss me off?"

He grinned. "To get you to stop obsessing about our assignment for a few minutes. Worked, didn't it?"

She blinked slowly.

"Now, eat. Then we'll go tackle access to that room."

29

Early Friday afternoon, Mike sat on the other side of Nate Black's desk, frustrated and weary.

Mike needed Coop back, but Nate had just broken the news that he'd had to divert him and Burns to Nevada. The team could use Coop's analytical mind here to deal with the investigation. Burns's, too.

"So how long are they going to be gone?"

"I don't know. I hope no more than a couple extra days. Orders came down straight from the Pentagon. NSA picked up some cyber-chatter with coded references to a high-value facility in the States."

"Which could be anywhere. Why Nevada?" He'd always figured that top secret testing was still going on at the Roswell facility, but power grids, nuclear plants, and any number of other targets could fall into the high-value category.

"Not sure," Nate admitted, "but they asked for your team specifically. Cooper and Burns were in the area, so they got elected."

"They're not going to run into something hot, are

they? Coop can handle himself, but this is Burns's first field assignment."

"No, the threat level is 'suspected,' not 'imminent.' Homeland Security's jumpy, waiting to find out when the next shoe's going to fall, and they want to make sure they're ahead of the game on this one. They decided they needed an immediate security threat analysis, and they wanted an out-of-house team.

"I've got more news," Nate added after a moment, "and it's not good, either. Barry Hill's been cleared. He had nothing to do with Monday's shooting."

"Bad news seems to be turning up all over." Discouraged and restless, Mike rose from the chair, tucked his fingers into his back pockets, and walked to the window. Five days ago, his wife had been near death's door, and they still didn't have the bastard who shot her. "We're absolutely certain Hill's not involved?"

They'd found Barry Hill on Wednesday night and had been interrogating him at Langley ever since. This morning, they'd had to let him go.

Behind him, Nate's chair creaked. "Even if his alibi wasn't skintight, he's too stupid to lie his way out of this. Too stupid to hide his amusement when he found out the team was on the ropes. The guys worked him from every angle—his known associates, their whereabouts as well as his. There's just no way to tie him to the shooting."

Mike shook his head. Hill had been the most logical suspect, and now that lead had gone bust. "What's happening on the La Línea front?"

"Interpol's all over it. Those guys are slick. But I really don't like La Línea for this, anyway. They've got a shitload of trouble right now. Between the arrest of four of their top lieutenants last week and the heat they're getting from DEA, I think their plates are full."

"So we're dead in the water."

"Never say never. The teams have been working their asses off, much of it on their own time, trying to get a lead. By the time they let Hill go, they had a whole list of other names they're working on," Nate said.

"We've got to be missing something. Something that's right in our faces," Mike insisted. "We're just not seeing it."

"We're going to get him. It's just going to take longer than we'd like."

Nate's office door flew open right then, and Carlyle flew in with it. "Mike, you need to get over to the ITAP briefing room right now."

On full alert, Mike glanced at Nate, then back to Carlyle. "What's up?"

"Package arrived in the morning mail."

"From?"

"No return address. Postmarked Toronto."

"What's in it?"

Carlyle shook his head. "No clue. But it's damn clear that it's meant for you."

Nate was right behind them as they headed out the door. "Clear how?"

"You need to see it."

All incoming mail was screened for explosives and chemical compounds before it ever made it through the front door; this included X-rays, advanced scanning techniques, and being sniffed by a bomb-detecting dog.

This particular package had been given special attention, because not a lot of people knew of ITAP's existence. So the fact that the package was addressed to ITAP, at their HQ, no less, had raised scrutiny to the five-alarm-fire level.

Both Nate's and Mike's teams were surrounding the conference table when Mike, Nate, and Carlyle rushed into the briefing room.

Remnants of their lunch had been scooped aside; the package took center stage in the middle of the table.

"The X-ray showed two indistinct metal shapes, and the chemical analysis revealed very slight amounts of burned nitrates, like those used in gunpowder and some explosives," Carlyle said. "The levels are too minuscule to be an explosive device."

Mike stared at the package. Wrapped in plain brown paper, it wasn't much bigger than a pack of cigarettes. Carlyle, already wearing latex gloves, picked it up, then turned it over. A jack of hearts with a bullet hole through the middle was taped on the back.

This was meant for him, all right.

Mike slipped on the latex gloves that had been laid out for him—lifting prints was doubtful but still a slim possibility—and fished in his pocket for his knife. Very carefully, he slid the blade beneath the tape, taking care not to do any more damage than necessary.

Long minutes later, the brown paper lay unfolded on the table, and Mike held a plain white jeweler's box in his hand.

He glanced at Nate, who nodded, and then Mike lifted the lid.

Inside, on a bed of white cotton, were two bullets.

One was a .223 Remington—at first glance, identical to the cartridge the team had found with the playing cards left behind by the shooter. The other appeared to be a 9mm.

"What the hell?" Taggart muttered as Mike set the box on the table so everyone could get a look.

"Somebody's playing games," Gabe Jones said, sounding grim.

"We need to get this over to ballistics right now." Mike looked at his team. "Carlyle, seems you've got your running shoes on today."

"On it, boss."

"Tell them to drop whatever they're doing and get us the specifics on both bullets within the hour."

"And make sure they know who's asking," Nate added, "so they'll know who's coming after them if they don't follow through."

• • •

Exactly forty-two minutes later, the ballistics report was hand-delivered.

"As we figured, the .223 is a match to the bullets found at the restaurant and at the shooter's hide," Mike told the team.

"And the other one?" Nate asked.

Mike handed him the report. "The 9mm is also an exotic designer bullet—blended metal, armor-piercing, and very antipersonnel."

"You want a quick and devastating short-range kill," Gabe said, "that's your ammo."

"It was also hand-loaded, like the .223, but that's where the similarities end." Nate handed Mike back the report.

Mike picked up the 9mm cartridge. Too many weapons to count fired 9mms. But this designer bullet would be easy to track if the shooter was in the database. Contract killers were very particular about their ammo.

"Nate, can we get B.J. on this? Though we came up blank on the designer .223, let's have her check for known shooters who may have used this particular type of load in hits within the last two to three years."

"Sure thing. Carlyle—"

"Already on the way." Carlyle lifted the report out of Mike's hands and sprinted away.

A former DIA field agent, B.J. Mendoza had resources and assets worldwide. Only a few minutes

later, the petite, pretty blonde walked into the conference room. "I got a match. There's a file an inch
thick on this shooter. Loves his hand-loaded nines; it's
definitely his signature. At least two dozen kills in the
last seven years."

"We got a name?"

"Can't name a ghost," B.J. said apologetically. "But
his mark is on hits all over the globe. No one's ever
lived to ID him, but one victim lived long enough to
give a fuzzy description." She referred to her tablet
and the report. "Short and slight, wearing black and
a hood that covered his face. That's it for physical details. But he ID'd the weapon as an H&K MP5K."

"Nasty bit of work, that," Taggart said.

"No question that it was an H&K?" Mike asked,
getting a sick feeling in his gut.

B.J. tucked a long corkscrew ringlet behind her
ear and consulted her tablet again. "Yup. The flutes
burned onto the brass from the chamber show that it's
from an H&K, and from there, we give it a very high
probability that it's from an MP5K, based on extrac-
tor marks and ejection pattern. That's apparently the
shooter's weapon of choice."

"Is either team tied to any of those hits?" Nate
wanted to know.

"Nope," she said. "The hits are a mix of good guys
and bad guys. Looks mostly political, cartel, and mafia-
related. Pick a country, he's done their dirty work."

Mike kept thinking about the MP5K. "How long
has it been since he's made a hit?"

B.J. scanned her tablet again. "A couple of years."

"What?" Taggart asked, watching Mike closely.

Mike shook his head. "I don't know. Something. Maybe nothing." *Maybe everything.* "I want to check something out. Where's Peter?"

"In his office," Santos said. "Want me to call him in?"

"No. I'll go to him."

Mike knew they were all watching him as he rushed out of the conference room, but he wasn't willing to share his hunch just yet.

In the first place, he had to be wrong. In second and third place, he had to be crazy and desperate, because what he was thinking couldn't possibly be right.

But he *was* desperate, and with Eva's life on the line, he was going to explore every possible lead until he was 1,000 percent sure it was a dead end.

"Peter."

He startled his operations manager so badly he spilled his coffee. Peter Davis spun his wheelchair around, dabbing at the front of his shirt. "What's up?"

"I need you to do something for me."

"Name it."

If Peter questioned Mike's request, he didn't say a word. He just nodded. "I'll get right on it."

"I'm heading for the hospital. Let me know the second you hear back."

"Will do."

"I need this yesterday. And Peter—for now, this stays between us."

● ● ●

Mike was at Eva's bedside when Peter called only two hours after what he'd thought would be an impossible task.

"I've got your intel," Peter said, then gave him the information Mike had both wanted and dreaded hearing.

Turned out he hadn't been wrong or crazy. Because they *had* been trying to find a ghost.

Feeling Eva's gaze on him, he turned to her. She knew him so well. Just by looking in his eyes, she knew that something big had broken on the case.

"Go do what you have to do," she whispered.

He leaned down to kiss her. "Count on it."

"When Eva found me in Lima," Mike told his and Nate's teams in the briefing room a short while later, "a shooter came after us in a hotel room on Calle San Ramón. A shooter wielding an H&K MP5K. She emptied the clip on us. Hit us with everything she had, but we nailed her—at least, we thought we had. Somehow, she got away."

"Wait." Gabe Jones held up a hand. "She? You said *she*?"

"That's what I said. When B.J. dug up the shooter whose MO was a designer 9mm bullet fired from an H&K, I asked Peter to contact one of our assets in Lima. He went to the hotel, and, as I'd hoped, not much had changed in that pit. There were still bullets embedded in the wall and the floor behind the bed in room two-oh-five."

Peter handed out hard copies of the photographs their contact had e-mailed, photos of the bullets he'd dug out of the floor in room 205 earlier today.

Mike picked up the 9mm cartridge that had arrived in today's mail. "Exact same bullets."

"Wait." Taggart looked as if a ghost had just stepped on his grave. "The shooter in Lima. Wasn't she Brewster's psycho girlfriend?"

"Yeah," Mike said grimly. "She was."

Not only had Brewster betrayed Mike, Taggart, and Cooper during Operation Slam Dunk in Afghanistan ten years ago, he had also tried to kill them at the UWD compound in Idaho two years ago.

"But she was with Brewster in Idaho. She was on the helipad when it blew." Taggart appeared more rattled than Mike had ever seen him. "I saw it blow up. You saw it blow up. Everyone on that pad died. She can't be our shooter, because she can't be alive."

"I promise you that she is." Mike set the photos in the middle of the table. "Those were bullets from her HP5K." Then he placed the full cartridge on top of the stack. "And this is a match to those bullets. She's alive—and she wants us to know it."

Then he looked at his team. "A move this bold tells me that she's done fooling around. She's coming after us again. And she's coming soon."

30

"I knew you could do it."

"Well, I *sort* of did it." Rhonda continued pecking away at the keyboard. It was closing in on three p.m., and she'd been at this for several hours. "You said you wanted to physically get into the room."

"And we will, eventually," Cooper said, peering over her shoulder at the monitor. "For now, a little covert camera surveillance is the next best thing to being there."

Since they'd been given full access to everything in the facility except the "No Admittance" rooms, as long as Rhonda could access a computer connected to the network, she could get into any part of the system she wanted—even the one place they'd been told was completely off limits.

She'd known there had to be cameras in the "No Admittance" areas. What if something went haywire in there? A test went wrong? A fire broke out? No way would they not have something in place to confirm exactly what happened.

"Hold on a sec, and I'll see if I can figure out how to control the camera."

After the long process of identifying the cameras and then isolating the one she wanted, this part was a breeze. She quickly wrote a simple script, then fed it to the camera so that anyone monitoring it would see only what she wanted seen: a shot of an empty hallway, which she'd created to block what was *really* going on while she manipulated the camera to scan the lab.

Piece of cake. Well, not for everyone. For whatever reason, hacking had always been easy for her. She'd never been able to explain her techy instincts, but when it came to computers and networks, she generally knew exactly what to do and how to do it.

"Okay." She keyed in the final command. "Here we go."

With the dummy shot in place, she guided the real-time camera and started panning the large room.

Six office cubes were lined up against the closest wall. Computers, the occasional plant, the messy desk, the OCD clean desk, and some in between. To the right of the cubicle, a long stainless-steel worktable was set up with more computer monitors, intricate robotics, and a variety of hand tools.

"Wait. Stop it there."

Rhonda stopped and squinted at the object that had caught Cooper's eye.

"Can you enlarge that shot?"

"Can a cow moo?" She zoomed in on the object and gave it a good once-over. "Is that what I think it is?"

"If you're thinking missile, you get the grand prize." Cooper leaned in closer. "Can you make a screen print of that? And a shot of the worktable?"

"Give me a sec."

She froze the frame, sent it to the printer, then zoomed in and froze several other frames, which she also printed.

"Can you access any of the computers in that room?"

"You don't ask for much, do you?"

He rubbed her shoulders as if she was a prizefighter about to step into the ring. And damn if she didn't feel one of those electric, sexual zings shoot through her. He must have felt it, too, or noticed when she stiffened, because he gave her shoulders a final squeeze and dropped his hands. "Can you do it?"

"Of course, I can do it."

He chuckled, probably because she'd sounded offended that he'd even asked. "All right, hotshot, check out the nameplates on the first cubicle. We want to look for the mad scientist who's creating this 'No Admittance' project. Holy shit—stop right there," he said abruptly. He not only sounded surprised, but he looked puzzled when she glanced up at him.

"What?"

"Does that say 'Corbet'? 'Dr. A. Corbet'?"

"Yeah. That's what it says. You know him?"

"Yeah, I know him. I'll tell you about it later. Right now, I figure we're running out of time."

"You figure right."

She didn't have to tell him why. While she'd been locating the camera that covered the inside of the lab and scrambling to get access, Cooper had been watching the hallway camera. He'd timed the fourth-floor guard's rotational pattern at every half an hour, which meant she originally had thirty minutes on her fake loop. If the surveillance team saw an empty hallway when there should be a guard making the rounds, they'd get real suspicious real fast.

"I've only got about five minutes left." She ran a quick search on the network's addresses, found Adolph Corbet, and scanned the directory for the most up-to-date files. Then she started copying.

"How's it going?"

"Almost got it," she said, willing the system to move faster.

"Better make it quick." He nodded toward the screen.

A balding, weary-looking man in a white lab coat and worn black shoes shuffled into the room.

"It's Corbet. And he's heading for his desk. Hurry up, Buttercup."

"I told you not to call me that," she muttered without looking away from the computer or losing focus. "Yes! I've got it."

She quickly saved the file, named it, and reset the

camera view to real time. Then she copied Corbet's saved files to a zip drive, deleted the logs and files she'd generated, along with her spoofing script, and backed completely out of the system. If staff security dug hard enough, they might find traces of her handiwork, but she'd covered her tracks pretty well. Even if someone found it, they'd never know what she'd been up to. Most likely chalk it up to some system glitch.

With a relieved breath, she leaned back and handed Cooper the drive. "That was a little too close."

"Welcome to the wild side."

She laughed. "Too late. I crossed over around four this morning."

To be more exact, she'd crossed over when she'd knocked on his hotel-room door, invited herself inside, and then attacked him. Libido, chemistry, abstinence—they'd all been in play. But she had never let her physical needs overrule her common sense before.

So why had she done it? And why with him? Because his story about what had happened in Afghanistan had touched her? Had made him real to her? Had made her remember what it felt like to relate and care?

Maybe all of the above. And maybe it had something to do with Cooper himself. He was more than she'd thought, more than she'd wanted him to be. And now she had more things to think about than she wanted to.

But it didn't matter what made her do it. It didn't matter what she felt or even if she thought he might care, even a little bit.

What mattered was what was real—and love wasn't. No matter how hard she'd once tried to make herself believe it, no matter how completely she'd given herself over to it, it just wasn't.

The only thing that was lasting and real was the pain that came with that truth.

Dr. Adolph Corbet. Coop could hardly believe it. A man he'd never thought he'd see again—at least, not alive.

"So what's the deal with Corbet?" Rhonda asked.

Her curiosity level was off the charts, but Coop wasn't ready to talk about Corbet yet. "Later," he said. "When we can be sure we won't be interrupted."

While he was itching to get back to their temporary living quarters and read the doctor's files, he suddenly felt an urgent need to run through some of their security.

"Can you keep yourself busy in the computer lab?" he asked Rhonda.

"Of course," she said, looking a bit perplexed.

"Then go do your thing. We'll meet up around 5:00 p.m., and I'll fill you in on Corbet then."

"You're the boss," she said, and headed for the elevator.

He stood and watched her go, suddenly filled with a niggling sense of dread for her safety.

Top-security facility.

"No Admittance" lab.

Credible threat.

Dr. Adolph Corbet.

His inclusion in this tableau was a game changer. His presence upped the stakes and the possibility of an imminent threat by about one hundred notches on the danger meter.

For that reason, Coop spent the rest of the afternoon running intense spot checks on security protocols. He poked for holes and felt only a modicum of relief when he found none.

He interviewed a number of staff about everything from food delivery to shift changes, all the time wondering about Corbet and what his role was in the "No Admittance" room. Unfortunately, he thought he had a pretty good idea.

By the time he was finished and met up with Rhonda in the computer lab, it was close to 5:00 p.m. Except for a small weekend crew, everyone else was making preparations to go home.

"I didn't think the military punched a clock," she said as several workers passed them in the hallway, heading for the elevators.

"I did some more extensive reading this afternoon, so I can fill you in on that. Most of the staff are civilian contractors. For them, it's a five-day workweek and an eight-hour day. It's Friday night. Except for a skeleton crew, this place will be a ghost town from tonight through Monday morning."

"The staff doesn't live on the base?"

"Through the week, yeah. But in about five minutes, they'll all be hopping on a jet and heading home
to Vegas for the weekend."

"A jet?"

"Special transport just for them. Most likely the
same one we flew in on."

"I'd have thought they'd be locked down here,
given the secrecy of the projects."

Coop shook his head. "Everyone on staff is fully
vetted before they even get an employment interview.
Once they're hired, they sign their life over to confidentiality clauses. And we're not talking fines for a
breach of confidentiality here. We're talking treason
if a leak is traced back to an employee. Treason and
very hard time.

"You've got to remember, too, that the facility is
highly compartmentalized," he continued. "Everyone has their place and job, and they are not to cross
boundaries into other people's business. There could
be a major project going on at one section and no one
would know anything about it at another section—or
admit it if they did. That compartmentalization is a
fail-safe in itself."

"So how many staff remain?"

"Inside, there'll be just one guard per floor, most
likely civilian contractors overseen by an Air Force
MP at the main door. Outside, they'll have one guard
positioned every eighth of a mile around the perimeter fence, which is five miles out. Another three

directly outside the bunker, patrolling the building, with direct radio contact to the AFB five miles away. If anyone tries to breach the outside perimeter, this place will be crawling with armed Air Force personnel within minutes. And some mighty big guns will be aimed at any vehicle not marked with paint that can only be ID'd through specially fitted lenses."

These security measures were reassuring, now that he knew Corbet was in the mix. If anyone came within a quarter-mile of the perimeter fence or dared to breach the no-fly zone, World War III would break out before a bad guy ever got close enough to try to get inside the building.

"So you think most of the staff are gone now?" Rhonda's question broke into his thoughts.

"There's one way to find out."

They hit the elevator and rode to the first floor.

"Access log, please." Coop waited for the MP manning Helen's desk to hand it over.

Coop scanned the list of personnel still inside the building, taking note of several things of interest before nodding his thanks. Then he gripped Rhonda's elbow and walked back toward the elevator.

"So?" she asked, once they were inside and heading down to level five.

"It's just us—except our names were removed from the log per Sec Def's request, so officially, we aren't even here. Only the MP and the five floor guards. And Dr. Corbet, who never logged out."

"Corbet's here? Isn't that unusual?"

"Apparently not. When I saw his name on the log, I looked back a few weeks. He works a lot of weekends."

"That's kind of sad. Why wouldn't he want to go home to his family?"

"Because he doesn't have a family to go home to," he said soberly.

He could see she was dying to know what he knew about Corbet, but she didn't ask again. So he gave her an opening.

"Before you dig into the data you 'borrowed' from his computer, why don't you see what you can dig up on Corbet and his family?"

31

"This is so sad," Rhonda said a little over an hour later.

They'd settled in her living quarters. Coop had plopped onto his back on her bed, his arms crossed behind his head, his eyes closed. She sat at the small desk, her tablet plugged into a network port that accessed the main network, acquiring data on Corbet.

"He was born near Ukraine. Taken away from his family by the Russian government when he was only ten and sent to a state-run school when his aptitude for science and physics caught the attention of one of his teachers. It's barbaric," she said.

"That's the good old USSR for ya." Cooper was clearly as disgusted as she was.

"You already know all of this, though, don't you? How he was rushed through accelerated classes, paraded around Moscow like some pet protégé? How he was running a government-sponsored weapons lab at the age of twenty-five?"

"Actually, the only part I knew about was the weapons lab."

That uneasy feeling she'd had ever since seeing the missile in the "No Admittance" room raised its ugly head again.

"What else did you find out?"

She read on. "He fell in love with one of his research assistants when he was in his late thirties and was only allowed to marry her after he refused to continue working for the state. That was thirty years ago. Her name is Svetlana. They have a daughter, Anna. She'd be twenty-five now." She turned in the chair to look at him. "I thought you said he didn't have a family to go home to."

"He doesn't." His face had hardened. "When he sought asylum and defected to the U.S., they didn't make the trip with him."

"How could you know that? I haven't been able to find any more information. Everything ends with him defecting."

His jaw clenched, and it was clear that he couldn't or didn't want to meet her eyes. And just like that, she knew.

"Oh, my God. You . . . you and the team. You made it happen. You got him out of Russia."

His silence was her answer.

And suddenly, she understood. There had been a cost involved in bringing Adolph Corbet to the United States. The cost had been leaving his family behind.

"Months of work. Careful preparation. Precision planning. Everything was in place," he said softly.

"But the day it went down, Anna missed her bus because of a flat tire. For sixty-eight consecutive days, that bus had picked her up from her job at exactly three forty-five p.m. and taken her to the library, where her mother would meet her, and then they'd walk the rest of the way home. On the one day that it mattered, Anna didn't make it to the library on time."

Her heart fluttered wildly. "So you left them there?"

Guilt filled his eyes. "We had no choice. Corbet was already with us. It had taken months to make that happen, and other lives were on the line. Good people had stuck their necks out for Corbet and would die if we didn't stay the course. We had to move him before he was missed. Uncle wanted him out of Russia as much as Corbet did. So we got him out."

"And Svetlana? Anna?"

"Were waiting at home when the Soviet police went looking for them."

Oh, God.

"We had a team on the ground that intercepted. They got them across the border and finally to Budapest and safety."

This was no spy story. This was real life. Agonizing, terrifying, real life in a Communist country. "How long ago was this?"

He let out a weary breath. "It'll soon be two years."

Two years. How horrible. How sad. "Why haven't they come to the States to join him?"

"Because there are eyes everywhere. They're in hiding. At least, I hope they are."

Her heart jumped again. "What does that mean?"

Again, he didn't look at her. But his tone revealed his anger. "You know what it means. If they're not hiding, then either they're dead or the Russians found them and are holding them in prison."

She was quiet for a long while, digesting it all, thinking of the suffering they'd been through. "Why do you think Corbet ended up here? At Area Fifty-One?" she asked. That, it seemed, was the million-dollar question.

"You saw the same thing in that room that I did."

The missile.

"Whatever he had in the works when we got him out of there was big. We made sure he escaped the lab with most of his research, and what he couldn't bring with him we destroyed. That's why we had to get him out that day. That moment," he added, and she knew he was again feeling guilt over leaving Svetlana and Anna behind.

He dug into his pocket, pulled out the zip drive with Corbet's copied files, and stared at it for a long moment before tossing it to her. "Now's as good a time as any. Let's see what's on this puppy."

"Here goes everything," she said, and plugged it into her tablet.

Corbet's files were thorough. And shocking. Just as shocking as the title of the first document she opened up.

"Eagle Claw," she murmured, not believing what she was seeing.

"Say again?" Cooper sprang off the bed.

"He's working on Eagle Claw. My God, I thought that was a myth."

"Scroll down. Let's see the overview."

Eagle Claw:
Hypersonic cruise missile
Speeds between Mach 5 and Mach 7
Range 500+ kilometers, the capability to reach
  any target on earth in less than an hour
Prototype includes advanced avionics GPS, radar
  terrain matching, and internal guidance
Semiautonomous terminal guidance, the ability
  to use heat signatures or radar to provide final
  targeting, results in extreme accuracy
Titanium alloy construction
Scramjet engine and a rocket booster power
Adaptable to conventional and nuclear payloads
Can launch from the ground, ship, or an aircraft

"Holy, holy hell," Cooper swore. "Do you know what this is?"

"A doomsday missile?"

"I was going to say Armageddon, but that's close enough."

"No wonder the U.S. wanted Corbet and his research."

"And what do you want to bet that the Russians

would do just about anything to get it and their scientist back?"

"Let's back up a sec." She scanned the overview again. "These are merely specs. This doesn't mean the project is anywhere near completion—or even operational, for that matter."

"You saw it. It looked pretty damn complete to me."

"Hold on. Let me check out some of these other files, see where they're really at with the production."

She quickly opened file after file. Most of them contained indecipherable equations and formulas, test runs, and databases. And there were hundreds of them.

"This is going to take a while," she said. "Looks like I'll be pulling an all-nighter."

Cooper walked restlessly to the door. "I need to figure out how to get to Corbet. I want to talk to him."

"What do you plan to do? Take out a guard?"

"It won't come to that," he assured her.

Yikes. She'd been kidding. "What if I find something here? Something you need to know about? How will I get a hold of you?" Cell phones wouldn't work in this five-level underground bunker designed to shield against electronic eavesdropping.

He dug around in his duffel and pulled out a small case. Inside were two earpiece radios. "The latest and greatest technology Uncle's money can buy."

"They're so tiny."

"Which means they have a pretty short range. Not

too sure how well they'll work in reinforced concrete, but we'll give it a go."

He turned one on and handed it to her before carefully fitting his in his ear, making sure the appropriate tab lay against his cheek.

When she struggled with hers, he reached up and helped her. "This tab stays against your cheekbone. It's a bone-conduction microphone. You don't have to key anything to transmit—just speak as clearly as you can."

"Pays to have spooky friends, huh?"

"Let's hope so. Don't wait up for me."

As he headed for the door, she said, "Don't do anything stupid."

Two minutes later, she heard his voice in her ear. "Hondo to Buttercup, do you read me?"

Despite herself, she grinned. "Burns to Cooper. Some nitwit intercepted our private line. If you see him, shoot him. Over and out."

32

She wasn't smiling an hour later. She'd finally found what she'd been looking for.

Big, scary stuff.

She touched a finger to the radio tab against her cheek. "Cooper. Get back here. Now."

"What's up?"

"Just get back here."

"On my way."

She paced as she waited, almost bursting with panic when he finally walked in the door five minutes later.

"Eagle Claw is way past its testing stage," she blurted out. "It can be ready to go into production in a matter of days."

He eyed her thoughtfully. "You sure?"

"I'm sure. That killing machine is ready to go." She ripped the earbud from her ear and tossed it onto the table. "What the *hell* is DOD thinking? Something this cutting-edge, with the capacity to elevate military power to world domination, and which the government has sunk billions of dollars into—why the hell wouldn't they already have security nailed to the wall?"

His expression had grown dark, and she could see he had the exact same questions.

"They'd *have* to have this wrapped up tight," she continued. "There can be *zero* chance that Russia gets this technology back. Or what if North Korea or Iran or any other badass regime got hold of any part of the working plans or the alloys?"

When he still said nothing, she let it all out.

"Why the *hell* don't they have this facility armed to the *gills*? I'm talking antiaircraft guns, Phantom jet patrols, hell, a battalion of Marines!"

He met her eyes then, and she knew she wasn't going to like what he had to say. "Because they don't know that Eagle Claw is ready to go," he speculated, his words hanging in the room like a black cloud.

"How can that be?"

"Maybe because Corbet hasn't told them."

She let that idea take shape, congeal, and finally form. "You got in to see him? Is that what he told you?"

He gave a quick shake of his head. "No. I didn't get in to see him. Short of explosives, no one's getting into that room unless Corbet gives them access. You need to keep searching his files," he said abruptly.

"What exactly am I looking for?"

"Anything in duplicate. Progress reports. Timelines. Any files that seem redundant."

"Now that you mention it . . ." She turned back to her tablet and scrolled through Corbet's files. "There *are* a lot of copies of the same files. I only opened the originals. Hold on."

She went to work and soon came up with a frightening pattern.

"He's cooking the books," she said finally. "Providing a progress timeline to DOD and keeping another timeline for himself."

"And?"

"And," she said, her alarm building, "according to the timelines he's been turning in to DOD, Eagle Claw is a good three months away from completion."

She looked up at Cooper, who had stopped pacing.

"Why would he do that?"

She could see him attempting to frame all the pieces they'd uncovered into a cohesive picture. When he turned to her, she could tell that he had it all worked out in his mind. "We were sent here because of a vague but credible threat, right?"

She nodded, giving him time to pull it all together.

"We find that security is tight but not on red alert. We've got ourselves a Russian scientist who defected with his plans for a doomsday missile. A scientist who apparently has attained his mission but fudged his reports to the Department of Defense, so they have no way of knowing that Eagle Claw is mere steps away from being operational."

She swallowed hard, afraid she knew where he was going with this.

"A scientist," he continued, "who hasn't seen his wife and daughter in two very long years and who, according to all the data you've found, has worked day and night to complete his task." He looked at her sharply. "The Russians got to him. That has to be it. Somehow they got someone on the inside and got to Corbet. What do you want to bet they're using his wife and daughter as bait for blackmail?"

"They want their Eagle Claw technology back," she said as the horrible realization gelled. "And the only way they can make it work is if they get Corbet, too." She looked him squarely in the eyes. "They're going to attack this facility to get it, aren't they? They're coming after Eagle Claw and Corbet. *That's* the credible threat."

He looked at her long and hard before reluctantly nodding. "Yeah. I believe it is. The big question is, when are they going to make their move?"

"We've got to get word to Nate," she said urgently.

"And how do you propose we do that? We're as locked in as the facility is locked down. We're not getting out of here until Monday morning, when the staff return from Vegas."

He was right. Once you stepped into the bunker, all contact from the outside world ceased. That had been built into the security program. Clever, and exactly what she would have done. Until she urgently needed to contact someone on the outside. "What if we don't have until Monday?" She hated even asking. They both looked at the wall clock. It was a little after nine p.m. The longest Friday of her life—and it was about to get a lot longer.

"I'm going to go talk to the guards and the MP," he said. "Give 'em a heads-up to be extra alert and see if any of them are in the loop on a contingency plan to bust our asses out of here or if the plan is to go down with the ship."

"I'll head for the server farm," she said. "Maybe I can find a way to circumvent the system and somehow reach Nate. Or even the nearby Air Force base."

"My money's on you," Cooper said.

"Normally, I'd agree. But from what I've seen, even though interior communication can be breached by someone who knows what they're doing, getting outside contact is a whole other ball game. If I manage to find a way, it's going to take a while."

"Keep something in mind, Buttercup, we're merely speculating here. What we've got is valid, and we should assume the worst and be prepared. But with the no-fly zone an exterior security, the odds of anyone even getting close to the bunker are almost nonexistent. There's every possibility that we'll spend a dull weekend playing gin . . . or strip poker?"

"Nice try, Hondo. But I've got a very bad feeling about this."

He picked up her earbud and handed it to her. "Don't leave home without it."

She slipped it into her ear and headed for the door. His hand on her arm stopped her. "You okay?" He searched her eyes intently. "I know you didn't sign up for this."

She was as okay as a woman who had applied for a desk job but had ended up in the middle of a possible siege situation could be. "Got my badass outfit on," she said with a weak smile. "How could I not be okay?"

He grinned and pulled her against him. "You *do* look pretty badass in black."

Then he kissed her. She moved into him, wrapped her arms around his neck, and pulled him close. He was the only thing that would hold her together if this weekend turned into something she had no preparation for.

When he pulled away from the kiss, he pressed his forehead to hers, still holding her. "Nothing's going to happen to you as long as I'm drawing breath, Buttercup."

"Gosh. I bet you say that to all the computer nerds."

He grinned. "Nah. Just the ones who smell good and wear my hickeys on their breasts."

She felt herself redden but wouldn't give him the satisfaction of letting him know he'd embarrassed her. "I'll be sure to think about that while I do my nerd thing."

Saturday

If the enemy is in range, so are you. When you're short of everything but the enemy, you're in combat.

—Infantry Journal

33

Twenty-five thousand feet above Nevada, twenty-five miles north of the Groom Lake Air Force facility, the Boeing 727 flew through the early-morning hours, following the route commercial airliners used going to and from Vegas. Vadar Melnik looked at the men assembled in the darkened hold of the jet. Only his second in command, Ivan Grachev, noticed his concerned scowl. Ivan nodded, his look saying, *They'll be fine. They are ready.*

They'd better be more than ready. They'd been training for months. Waiting to get the call. Not, however, expecting the timeline to be stepped up this quickly and on such short notice.

He thought of the assassin he knew only by the code name Anya.

She had too much influence. She'd altered the plan by not eliminating the U.S. government's biggest thorn in his side. Cooper, Taggart, Brown, and their friends should be dead by now. But no. Anya had thought it unwise. Worse, his employers agreed with her that it was much smarter to pick them off one by one over time, to keep the attention away from Mother Russia.

She also had too much control over the soon-to-be-dearly-departed Dr. Corbet, who had had the bad sense to defect to America and to take his Eagle Claw research with him. Once they got what they needed from him, his reward would be death, the same fate that his wife and daughter would meet.

That was what this raid was all about. In the early hours of this Saturday morning, they would bring home both Dr. Corbet and his technology and ensure Russia's military domination. And it was happening tonight because Anya had said this was their only window of opportunity.

He didn't trust her. But he had no choice.

He glanced again at Ivan, who looked secure in his place, secure in their mission. And he put his trust in Ivan's assessment of the team's readiness.

Ivan had been at his side since they were both Spetsnaz, Soviet special forces. At the end of the Cold War and with the collapse of the Soviet Union and the turmoil following, their skills had no longer been required. At least, not for many years.

But there were new games to be played in the twenty-first century. And the Russian mafia, working closely with Putin's enforcers, had once again made Vadar a key figure in the order. An order that paid him well to deliver, instead of the pittance of a soldier's wage.

The men with him tonight were hand-picked for this mission. All had advanced parachute infiltration skills, except for the two technical support specialists, who were merely baggage as far as he was concerned but necessary according to his employer.

For the jump, the two techs would be strapped to Nikolai's and Pavel's backs, like the explosives and weaponry the other jumpers would be carrying. Vadar shifted in his seat, where the parachute harness dug into his ass. Like his men, he carried seventy pounds of gear. It was a challenge. He wasn't as young as he used to be. And he hated the metallic taste of the oxygen that flowed into his mask. He looked forward to switching to the bailout bottles strapped to his harness which would be used to get them down to where the air was thicker.

He checked the altimeter on his wrist. Altitude twenty-five thousand feet. Air temperature minus forty-one Celsius. He went through the operation plan in his head for the hundredth time—there could be no room for mistakes. When given the go, they would jump, deploy their parachutes, group together in a "stack," and guide themselves onto the target base using GPS. The high-altitude, high-opening, HAHO, jump was necessary for this mission. If they flew in low, radar would pick them up. By flying high above the no-fly zone surrounding the base, they'd be too small to detect on radar. And by landing precisely at their planned coordinates well inside the perimeter fence, they would avoid all but a handful of exterior guards.

Once at the base, the plan was to get in, get Dr. Corbet and all technology related to Eagle Claw—the technicians were insurance, in case Corbet refused to cooperate—and get out, commandeering vehicles from the base to drive to the preset location, where a team would be waiting to extract them.

This jump would be Vadar's forty-second combat jump. The rest of his team had similar experience, some in Chechnya and others as far back as Afghanistan. Mavriky Shirshov, his team sergeant, was a veteran of brutal combat and an animal in battle.

His second in command, Ivan Grachev, had fought alongside him in Chechnya and had once taken a bullet for his commander. Ivan was smart, tough, adaptable, and quiet; the fact that he also liked to torture prisoners was a plus. He could get a stone to talk with the tip of his blade, if the need arose.

Vadar fingered the M4 rifle strapped to his harness. American-made, all the way. They were to leave no trace that Russia was involved in the attack. Which also meant no witnesses. With Mavriky carrying the M249 machine gun and the rest of them with M4s, that was ensured.

Intel on the staffing had been thorough. The perimeter security would be tight and fully manned, but he had no concern about that. They wouldn't drop within four miles of it. Since the manned fence was the first line of resistance, the security around the actual building would be light. Only a skeleton crew, inside and out, during the weekend.

This obsession with weekends would become America's downfall.

The red light above the door lit. Five minutes to jump.

The men struggled to their feet, fighting the heavy loads, then disconnected from the plane's oxygen system to their bailout bottles. Without prompting, they checked one another's gear, making sure that it was tight and strapped right. Yes, he had a good team. He'd paid a lot of money for the best in the business and fully anticipated both the rush from the jump and the money he'd net from this job.

Using hand signals to communicate over the roaring jet engines, Nikolai and Pavel strapped on their unwilling technicians. Pavel had to cuff his behind the ear to get him to stop struggling.

When everyone was upright, he motioned for them to put on their night-vision goggles as he shut off the cargo hold lights. Another good American piece of equipment. The NVGs in the Russian military tended to freeze solid at this altitude. It was difficult enough to jump out of a plane in the dark, and restricted vision meant you couldn't see the team. It gave jumpers nightmares, because collisions at the speeds at which they were going to fall could be fatal.

In the greenish glow of the NVGs, Vadar made his way to the cargo hatch door and opened it. Wind tore at his body, threatening to rip him out the door. The sky was lit by the moon and stars. He couldn't see the ground, but that was never a problem; it was always down.

Ivan made his way to the front so he would be the second one out the door. Vadar checked Ivan's gear, then turned so Ivan could do the same with his.

Satisfied that they were both strapped in tightly, Vadar glanced back at his men. They all gave him a thumbs-up.

Then he stepped back far enough to see the jump light that glowed white instead of green through his NVGs.

When the light changed color, he stepped out into the icy darkness and into free fall.

34

Rhonda had always looked at a computer system like a big jigsaw puzzle. Once you had the corners in place, then the borders, you could figure out a general picture. Even if the important details were jumbled, it was always solvable, given enough time. And the computer system at the Area 51 facility consisted of layers upon layers of puzzle pieces, all of them mixed up, all of them testing her patience and her stamina.

It had been a long day after a short night — although she wouldn't have traded that night with Cooper for more sleep. At least, that was how she felt at 1:30 Saturday morning. Fatigue had done a damn fine job of mellowing her out in the Jamie Cooper department.

The problem was, that mellowness was also a sign that she was losing her edge. And it was slowing her down.

She'd been working the system for over four hours, and she was close, she thought, as she suppressed another yawn and continued to tap away at the keyboard. She knew that she was close to finding the

worm hole that would allow her to burrow out from
under all the security blocks and make contact with
the outside world. But repeated attempts that resulted
in slamming into brick walls finally had her frustrated
to the point of pulling her hair.

Literally.

She shoved herself up out of her chair and glared
at the computer monitor. "You are the queen bitch
of the world!" When she realized she was yelling at a
machine, she settled herself down.

What was she missing?

And where the heck was Cooper? He should have
schmoozed those guards by now. Should have been
back with some good news. Like he'd found a trap
door that led outside. Or he'd discovered a time con-
tinuum that could transport them back to Langley
and reinforcements.

"I've got to get out of this room and make a fresh
pot of coffee," she muttered. And maybe take a quick
shower to wake herself up before digging back into
the system again.

Where *was* that man?

She'd tried to reach him several times just to see if
they could keep in touch. Another go at it wouldn't
hurt. "Hey, Cooper. You out there?"

When she stepped out of the room, she saw that
the lights had cut to half power in the hallways. Probably because it was night and a weekend.

She went back into the computer room, rum-
maged around until she found a flashlight, then re-

turned to the hall, more jumpy than she'd like to be. And because she knew she'd probably panic alone in a semidark elevator, she decided to take the stairs. Not that the dark, shadowy stairwell was much better.

"Cooper? Where the heck are you?" she asked again, feeling more uneasy as her boot heels echoed in the long, empty corridor.

This place was spooky enough when it was fully staffed and knowing it was daylight aboveground. In the middle of the night, with nothing but her own shifting shadows dancing against the stairwell walls, it was enough to make a grown woman downright jumpy.

When he finally answered, she did jump. "What's up, Butter—"

"Do *not* call me that," she snapped, cutting him off as she pressed a hand to her racing heart. "I'm tired, I'm cranky, and I'm a failure to boot."

"Poor Bombshell," he soothingly. "You've had a long, hard day."

She waited several beats. "What did you just call me?"

A guilty silence rang over the line. "Call you? I didn't call you anything."

"You called me Bombshell."

"Oh . . . oh, that. No. No, what I said was, it would take nothing less than a bombshell to break us out of this bunker."

She didn't buy it, but she was too tired to raise a fuss. "Whatever. I'm heading for the commissary. Putting on a fresh pot of coffee. Then I'm taking a quick shower to wake myself up before hitting the system again."

"I could use coffee," he said. "And I could use a shower myself. Maybe we could—"

"Conserve on energy and shower together? That's not happening."

"Actually, I was going to suggest that maybe we could take turns with a short combat nap."

She finally smiled. "That is *not* what you were thinking."

He laughed. "I guess my mind's not nearly as complex as those computers. See you by the coffeepot."

The jump went exactly as planned. There had been no radar detection; otherwise, the entire compound would be lit up, with horns blaring right now. They'd landed a little farther from the planned drop zone than Vadar would have liked, but taking the wind into account, a slight deviation was to be expected. The good news was that they were a quarter of a mile closer to the target building than had been planned.

And when humping fifty to seventy pounds of gear, a mile hike was much preferable to a mile and a quarter.

Once all the men had gathered, they fell in line in single file behind him, with Ivan pulling up the rear. No words were spoken. Everyone knew his assignment.

Even in the bitter cold night and with the shorter walk, Vadar was soaked with sweat inside his American fatigues. Adrenaline still ran high in the wake of the jump—falling twenty-five thousand feet never became routine—so despite the uneven terrain and their heavy loads, they easily hiked what would normally be an arduous trek. It took less than twenty minutes to reach the target.

He checked his watch as they bellied down behind a berm at the rear of the low building. They were exactly on their timetable.

First course of action: take out the three guards patrolling the exterior of the building. Vadar lifted a hand, and three members of his team immediately crept forward, low and slow.

He waited for the first cough of the sound-suppressed M4 rifles. The second and the third shots were mere seconds behind. Three shots, three down. Now nothing remained between them and the inside of the building but a little finesse.

He took a measured look around. Other than a tumbleweed blowing past, there was no activity. Assured that they'd raised no red flags, he stood and motioned for the remaining team to follow.

As a group, they approached his three gunmen. Along with the guards' uniforms, each held a badge and the bloody forefinger of the guard he had killed.

Vadar selected a uniform that fit, took the badge and the finger that went with it, and slipped on the uniform. Quickly moving to the security scanner, he slid the badge through the magnetic reader and was prompted to verify with his fingerprint. He pressed the dead guard's finger against the scanner, and the lock clicked.

He quickly opened the door and held it for all but the three team members who were hiding the bodies of the dead guards. Then they would keep watch outside, posing as facility security.

"What the hell are you doing in here, Leonard?"

The MP behind the desk couldn't see who had entered, but he knew the exterior door had been opened.

Vadar walked to the desk and shot the shocked MP between the eyes before he could reach for his gun.

Behind him, Ivan quickly checked the rooms directly off the security desk and nodded to Vadar. "No one else."

"Matvey."

The computer tech, still out of breath from the hike and his first experience at jumping—not to mention witnessing the cold-blooded execution of four men—shook as he stepped forward. "Sir."

"You know what to do."

Matvey Polzin shrugged out of his pack and sat down shakily in front of one of the computers in the security room. Ivan had assured Vadar that Polzin knew his tasks and had been instructed in exactly what he needed to do: take control of the security system, and allow the rest of the team into the areas they needed to access.

"How many more guards in the building?" Vadar asked.

Polzin scanned the printed log for any employees who remained in the bunker.

"As our sources reported, one for each floor, sir. Plus the military policeman who has been . . . taken out of commission."

"Anyone else?"

"No one except Dr. Adolph Corbet, who is in his lab, as anticipated."

Vadar smiled. So the doctor did not break his promise. Amazing what a man would do when he believed he could prevent the death of someone he loved. And Corbet, it seemed, would do anything, including betraying the country that had given him asylum.

Ivan had opened a secure cabinet and taken out several pairs of radios. He handed them out to the men, who set them to a common frequency.

One man was then assigned to each floor. Their mission was to eliminate the single guards roaming each hallway. Matvey would assist them by monitoring the cameras and alerting them of each guard's position, using the main radio.

Vadar glanced at a diagram of the facility. As their mole had told them, Corbet would be in his laboratory on level four.

"Quickly," Vadar said, and his team scrambled after him and gathered in the hallway outside the security office. He held up his watch. Fifteen minutes was all the time they should need to accomplish their task.

Vadar felt a flash of satisfaction as he watched his men deploy, heading for the stairway to execute their mission.

Keeping Ivan and the other tech, Iosif Yakovlev, with him, Vadar returned to the security desk. There he waited, watching the cameras. He anticipated that it would take no more than ten minutes for his men to eliminate all five guards.

However, he had learned long ago that all was not always as it seemed. He would wait until he was assured that all threats had been eliminated. And then he would head down the stairwell toward the fourth floor and the prize that would make him a wealthy man.

Rhonda had revived herself on fresh coffee, then ducked in and out of a quick shower. Marginally refreshed, she set up shop at the small table in her assigned room instead of trudging up to the server room. Since there were no in-house computers in the living quarters, she plugged her tablet into the data port.

In his own room, Cooper was still in the shower. She would have figured he'd fallen asleep in there, if she didn't know he was as ramped up as she was trying to figure out a contact to the outside—

Whoa.

She sat up straight, fingers frozen above her keypad, her gaze locked on her tablet.

What the heck?

Maybe she was seeing things. Maybe her screen hadn't just gone black, then popped back to life—but on a totally different drive from the one she'd been on.

She closed the program, keyed in the commands to return her to—

Startled, she blinked. There it was again. The black screen, then an instant return to a setting that took her to the security cameras.

What the hell? She'd lost control of her tablet.

She sat back, staring, thinking. Had the "worm" she'd planted to test cyber-security tomorrow morning gone glitchy? Started up before she'd given the command?

There was only one way to find out.

She accessed the "worm," removed it, and started in again.

And again, she went somewhere she didn't want to go.

Okay, she was tired. Maybe she'd left something open when she'd been working in the server room. Maybe the network port here in her room wasn't as fully connected to the main servers as she'd been told.

Whatever it was, she couldn't work like this. It was as if someone had taken control of her programs . . .

Her thoughts snagged—and stopped.

But that couldn't be. Someone couldn't have taken over her programs. There was no one here with a reason to do it.

"Wake up and figure it out, Burns," she muttered. "This ain't rocket science."

Still, she couldn't shake the feeling that something bigger than a faulty network port was the problem. It was as if the system was fighting her once she had gained access to it, but it seemed as though there was another presence on the network.

Just for giggles—at least, that was what she told herself—she grabbed her badge and the flashlight. Then she headed down the dim hall to what she knew was a janitor's office.

Her badge got her into the room. The tiny office reeked of stale coffee and, except for the nude pinup of a buxom blonde on the bulletin board, was pretty much standard government issue.

She settled down in a battered chair and fired up the desktop computer. If it worked the way it should, then she'd know that the network port in her living quarters was the problem. Or that her tablet couldn't, for some reason, handle the magnitude of the data she was attempting to access. Since all the in-house computers were on the same network, she should have full access to everything in the building.

She opened up another window on the screen and checked the network usage map. And found something *else* odd. The security office on the first floor was utilizing a lot of the network resources—too much for a weekend skeleton security crew and no apparent physical security breaches. Was the MP on duty up there bored and playing solitaire and masking it with some data manipulation?

She watched for several more minutes, then keyed up a program—and *bam!*

It reverted back to something she hadn't even tried to access.

What the *heck* was going on?

She keyed in the part of the network that ran the cameras and saw what appeared to be a great deal of camera activity—as if someone was searching the facility the same way she and Cooper had searched earlier today, when they wanted to get a look into the "No Admittance" room. Was this activity preprogrammed as part of weekend surveillance?

Then an unfamiliar command scrolled across the screen. Based on her previous explorations, it might have something to do with the fourth floor. Corbet's lab?

Was Corbet somehow manipulating the cameras? Or was he using such a large volume of the server's capacity that the system couldn't function properly? It hardly seemed likely, but she was going to find out.

But first, she had to go back to her room for the notes she'd taken when she'd isolated the camera for Corbet's lab. Without them, it could take hours to find that specific camera again.

Flashlight in hand, she opened the door and stepped out into the hall.

And stopped cold when she heard footsteps. In the stairwell. Where none should be, in the almost-empty facility.

Heart slamming, she eased back into the janitor's room, turned off the lights and the flashlight, and stood there, the door open a crack, her heart beating so hard and fast she felt light-headed.

The stairwell door opened. Then closed.

Relax. Relax. It's only the security guard.

But some sixth sense told her to stay quiet. So she did—and she thought about the computer glitches and the cameras searching the floors.

Feeling a sudden urge to contact Cooper, she reached for her earbud—and realized she'd left it in her room after her shower.

She squinted through the tiny crack between the doorway and the frame . . . and saw a dark figure. Carrying a big gun.

Then he spoke.

And it sure as hell wasn't English.

She didn't know what he'd said or whom he'd said it to—maybe he had a radio—but that language had no place in the bunker.

So close to panic now that she thought she'd pee her pants, she forced calming breaths, waiting for him to continue down the hall.

When she no longer heard footsteps, she counted to ten.

Then she counted again.

Only because she had to get to Cooper did she find the courage to leave the room. She inched the door open, carefully checked to make sure the hall was empty, searched and found the little red eye that was the surveillance camera, and waited until it swiveled in the opposite direction from the living quarters.

And then she ran like hell.

35

"Wake up!"

He wasn't asleep, for Pete's sake. He'd just lain down to rest his eyes for a sec.

"Cooper! For God's sake, Cooper. Wake *up*!" A hand smacked his face hard.

He reared straight up in bed. "What?"

Then he saw her face, and the cobwebs cleared real quick.

He shot off the bed, gripped her shoulders with both hands, and held her steady. "Settle down. Tell me what's got you so spooked."

"A man. In the stairwell."

"Yeah. Probably the gua—"

"*Not* a guard," she cut in sharply. "Not *our* guard, anyway. He wasn't speaking English."

He instantly clicked over to red alert. "What was he speaking?"

"Russian."

He slid into his pants, stepped into his boots, and pulled a shirt over his head. "You sure?"

"Had to be. I was in the janitor's office, checking whether the computer worked there, because something hinky was going on with my tablet."

Hinky did not sound good. "Hinky how? And make it fast."

"I couldn't keep control of it. I thought maybe there was a problem with the network port in my room. But now I think someone's manipulating the computers, because the same thing happened when I tried to use the computer in the janitor's room. The surveillance cameras are being manipulated, too, so that means there's more than one unknown person here."

Coop swore under his breath as he quickly tied his boots.

"What do we do?"

"*We* don't do anything. You stay here. I'm going to go check it out. Lock the door behind me. Don't open it for anyone but me. Got it?"

She nodded like a bobblehead.

"Deep breaths, Rhonda. And put in your earbud."

Coop didn't travel with weapons on security gigs, and he sure as hell wished he had one now. He made sure his Emerson knife was in his pocket, ready to go. The blade was short but tough enough to cut himself out of a crashed airplane if the need arose.

Conscious of where the security cameras were

pointing, he slid into the hallway, eased along the wall, then hotfooted it to the stairwell door.

He cracked open the door and listened carefully. He hated stairwells and this was his second "fatal funnels" of the week. Even someone shooting blindly could get lucky with a wild shot. They also had a lot of dead spaces to set up an ambush.

And there it was.

The sound of someone breathing. Then muttering into a radio. Rhonda was right about the language. Coop's Russian vocabulary was fairly limited, but he recognized it when he heard it.

Sonofabitch.

Somehow this guy had breached the building. And Rhonda was right: if there was one, there were more. The facility was under attack.

He dragged a hand roughly over his jaw, assessing his options.

Slim and none. He had a single-blade knife, the element of surprise, and a woman with no experience in hand-to-hand combat.

So, bottom line, he was on his own. First order of business: reduce his opponents by one. Then arm himself with more than a pocketknife.

The Russian was on the landing above him, still speaking into a radio. Had he lifted it from the main entrance, or had he taken out one of the weekend guards? His money was on the latter, which meant he was most likely dead.

Very quietly, Coop pulled out the Emerson, then ran the back side of the blade across the metal framework of the stairs just above his head, making a scratching noise.

That should do it.

The Russian went silent and then started down the stairs. When he hit the last step and wheeled around the corner, Coop jumped out from under the steps, startling him enough that he lost focus.

Coop chopped the rifle barrel of an M4 away, stepped into the Russian, and jammed his knife into the soft spot beneath his ear. He twisted the blade, and the man sagged against him, dead before he hit the floor.

He quickly searched the body—standard-issue gear from the U.S.A.—and felt sick to his stomach. Had he killed an American soldier?

Then he ripped open the dead man's shirt, saw the tattoo on his chest, and knew exactly what he was dealing with.

Spetsnaz. Former Soviet Union special forces. They made the KGB look like newborn puppies.

The radio crackled.

He was fluent in Farsi and Arabic but knew only a little Russian—but he'd bet his life that this was a routine check-in. On a deep breath, Coop picked up the radio, keyed the mike, and took a shot at it. "Yes, I am fine," he said in Russian.

At least, that's what he hoped he said, and he counted on the static from the mike covering his horrible accent.

After a lengthy pause on the other end, the radio squawked again.

Okay. Whatever the guy said was beyond him. Time to beat feet.

He slung the dead Russian's rifle over his shoulder, grabbed his extra magazines, and, dodging the camera, dragged the body back down the hallway of the living quarters.

"Oh, my God."

He looked up and saw Rhonda in the hall.

"I told you to stay inside. Since you didn't, hold the door open."

She stood back as he dragged the body into the room. "Russian?" she asked in a shaky voice.

"'Fraid so. Former Spetsnaz."

He pulled back the man's shirt and showed her the tattoo of a bat on a yellow and blue field with Cyrillic letters surrounding it.

"That's their gang tat. These are hard-core warriors, the Russian equivalent to the Navy SEALs but a lot meaner and without any integrity."

"So we're under attack."

"Hell, yes."

He quickly stripped the body of the harness containing more ammo pouches and put it on. Then he slid the dead Russian under the bed. He'd hoped to find a handgun so he could arm Rhonda, but no such luck.

"How did they get in here?" she asked.

"Best guess? High-altitude, high-opening parachutes. Radar can't detect them. They land inside the perimeter—don't have to deal with the guards on the fence that way. Take out the three guards patrolling the building, use their ID to gain entry. Done deal."

"I don't suppose now is a good time to point out that you're the only thing standing between God knows how many Russians and Eagle Claw?"

He had to grin. "You stated that obvious point very well."

"What are we going to do?" she asked, clearly scared to death but with enough fire in her eyes that he knew she was hanging in there.

He looked at her. Really looked at her. Past the wild eyes and the messy hair, past the natural beauty that would always take his breath away. He had to get her out of this. He had to get them *both* out of this, because he damn sure wasn't through with this woman. And he had to keep the Russians from getting Eagle Claw, or there wouldn't be a world left for him and her to really get to know each other in.

"Okay," he said, coming up with a plan. "I don't know how many we're up against, but if I'd planned this op, I'd run it lean. Maybe three men positioned outside. One man on each floor to take out the guards. A couple of computer techs to gather data off Corbet's computer. Two, maybe three more, just for insurance. So maybe thirteen. Now twelve. And I'd want to get in and get out fast."

He thought for a moment. "If I can get you to a computer, can you gain control of the cameras and the system again?"

"Damn right I can."

"Then that's our first priority. You man those cameras, help me find our bad guys, so I can take them out, and let me know if they're getting close to Corbet. We can't let these bastards get their hands on him or anything to do with Eagle Claw."

"You're going to take out thirteen . . . or, for all we know, thirty men? By yourself? What about the guards? If I can locate them, they can help."

He didn't want to tell her but didn't have much choice. "The guards are dead, Rhonda. Otherwise, the Russians wouldn't have control of the computers and feel free to roam the halls. And they're going to come looking for their silent friend here real soon, when he doesn't check in."

Her eyes got wider—then she threw herself against him, wrapped her arms around his neck, and kissed him like there was no tomorrow.

Please, God, let her be wrong. "Steady, now," he said.

She gave him a firm nod.

"Atta girl. Now, stay with me. We've got to move fast to have any chance of getting on top of this."

Watching the camera, they slid out into the hallway, keeping along the wall. When it was clear, he hustled toward the stairwell door, opened it slowly, and, satisfied that the landing was empty, ducked inside. Like a good soldier, she stuck to him like a shadow.

"Stay here," he whispered, then made sure the

stairwell and the next landing were clear before he motioned for her to join him.

He followed the same process up to level three, where he found another Russian standing guard in the hall outside the stairwell door.

He motioned for Rhonda to stand back. Then he cracked open the door and rattled out the only Russian phrase he knew with rock-solid certainty. "Hey, baby, come here often?" And he let the door click shut.

Half a heartbeat later, the Russian ripped open the door and burst into the stairwell.

Coop cracked him on the head with the rifle, then spun him around, grabbed his mouth to keep him quiet, and jammed his Emerson knife into his kidney and twisted, severing the abdominal aorta. The Russian shuddered, then went limp and bled to death internally. One fewer bad guy to hunt.

Coop lowered the body to the floor, then stood and saw Rhonda's horrified stare.

He knew that look. He'd worn it the first time he'd seen an enemy combatant killed. Couldn't be helped.

They had to keep moving. He quickly stripped the body of ammunition and handed Rhonda the guard's rifle. He'd expected her to hold the M4 at arm's length like it was a snake, but she pulled herself together, expertly checked to see if it was loaded, and slapped the bottom of the magazine to make sure it was fully seated.

"Oh, man. Now you've done it. I am *so* turned on."

She ignored him. "What's next?"

"We get you to a computer." *And out of harm's way.*

He glanced out into the hallway to the administrative floor. All was clear.

"Let's go."

Using his key card, he opened the door to the first room he came to.

"This guy has a high pay grade," he murmured as they walked into an executive suite, complete with an aircraft-carrier-sized desk, wood paneling, an "I love me" picture wall, and other executive toys.

"This'll do," she said as she crossed the room, set her rifle on the desk so she could get at it quickly, and piled the ammo pouch next to it. Then she settled into the plush chair and turned on the computer. "I'm going to *own* this network. These guys are toast."

God, he loved her grit. "I'll be back in time for cocktails, darling."

"Just take care of you," she said sternly.

He tapped his earpiece radio. "Keep in touch. And keep that rifle in arm's reach."

With that final order, he slipped out the door and went on the hunt.

36

Vadar was perspiring inside his uniform again; rage always elevated his body temperature. "The facility guards are all accounted for, is that correct?"

"Yes, sir. All five interior guards have been eliminated."

"If that is so, then who is killing my men?"

"I do not know, sir."

"Unacceptable." Vadar raised his Walther and shot the messenger in his left temple.

"We might have had use for him," Ivan said in a low voice after the man crumpled to the floor at their feet. "We are now three men down."

"What the fuck is going on?" Vadar screamed.

"Clearly, there is someone in the facility not accounted for on the entry log."

"Find them. Eliminate them. See to it," he ordered Ivan, who bowed his head in compliance. "Take Vasin and Goraya with you. Make quick work of it."

"On my honor," Ivan said with another clipped bow. With Vasin and Goraya by his side, he rushed toward the stairwell.

Vadar glared at the clock. He'd designed this mission to be in and out in fifteen minutes. They were nearing fifteen minutes now, and he hadn't yet descended to the fourth level and collected the Russian scientist and Eagle Claw.

"You!" he shouted at the tech manning the computers. "Use those cameras. Find whoever is behind this, and direct my men to that position. And you," he said, turning to the remaining three men assigned to the team and the second technician who might be of value when they confronted Corbet. "Come with me."

He had to chance going after Corbet, even though the facility wasn't secure yet.

"Cooper. I've lost you."

Coop ducked lower under the stairwell on the second level and whispered, "Good. That means no one else can see me, either. Where's our Russkie on the second floor?"

"Hold on." She replied less than a minute later: "By the stairwell door. But there are two of them, and judging by their constant radio communication with their team, they're clearly on high alert."

"They'd better be, if they know what's good for them. Let me know if their location changes."

"Damn. I just lost control of the cameras again. You're on your own until I figure out how to get it back. Be careful."

"Always."

So far, he'd been lucky. Rhonda had come through

in spades, manipulating the cameras and locating the threats on the third floor. The Russians had doubled their efforts there. Good call on their part. Bad call assuming he wouldn't find them.

Five minutes later, two more Russians were down, and he dragged the bodies beneath the landing. He felt better about Rhonda's safety now that this floor was cleared—at least, for the moment. The fact that all four men he'd taken out were Spetsnaz didn't bode well for his continued survival or for Rhonda's.

So, if he was a bad guy, with an unknown force picking off members of the team, where would he start the sweep-and-destroy mission?

They'd want to control the access points, and then they'd control the facility, which was why every bad guy he had run across had been positioned near a stairwell or the elevator.

That left the elevator. He headed that way.

The problem with the elevators was that they also had cameras inside. He couldn't count on Rhonda to shut them down. Not when the bad guys were intercepting her commands as soon as they realized there was someone else maneuvering the system.

So if he wanted to move between floors, the only option left was the elevator shaft. Which meant he'd need an emergency elevator key. He knew of only one place to get one: the dead guard at the other end of the hall. Keeping clear of the camera's roving eye, he made his way back to the body and found the hex key on his key ring.

Then he lit out fast for the elevator. The hex key opened it easily. He gently pried the doors open and saw the elevator suspended above him. Quickly, so he wouldn't be seen, he squeezed through the opening, then reached out and grabbed the maintenance ladder that ran along the greasy shaft wall just as the door pinched shut behind him.

Now, up or down? If he was in command of this siege, he'd leave most of his operators up top to cover the exit. So he opted for down, since the odds were better there—until somebody figured out that was where he was.

He started descending the ladder.

It had been over five minutes since Rhonda lost control of the cameras. Frustrated, she continued to work the system. Whoever was manning the keyboard knew what they were doing. It was computer geek against computer geek, and by God, she would *not* be beaten—even though she was at a disadvantage, since she had to be careful not to reveal her location.

Then, *bam!* She broke through. She had control again.

"Take that, you dog!" she crowed, and quickly started searching for Cooper.

"You calling me a dog?" he asked through the earbud.

"Oh, thank God. Where are you?"

"Looking for a midnight snack."

Which meant level five. He was such a damn

smartass. She was glad when she finally located him on camera. He was crouched low to the floor. Searching another body, she realized, and swallowed back a rush of nausea. It was us or them—there was no other way.

She sat up straight when the camera caught a door open at the other end of the hallway and two big, heavily armed men creeping in.

Cooper was so focused on his search that he didn't hear them.

"Cooper," she whispered, so as not to startle him. "You've got company. Two big guns coming up behind you."

He didn't move. Hadn't he heard her? Had the radio stopped working?

"Cooper!" she screamed, just as he leaped up and swung around, firing and dropping both shooters like stones.

"You broke my freaking eardrum," he grumbled as he scrambled over to search the downed Russians.

"I didn't think you heard me." Her heart still raced like a freight train.

He grinned up into the camera. "No problem. Thanks for having my six."

"Your six?"

"My back. You had me covered ten ways from Sunday. You might make a field agent yet."

"Not in this lifetime."

"If there's anyone else on this floor, those shots are going to bring them running."

"Let me have a look." She quickly checked each camera, then breathed a huge sigh of relief. "None that I can see."

"Our odds are getting better, but I've got to get to Corbet. These guys aren't about to cut their losses and run."

"Hold on. Let me search level four."

She'd barely gotten the words out when a loud, reverberating boom shook her desk.

Coop's shocked expression filled the camera screen. "What the fuck?"

She found the camera that guarded Corbet's lab door, and all she saw was smoke.

"I think they blew up Corbet's lab. Or at least blew the door."

"On my way."

Fear for him coiled in her chest as he ran straight into the belly of the beast.

Vadar choked and coughed as black smoke filled the fourth-floor hallway. He'd found no way to circumvent the lock, so he'd ordered Nikolai to blow it. After the man set a breaching charge over the door latch, Vadar had stepped well back from the door and nodded for Nikolai and his other two men and the technician to cover their ears.

The smoke was still thick but clearing as Vadar walked over the ruined door and stepped inside the lab.

Dr. Corbet was on the floor, clearly knocked there by the force of the blast.

"Get him up," Vadar ordered.

Pavel and Mavriky picked Corbet up under his arms, then held him steady on his feet.

Vadar approached him. "Hello, Adolph," he said as the older man gasped for breath and pressed his palms to his ears. "Sorry about the extreme methods, but we're in a bit of a rush. Now, tell me that you've compiled all of your data and are ready to go."

Corbet looked back at him with the eyes of a beaten man. "Svetlana . . . my daughter—"

"Are both awaiting your return to Moscow," Vadar assured him. "That was our arrangement. One we will honor. Now, do you have the data compiled?"

The old man nodded reluctantly and handed Vadar a memory stick. "It's all here."

"It's all here, *comrade*," Vadar corrected, unable to resist the opportunity to goad this man, who had been not only a traitor to his country but also a pain in the ass to retrieve.

Corbet lowered his head, clearly shamed.

"Say it," Vadar commanded.

"It's all here, comrade," Corbet repeated in a monotone.

"You will understand if I have our technician verify that for me."

He nodded to the tech, who quickly inserted an empty memory stick into Corbet's computer and copied everything on his hard drive.

"Wonderful. Then let's go."

37

She'd lost Cooper when he took off running for the elevators.

"No, no, no!" she told him. "There are cameras inside. They'll spot you."

"I forgive you for underestimating me."

Instead of pressing a button and calling the elevator, he used something that must be a key, pried open the doors, and disappeared into the shaft.

Okay. So he'd have the element of surprise on his side, but who knew how many men were on the fourth floor? And who knew if Dr. Corbet was even alive after that explosion?

She rapidly flipped through the camera feeds, intent on getting a view of the lab door.

But when she landed on the fourth-floor hallway that was sixty yards from the lab, she stopped. And gasped.

A man lay dead, facedown on the floor. The good news was, it wasn't Cooper. The bad news was, Cooper was also down.

"Cooper," she whispered, overwhelmed with fear for him.

No response.

"Cooper. Damn it. *Please* . . . please answer me."

Still nothing. He slouched on the floor, leaning against the wall, his legs sprawled out in front of him. His head lolled down on his chest. Blood oozed between the fingers of the hand he'd pressed against his shoulder.

Pressed against his shoulder.

That vital detail finally registered. He wasn't dead. He couldn't be dead if he had lifted his hand and could hold it against his shoulder.

"Cooper!" She tried again.

Maybe he didn't hear her. Maybe his earbud had fallen out when he'd gone down.

And then she saw them: five men, one of them Corbet. He was being led down the hall by a man with a gun. Three in all had guns, and they were heading directly for Cooper. They might not see him yet in the dim hallway, but she wasn't taking any chances.

She was in the office of one of the system directors, so there was probably a facility-wide intercom. She studied the phone, quickly found what she was looking for, hit the "Emergency facility broadcast" button, and shouted at the top of her lungs.

"Cooper! Three shooters straight ahead!"

His head came up—*thank you, God*—and he lifted his rifle.

Then, to her horror, the camera feed went black again.

• • •

Rhonda's intercom blast shocked Coop awake. He managed to focus on five men and fired. It was a wild shot, but they quickly ducked for cover. That wasn't going to last long.

He had one good arm and a half-full magazine and was short on blood. That officially made him a damn sitting duck.

Worse, Rhonda had just outed herself. It wouldn't take them long now to realize he hadn't been acting alone or where she was when she'd accessed the intercom.

Damn it. He'd held out hope that even if he didn't come out of this alive, she'd escape unharmed because they wouldn't know she was here. That they'd just leave quickly once they had their prize scientist and the Eagle Claw data.

Cradling the M4, he scooted left as fast as his bleeding body would let him and almost fell through a door into a room. He dragged himself inside, flipped over onto his belly, and, gritting past the pain in his shoulder, propped his rifle on the floor. Ever so slowly, he eased his head out into the hallway—and saw a head pop around the corner. This time, he didn't miss. The Russian went down, his head hitting the floor like a watermelon.

He ducked back into the room and quickly looked around. Lab tables, computer desks. Too flimsy to stop any bullets.

If only he had a couple of hand grenades. They'd

come after him soon, realize that they had him cornered, and probably call for reinforcements.

So this was where it ended. He was okay with dying; he'd made that decision years ago when he'd signed up with the Marines. But he wasn't okay with what was going to happen to Rhonda.

He'd promised her that he'd protect her.

But he hadn't saved her. He'd as good as killed her.

A blast of noise, so piercing it nearly made his ears bleed, broke out through the halls.

Fire alarm, he realized. Then the strobes came on, disorienting and blinding, while the shrill scream of the alarm echoed off the walls and tore through the halls.

Holy hell—it was Buttercup to the rescue! She was creating a diversion, giving him a chance to escape. This wasn't over yet!

A renewed surge of adrenaline shot through him— just as two hulking silhouettes appeared in the doorway.

He tried to lift his M4 but didn't have the strength.

He steeled himself to die.

Then the rattle of another M4 cracked through the hallway, and he watched, mystified, as both Russians dropped to the floor.

"Cooper?"

Holy shit—Rhonda?

He looked up. And there, through the haze of gunsmoke, stood the Bombshell, a shocked, victorious, and horrified look on her face and a smoking M4 in her hands.

● ● ●

"Can you stand up if I help you to your feet?"

Coop still couldn't believe he was alive. And alive because of this amazing woman. "Sweetheart, I can do anything for you. Except maybe stop bleeding."

She walked him back into the room, catching him when he stumbled, then leaned him against the wall. She quickly stripped him of his shirt and assessed the damages. "Hold this," she said, handing him his rifle. "And don't fall over."

Then she raced across the room, rummaging through drawers, tossing things aside until she found what she wanted. When she returned, she had a bottle of alcohol and a stack of gauze.

After she'd unceremoniously dumped the entire bottle of alcohol over his bullet wound, upping the excruciating factor by about one hundred, he gritted out, "Could have . . . warned me."

"Like I've got time." She pressed the gauze pads over the open wound, then used his T-shirt as a stretch bandage to keep them in place. "Stay there," she ordered, picked up the M4, and peeked out the door. "Shit," she swore, and backed into the room. "He's holding Corbet at gunpoint."

"He? Only one?" Cooper asked, fighting to keep his head in the game.

"Yeah. Only one."

"If you want the doctor alive," a heavily accented voice said in English, "you will toss your weapons out into the hall and come out with your hands up."

She looked at Coop for guidance.

"You're not going to shoot Corbet," Coop said as loudly as he could. "You need him if you're going to salvage any part of your mission."

"Do you really want to take that chance?"

Before Coop knew what she was going to do, Rhonda flew out the door, rolled to the right, and came up on one knee, firing.

Coop shot out the door after her, if only to throw himself on her and protect her. All he managed to do was land on his face.

"What are you doing?" She helped him get upright.

He glanced down the hall. Dr. Corbet was on the floor, clutching his leg. The Russian was spread-eagled on his back, moaning in agony.

"Making a fool out of myself, apparently." He looked at her then. "I thought you didn't know—"

"Anything about close-quarters combat? I never said that. I said I'd never been involved in it. I had to take the same weapons classes you did. Aced them, by the way."

She walked over to the moaning Russian and kicked his gun out of his reach. Then she tended to Dr. Corbet, who, Coop now suspected, she'd intentionally wounded in the leg so he would fall and give her a clear shot at the Russian.

Before he could digest that amazing decision on her part, a small man stepped out of the shadows, hands raised.

"No shoot," he pleaded in broken English. "I surrender."

• • •

He turned out to be one of two technicians the team had brought along against their will. He also ended up being a wealth of information, more than willing to cooperate.

He radioed the other tech on level one—who was also more than ready to surrender—and discovered that the tech was the only man left on that level. Based on the body count and the numbers the techs provided, that left only three Russians outside guarding the building.

"Now what?" Rhonda asked as they rode the elevator to level one.

"Now we wait." His vision was for shit, and he tried to blink away the cobwebs. "The guys outside, they're going to start to wonder what's . . . taking so long. Sooner or later, they're going to send one in . . . to find out. Shouldn't be . . . much of a problem . . . picking them off."

He felt Rhonda's arm wrap around his waist. Damn good thing. He was about to go down for the count.

She turned him over to the tech when the elevator hit the first level and lifted her rifle to her shoulder, just in case.

The elevator doors opened, and waiting for them was what looked like the entire U.S. military, rifles pointed directly at their heads.

"Thank God," Rhonda said, lowering her weapon.

Coop grinned. "Glad you could make it, boys. We need . . . cleanup in aisle three."

Then he passed out cold.

Sunday

Bravery is being the only one who knows you're afraid.

— David Hackworth

38

11:37 p.m., United Flight 383, Eastbound

Helluva wake-up call, Coop thought as he sat beside
Rhonda on the flight back to Langley late Sunday
night.

During the thick of the siege, when he'd thought
he was going to lose her, when he'd thought he was
going to die, he'd come to terms with something unexpected. And he'd known that if they got out of that
mess alive, there were going to be some huge changes
in his life.

And all of them started and ended with her.

Beside him, Rhonda thumbed through a Skymall
catalog. She'd been quiet since this whole thing finished. Processing, he supposed. Violence was never
easy to witness. And killing a man, no matter how bad
he was, wasn't something she'd shake off in a week.
Or even a month.

Staying with him at the trauma center while they
filled him back up with blood and patched him

couldn't have been easy for her, either. She hated hospitals. And because of him, she'd had to wait in one for hours.

So he knew she needed time. But there'd be plenty of that, he assured himself. Plenty of time to say what he wanted to say to her.

He closed his eyes and drifted, letting the pain medication ease the way. A week ago, he'd have said no way. Denied it like a star goalie denying a line-drive puck. But not anymore. He was ready to admit that with Rhonda, he might just want to have what Mike had with Eva. What Joe Green had with Steph. What any of the other guys had with their wives. They couldn't all be wrong.

But *he'd* be dead wrong if he walked away from this woman without letting her know that for the first time in his life, he wanted more.

Though his eyes were heavy, he found himself grinning. He, a confirmed bachelor who'd never met a woman he couldn't walk away from, had finally taken the fall. If he was being honest, he'd fallen the first time he set eyes on her six months ago. It had just taken him this long to figure it out.

"You doing okay?"

He jerked his eyes open at the sound of her voice. "I think so, yeah."

She didn't look convinced. "Are you taking the pain meds the doctor prescribed?"

He smiled over at her. See? She cared.

Luckily, the bullet he'd taken hadn't done massive

damage. It hurt like hell, and healing would take him out of commission for a while, but he'd be back to full speed in a few weeks. Blood loss had been his main problem, and once they'd filled him back up, his strength had returned to about 80 percent.

But right now, he was tired. Really tired.

"Cooper? Are you with me?"

He must have drifted off again. He forced his eyes open and grinned at her.

"Judging from the loopy smile on your face, I'd guess that yes, you're taking the pain meds."

"Only because they made me."

She smiled. "Why don't you try to sleep? The doctor said rest is the best thing to help you heal."

"Yeah. Rest." He yawned; his eyelids weighed a ton. "I'll probably need a full-time . . . nurse when we get back to McLean. Someone to . . . tuck me in at night." Another yawn had him closing his eyes again. "Change my dressings. Hold me . . . if I have a bad dream. Any . . . volunteers?"

She mumbled something that didn't sound like a yes but he refused to believe was a no, and he didn't have the stamina to figure it out.

And then he fell asleep.

Rhonda had given Nate a full report from the military hospital while the doctors had worked on Cooper's shoulder. She'd called again before their flight left for home, telling Nate that they'd arrive on the red-eye, so there was no sense in him meeting them at the airport. She'd get Cooper to his apartment and to bed, where the docs had said he needed to be.

Afterward, she second-guessed herself. Maybe she should have let Nate take over with Cooper. But she was half afraid that in his medicated stupor, Cooper might make some grand announcement. Let it slip that they'd "been together."

She was probably being paranoid, but she wasn't willing to risk it, so that's how she'd ended up helping him to bed around 2:00 a.m.

His apartment was neat and clean and tastefully decorated in grays and silvers, with a few pops of red for color. The living room was understated and masculine but not macho, and his bedroom was far from the den of iniquity she'd half-expected to find.

More muted grays, this time accented with black, charcoal, and a stunning shade of steel-blue, all of which she was peripherally aware of as she supported him with his good arm looped over her shoulder and her arm around his waist, while walking him carefully to his bed.

Which was king-sized, covered in a plush cream and blue duvet, with a soft black throw tossed over the foot of it.

"You're an angel," he muttered as she helped him slip his arm out of his jacket—the other one was in a sling—and eased him down. "A Buttercup Bombshell Angel. You know that, don't you? You know that—"

"Yeah, yeah." She cut him off, not wanting to be

swayed by the gentle affection in his voice. "Exactly how many of those pain pills did you take?"

She gently helped him lie back, carefully squaring a pillow under his head, but he still winced when his shoulder met the mattress. "How many *did* I take?"

"Um . . . that's what I asked *you*."

"I don't do well with narcotics. Did I mention that? Don't usually . . . take them. Sometimes they make me a little stupid."

She couldn't help but smile. "Imagine that. Let's get your boots off."

"You're so good to me. I love you for that."

She froze, his left boot in her hand, then told herself to chalk the L word up to the medication and started on the laces.

"Was gonna wait. Was gonna give you time, but life . . . life's short, right? Didn't we just learn . . . firsthand . . . that life is . . . short?"

Her heart did a little stutter kick, and she knew she wasn't going to want to hear what was about to come out of his mouth. Medication talking or not. "Shush, Cooper. You need to sleep."

"There never was a man—me being the man. You understand?" he asked, then kept on rambling as his eyes drifted shut. "Never was a man more aware . . . of how short life can be. I almost . . . lost you. My beautiful Buttercup Bombshell. You saved my life. Do you know . . . how much my . . . mother is gonna love you . . . for that alone?"

"Go to sleep, Cooper," she insisted, and covered him with the soft woven throw.

"Almost . . . lost you," he repeated, reaching blindly for her hand.

His words were slurred from the meds, and his mind wasn't filtering them the way it normally would, but there was an intensity in his tone that cut a little too close to the heart.

"I love you, Rhonda. I . . . I think I should . . . marry . . . me. Wait. No." He cracked open an eye. "That was wrong, wasn't it?"

Everything about this was wrong. "Shut up, Cooper," she said, but she couldn't make herself pull her hand away from his.

"Don't go. Please sit by me," he pleaded, with so much need she felt she had no choice but to sit beside him. "I need to say this right." His eyes drifted closed again, but he snapped them open, fighting to stay conscious. "Me . . . marry . . . me. No. Damn. Not me marry me. You. You marry . . . you. Oh, God. I can do this. You. Marry. Me." He heaved a weary, relieved sigh. "That's it. Can you? Will . . . you . . ."

His eyes finally closed for good this time—and thank God, so did his mouth.

Because she didn't want to hear that question from him. She didn't want to believe he meant to ask it. It was the meds. The trauma. The full moon. Whatever.

She *didn't* want to hear it. Yet her heart beat with something that felt very much like longing. And very deep regret.

He'd forget about it in the morning.

He'd have to. Because what he thought he wanted could never happen.

Saddened, and angry with herself because she'd let him get to her, she turned on a bedside light in case he needed to get up in the night, then turned off the overhead light and closed his bedroom door behind her.

Then she made a phone call. "Hi, Bobby. It's Rhonda. Yeah. We're back. Thanks," she said when he told her he'd be over in five minutes to spend the night with Coop.

Because she just couldn't stay here. Not now.

A quick trip to the kitchen assured her that someone had stocked the fridge with fresh fruit, milk, and a couple of takeout meals to tide him over for a day or so.

Then she checked in on him one last time, made sure his pain pills and a glass of water were within reach, and resisted the urge to crawl into his bed and sleep beside him.

After she let herself out of his apartment, she ignored the burning tears in her eyes as she got into the cab that she'd asked to wait for her.

She'd known for years that happily ever after would never be a part of her life. Even though Cooper had turned out to be so much more than he was supposed to be.

Because she could never be the woman a man like him needed.

Monday

There's no honorable way to kill, no gentle way to destroy. There is nothing good in war. Except its ending.

—Abraham Lincoln

39

Monday morning came early. Rhonda had only caught about two hours of sleep and was beat, but she needed to go into the office, even though Nate had told her she should take the day to rest up and then report on Tuesday for a debriefing and an appointment with the staff psychologist.

"Standard operating procedure," he'd told her. "When a rookie discharges a weapon that results in a kill, they've got to see the shrink."

She got that part. And she knew she needed to talk to someone about it. But she wasn't ready yet. Neither could she stay home, constantly fighting the urge to answer Cooper's repeated calls. Or, worse, go over to his apartment and see him.

She couldn't talk to him yet, because she remembered every word he'd said last night. And she was afraid that he might remember, too.

When she walked into the briefing room, she found Mike leading the charge.

"Rhonda, welcome back!" Santos, still wearing a bandage on his upper arm, shoved himself out of his chair and gave her a one-armed embrace. Then he pulled back. "What are you doing here?"

"Last I knew, I worked here." She forced a smile for all the guys, who'd lifted their hands in greeting. They all had a look in their eyes—acknowledgment, even pride. She'd been through the fire, and their respect had never been more apparent. She was truly one of them now.

"You aren't supposed to report in until tomorrow," Carlyle insisted. "We heard what a badass you were in Nevada, but even badasses need a little time to decompress."

"I want to be here." She looked past Carlyle's concerned eyes to her boss and willed him to understand.

He considered her thoughtfully. "You sure this is where you want to be today?"

"It's where I *need* to be."

As the words came out, she realized that it was more than the desire to keep herself busy. She was here because she needed to be with these men. Her teammates. Her friends.

After what felt like an eternity, Mike gave her a nod. "Take a very quick five, everyone. Get your curiosity satisfied, hug her if you must, then get your heads back in the game."

She felt like a rock star by the time the guys had

"atta girled" her, hugged her, and teased her about whether Cooper's wounded ego was giving him more trouble than his gunshot wound, since she'd had to save his sorry self.

Of course, they all knew what an amazing feat Cooper had pulled off, taking down a crack team of Russian Spetsnaz, and she was quick to tell them that she was merely the cleanup crew.

After they'd all had their shot at her, she made her way over to Mike. "How's Eva?"

"First time out of bed yesterday. Only a couple of steps, but she promises there'll be more today." Then he hugged her, too. "Glad you're okay."

"You and me both. By the way, any word on Dr. Corbet?"

"He's going to be in the hospital for a while. Might need a second surgery on his leg, but he'll be fine."

"I know he was in on the deal, but I feel so bad for him. Cooper told me about his wife and daughter. He just wanted to be with them."

"We don't even know if they're alive. Sadly, we probably never will."

"What happens to Corbet now?"

"That will be up to the Department of Justice. I'm hoping his age, his physical condition, and what he's done for us on the Eagle Claw project will weigh in his favor."

She hoped so, too. But no matter how lenient the courts were, that still wouldn't reunite him with his family.

"Hey," Mike said, snapping her out of her melancholy thoughts. "Nice work out there. We may have to make a field agent out of you yet."

Déjà vu. She made herself smile. "I'll stick with my computers, thanks anyway."

"Speaking of which, selfishly, I'm glad you came in. We can use your help."

"What's going on?"

"Yeah, boss. What's going on?"

Rhonda spun around at the sound of Cooper's voice.

Taggart stood beside him, an exasperated look on his face. "He was going to walk here if I didn't bring him."

"Oh, for Pete's sake," Mike said. "You don't have the sense God gave a rock. What the hell are you doing out of bed?"

Although the corners of his mouth were pinched tight with pain, Cooper managed to smile. "You didn't really think I was going to let this go down without me?"

Mike narrowed his eyes and scanned the room. "The idea was to keep him out of the loop so he wouldn't pull this stunt. Who let the cat out of the bag?"

"Taggart," Cooper announced as cheerily as a man with a bullet wound could.

"You just couldn't stand to be on the shit list by yourself, could you?" Taggart grumbled, but the concern for his friend was very evident.

"It's lonely at the bottom," Cooper said.

Rhonda finally recovered from the shock of seeing him and keyed in on what had been said. "Wait? Go down? What's going down?"

"They found Eva's shooter." Cooper's words forced her to meet his eyes.

She saw no sign that he was on pain meds today. His eyes were clear, though bright with pain. Physical pain . . . and something more? Something that said she'd hurt him because she hadn't returned his calls?

Unsettled, she turned back to Mike. "Am I the only one who doesn't know what's going on?" She'd thought she was finally part of the team in every way, yet no one had thought to tell her this huge revelation about finding the shooter.

"Sit down," Mike ordered firmly. "Everyone except you, Coop. You get your ass back home to bed."

Cooper pulled out a chair and eased down into it. "You're going to have to make me. Sir."

Mike glared at him. "I don't need this today."

"Then let's not make it an issue. I got pulled off this investigation once. It's not happening again. If you insist that I walk out that door, I'm not coming back. Your call."

The room went deadly silent.

Rhonda held her breath. She knew Cooper well enough to know that he meant it. If Mike made him leave, he would not be back.

She also knew a bit about her boss. He was fair but firm. If he issued an order, he expected it to be obeyed.

But these guys had a long history together. A history that made them brothers in every way but blood, though it hadn't always been easy.

All eyes were on Mike. No one even blinked.

Mike never looked away from Cooper. "Are you on pain medication?" Mike asked after a long silence.

"Don't need it," Cooper said firmly. His washed-out color and the pinched look around his mouth proved him a liar.

"Just so we're clear, is that a no? You're not on medication?" Mike lifted a brow.

"I'm not on medication."

"Too bad," Mike said. "Otherwise, I might have overlooked your blatant defiance of a direct order."

Cooper waited a long beat, pushed back his chair, and stood. "It's been real," he said, and headed toward the door.

"Sit your ass back down," Mike ordered. "No one said you could leave."

Rhonda's heartbeat rose several ticks. Mexican standoff, anyone?

Mike let out a "why me?" sigh, then glared at Cooper. "You do what I say, when I say it, or your ass lands on the DL before you can complain about your boo-boo. Understood?" His choice of words might have caused a snicker or two, but the tone in which he delivered them and the graveness of the moment made it clear that this was no laughing matter.

"Yes, sir." Cooper sat back down.

The tension in the room relaxed by about ninety turns of a tightly wound spring.

"Burns."

"Yes, sir." Rhonda met her boss's hard gaze.

"It was my oversight for not briefing you. Taggart. Nutshell it for her since you've got such loose lips."

It took less time for Taggart to relate the startling information that their would-be assassin was their former CO's psycho girlfriend than it did for Rhonda to get over her shock.

"But . . . I thought she died in Idaho."

"We all thought she did," Taggart agreed, "right along with Brewster and a boatload of UWD followers and La Línea cartel members."

"Then . . . how?" she asked, dumbfounded.

"The bitch apparently has nine lives. And we found out it was her because she practically drew us a map."

Taggart told her about the package containing the bullets and how Mike had traced the designer 9mm back to the gun the paid assassin had used to try to kill him and Eva in Lima.

"Why would she lead you to her?"

"Because it's a game to her now," Mike put in. "In the beginning, it was about revenge because we killed her boyfriend. She was supposed to take us all out last Monday. She failed.

"And now she knows she's failed again. The attack on the Area Fifty-One compound? She had her finger deep in that pie, too."

"How do you know this?"

"The Russian ringleader you shot? In the hospital, he sang like a wounded canary. The attack had been orchestrated by a woman he knew only as Anya."

"Our shooter?"

"None other. She was supposed to knock off the One-Eyed Jacks for them—something she'd probably have done for free—and clear the way for the Russians to scoop up Dr. Corbet and Eagle Claw. Thanks to her mole in the CIA—"

"What?"

"B.J. and Steph, pretending to be the assassin, smoked him out online. We arrested him yesterday," Mike told her.

"Looks like Rhonda and I weren't the only ones playing 'get the bad guy,'" Cooper said, not doing a very good job of masking his pain.

"Yours had guns," Mike pointed out. "This pissant was a communications clerk with an expatriated father who persuaded him to aid Mother Russia. Anyway, B.J. and Steph went to work digging for photos of Brewster. They finally found one with the woman at his side, and that led us to an ID and a profile."

Mike's eyes were hard, and Rhonda could read his thoughts. He wanted this woman. He wanted her a week ago, before his wife had almost died from one of her bullets.

"Marjorie Reynolds, a.k.a. Jane Smith and a dozen other aliases. Blond, blue eyes, plain, average build. She'd blend in with any crowd. But not anymore—now we have a way to find her."

"Facial-recognition software?" Rhonda's heart beat with excitement.

"Damn straight. Her photo is rolling through intelligence agencies around the world, along with an APB. If she shows up in any airport, any train station, hell, on the streets of New York City, some camera somewhere is going to spot her."

"But the trick will be spotting her before she comes after another one of us," Cooper said.

40

"I'm going to see if I can help B.J. and Steph with their search," Rhonda said once Mike called an end to the meeting.

She didn't waste any time getting out of the briefing room, Coop thought.

Then his teammates crowded around him, pronouncing him an idiot for not taking advantage of sick leave, as ugly as ever, a pansy-ass for letting a woman save him, and generally making him feel loved. His brothers.

By the time the room cleared out, he felt like shit. Yeah, he probably should go home to bed. But the guys felt really solid that Marjorie Reynolds was going to make a play soon, maybe even today.

And he didn't want to miss that action, even if Mike decided to stick him in a surveillance vehicle with a pair of field glasses, covering their backs while they closed in on her.

Then there was the issue of Rhonda. He wanted to talk to her. Problem was, she clearly didn't want to talk to him.

Tough noogies.

He walked down the hall to her office, rapped on the door, and let himself inside.

"Hey. How are you doing?" she asked after a moment of surprise clearly mixed with discomfort.

"Well, if you'd answered or returned my phone calls, you'd know exactly how I am. Let's start with confused. Then cut through all the rest of it and go straight to pissed."

She folded her hands together on the top of her desk. "I'm sorry. I was going to return your calls. But I was afraid you might be sleeping and didn't want to bother you."

He stared at her for a long moment. Long enough that she actually started to squirm. "Don't try to bullshit a bullshitter, Buttercup. Tell me straight. You're avoiding me."

"I'm working," she insisted.

"Goody for you." He sat down grumpily in a straight-backed chair across from her desk. "I remember every word I said last night."

She looked at her folded hands. "It's okay. The medication—"

"Had nothing to do with it," he interrupted. "So talk to me. Tell me what you would've said if I'd said that I love you just now."

His voice had softened. So had his eyes. His sad and angry eyes. And Rhonda felt as though a fist had wrapped around her heart and squeezed.

"You don't really want to have this conversation here. Not now."

"Oh, I do. I really, really do. Now, tell me. What would you have said?"

She'd never anticipated that this moment would come. That he'd tell her he loved her. That he'd want her to love him in return.

That she'd want to tell him that she loved him.

"We had an arrangement," she said, collecting herself.

"Screw that. That was then. That was before—"

"Before we had blistering-hot sex, then almost died? Yeah, we had some really intense, life-changing moments. But you knew from the start that I didn't want to get involved in a long-term relationship. You didn't, either."

"I repeat, that was then." He leaned forward in the chair, wincing when it jostled his shoulder. "Are you honestly going to try to convince me that you don't have any feelings for me?"

"Of course, I have feelings for you. My God, Cooper. We went through a small war together. We almost died together. How could I not have feelings for you after that?"

He leaned back again and slowly shook his head. "So . . . you're saying this is like a band-of-brothers feeling."

"No. Yes. Cooper, don't make this any more difficult than it has to be."

"Difficult. Good word," he said. "Tell me about

difficult. Tell me why, when we have this amazing thing going between us, it would be difficult to ride it all the way to the end."

She felt tears sting her eyes. She *never* cried. Not anymore. She swiveled around in her chair so her back was to him. Grabbed a stack of folders from an open drawer and . . .

"Rhonda."

His voice was so soft, so concerned, she almost lost it. She clutched the folders to her breasts, not even knowing how they'd gotten into her hands.

Then he was beside her. Squatted down on his heels, his hand on her arm, his eyes as full of pain as her chest. "Baby, what happened to you? Who hurt you so badly that you're scared to death to believe what you're feeling?"

She wasn't a babbler. She was a thoughtful and guarded woman, and she didn't share details of her life easily.

But he wasn't going to back away until he knew.

She battled her decision for several long moments, then finally gave up. "You wanted to know why I have a fear of hospitals," she began, not looking at him. "I don't fear them. I hate them. I spent too much time watching and waiting for someone to die in a hospital bed."

She waited for him to say something. To ask who, when, how. But he didn't. He just stood, eased a hip onto the corner of her desk, and took her hand in his.

"I was engaged once. Eight years ago. The wedding was just weeks away when Dan was in a car accident. He was late for our date and ran a red light. It was a miracle that he didn't die at the scene.'"

He squeezed her hand tighter.

"I spent weeks at the hospital, watching him on life support, nauseated from the overwhelming fragrance of flowers. Weeks where I mourned and grieved and blamed myself because he was in that horrible condition. He knew he couldn't be late that night; we had tickets to a show. Tickets I'd worked to get for months. He'd hurried so he wouldn't upset me. Four weeks and three days later—the week before our wedding— he died."

She stopped, then steeled herself to continue. "And there I was. Almost a bride. Not even a widow. But the man I'd planned to live my life with was dead."

"I'm so, so sorry."

"Yeah. I was, too. I grieved for over a year. Blamed myself for over a year. Then my best friend, who would have been my maid of honor, came to me one night, drunk, crying . . . and admitted that she and Dan had been together that night. That's why he was late. He'd left her bed . . . to be with me. And she couldn't live with the guilt any longer."

She paused again, feeling oddly suspended above the pain now. "Apparently, they'd fallen in love. Oh, they hadn't meant to; they didn't want to hurt me. They'd planned to tell me, but the time was never right. Then, while he was dying, she didn't want to burden me with the truth. After he died, same story.

So she waited. A full damn year. She let me live with the guilt and the loss for a *year* before she could bother to tell me the truth."

He tried to pull her into his arms, but she stood, needing space. She crossed her arms over her breasts and paced to the glass window that looked out to the hallway.

"So then I got to grieve all over again. Over the fact that my best friend had betrayed me. That the man I'd loved had no longer loved me. And I got to grieve for the full year of my life that I'd lost wallowing in a guilt I hadn't deserved to feel."

She shook her head, remembering. "I felt humiliated and stupid and naive for not seeing it. And that's when I'd started hating him. A dead man. How small and petty is that? And I hated her, too. I hated my friend, who was in just as much pain as I'd been in."

She turned to face him, made herself look past the empathy and concern in his eyes. "And once I got past that, I made peace with the truth. I was never going to let myself in for that kind of heartache again. It changed me, Cooper. I'm not a person who can love anymore. I can't take that chance. I *won't* take that chance."

He was quiet for so long. So long that she finally made herself meet his eyes and realized that's what he'd been waiting for. "I'm sorry. I'm sorry for all you went through. But you're wrong about love."

She slowly shook her head. "I'm not wrong. Love isn't worth the pain."

Another long, searching look. "So what you're saying is that I'm not worth it."

Weary, she closed her eyes. "Don't put words in my mouth. That's not what I said."

"The hell it isn't." He was angry now.

Fine. Let him be angry. "You've twisted it."

"No. I've clarified. And while I'm at it, let me clarify something else, in case it didn't register the first two times. I love you. Do you want to know how many other women I've said that to?" He held up his index finger. "One: my mother. I say it every time I talk to her. Because I mean it, just like I mean it when I say it to you. I want to spend the rest of my life with you."

"You don't need me in your life," she challenged. "You just think you do."

"Wow. Thanks for clearing that up for me. I never dreamed you'd know my mind better than I do."

She walked back to her desk and sat down, needing a barrier between his anger and her resolve. "You need to think this through. This . . . feeling we have for each other. It's nine parts chemistry and one part wishful thinking. You want to love me. I understand that. I might even want to love you."

"That's good enough for me."

She pressed her closed fists on the desktop. "No. It's not. You deserve more."

"So do you. I'll give you more."

"Do you not understand?" she shouted in frustration. "Did you not hear me? I'm damaged. I *can't* love again. I've known that for a long time. I accept it. Now you need to."

He opened his mouth to reply, but her office door flew open, and Santos burst into the room. "We've got her!"

Startled, even relieved for the interruption, Rhonda jumped to her feet. "What?"

"We've. Got. Her! She landed at Reagan on an Air Canada flight about an hour ago. I could freaking *kiss* the guy who invented facial-recognition software, because TSA was locked in, and *boom*. Caught her at a rental-car agency. We've got the make, model, color, and plate number of the SUV she's driving."

"And?" Rhonda knew there was more.

"She's headed toward McLean."

"I think I know where she's going," Rhonda said as a revelation hit her. A sixth sense told her that she was as right about this as she'd ever been about anything.

Except maybe Cooper. Who looked as if she'd delivered a bullet to his heart.

She couldn't . . . she just couldn't think about it now.

"Where's Mike?" She skirted around her desk and headed for the door. "I've got to talk to him."

41

They wouldn't expect her to return to McLean.
They'd expect her to hide.

That worked for her; she wanted to hit them hard
and fast. Take out as many as she could before she
went to be with Ray. She hoped he'd understand.

She was weary.

She was lonely.

And she'd failed again.

The Russians would be after her, once they re-
grouped and decided she was the perfect sacrificial
goat for the failed Area 51 raid.

Time was limited. Brown and his team might know
her name by now, and they'd be using all the weapons in their arsenal to intercept her. Surveillance
cameras, facial-recognition software—they'd find her.
And if they didn't already know where she'd set up
shop to make her final stand, they'd soon figure it out.

God, she would have loved to see the looks on their
faces when they realized she hadn't died in Squaw Valley along with her beloved Ray, who had been blown

into red mist and ash. Just before the missile hit, he'd sent her to retrieve a gift he'd brought for the cartel. So her survival was a sign as big as any neon sign in Times Square: she was meant to avenge Ray's death.

He'd been the one person in her life who had seen her as more than a pawn. Her parents had deserted her. Her foster parents had abused her. The courts had failed her. Killing the man who'd proclaimed he loved her like a daughter, then violated her while his wife watched, had been the first thing in her life that had felt right. The next kills had been easy, even profitable. And when she'd hooked up with Ray, she'd felt as if she mattered for the first time in her life. And he became the one person who had ever mattered to her.

But Ray was gone . . . and Eva Salinas, Jamie Cooper, Bobby Taggart, and Mike Brown were responsible.

She knew how to get to them now. She knew their habits and their weaknesses, like she knew the cold blue eyes that stared back at her in the mirror each morning.

She glanced in the rearview mirror after she parked the SUV, stunned to see tears running down her face. Everything twisted and dead inside her had taken any emotion out of killing. But that emotion was alive again because Ray was dead, and so was the pain. And pain, she'd discovered, was a much greater motivator than mere money.

After retrieving her weapons from the backseat, she stepped onto the sidewalk.

By the time she'd climbed the stairs and reached

the sixth floor of the building where she'd fired the shot that hit Eva Salinas, she was breathing hard. She would always regret not killing her. Taking out her husband today would have to do.

As it had been eight days ago, the building was as empty as a confessional in a thieves' den. She walked toward the room where she had originally set up her hide. Crime-scene tape, plaster dust, and chunks of concrete from her grenade blast still littered the floor.

They'd figure out that this was where she would be. And she wanted them to find her here. She'd armed herself with enough ammunition to eliminate them all, starting with Brown.

She stopped, listened, and heard only silence. Confident that she was alone, she walked into the room.

The rattle of several rifles being raised immediately reverberated around her.

She stopped in her tracks. Cooper, wounded but alive, like Taggart, who stood beside him, their Glocks pointed at her heart. And Brown, rifle shouldered, pointing directly at her center mass. She recognized Santos because she'd managed to hit him. Carlyle and Waldrop. Faces hard. Jaws set. Safeties off.

"You surprise me, gentlemen," she said conversationally.

"Yeah." Brown seemed barely able to contain his rage. "That was the plan."

Her heart rate spiked with anticipation. "How's your bitch of a wife? I truly hope she's suffering."

"Drop your weapons," Brown said, his mouth

tight, his eyes glazed with hatred, and she wondered what kept him from pulling the trigger. Sense of fair play, she supposed. It was generally the downfall of men like him.

She held his gaze, staring straight into the eyes of the man who'd killed Ray.

"You're going to die here today." She pulled her MP5K out from under her jacket and aimed it directly at him.

The first bullet hit her in the chest just as she squeezed the trigger. And kept on squeezing, screaming like a crazed animal as bullet after bullet ripped into her body.

She dropped to her knees. The pain. Oh, God . . . the pain was unbearable.

And still she fired. Ready to be with Ray, a blood-curdling cry still spilling from her mouth, she fell facedown on the cold cement floor.

The screaming finally stopped.

The roar of gunfire stopped with it.

And the men who had delivered her to the end she'd so desperately wanted stood over her body in a silence that still vibrated with her hatred and insanity.

"Sit rep," Mike barked, his gaze never leaving her prostrate body.

Only after every one of the men flanking him had assured him he was okay did he lower his M4.

There was no pleasure in killing. But there was peace in knowing that it had come to an end.

42

Rhonda's apartment had always been her refuge, but it didn't feel like a haven tonight.

It felt empty. And even though a gas fire burned in the fireplace, it felt cold.

It had been three days since Marjorie Reynolds had committed suicide by cop. There'd been no doubt that she'd wanted to die. And there'd been no question that the world was a better, safer place without her.

And Rhonda had felt it was finally time to read her file.

Sitting on her sofa, an untouched glass of wine on the table beside her, she held the file she'd just read. She'd wanted hard copy, something tangible to hold on to. Something more personal than a scrolling screen that disappeared when you were done.

Marjorie Reynolds's story was excruciatingly sad. It read like a tutorial on how to make a killer. Abandonment, sexual and physical abuse, drugs, and alcohol.

Petty theft that paved the way to stealing a gun—and to killing the man who'd been entrusted to give a child a loving home but had violated her in the most heinous ways possible.

But although the events of Marjorie's life had influenced how she'd lived, it was the decisions, the choices she'd made, that led to her evolution into a monster.

After reading the file, Rhonda had realized that she'd let herself become a product of *her* environment, too. And she couldn't stop wondering if she'd also made poor choices. Although she wasn't a monster, she'd felt like one the last time she'd seen Cooper.

"So what you're saying is that I'm not worth it."

"Don't put words in my mouth. That's not what I said."

"The hell it isn't."

She'd seen the look on his face, had known she was hurting him, but didn't try to stop. And look where it had gotten her.

She was determined not to risk love, to protect herself from pain. Yet here she was, tears blurring her eyes every time she thought of going through life without Jamie Cooper.

She swiped a tear angrily from her cheek. She *didn't* cry.

But she was crying now. And didn't seem able to stop. Grabbing a sofa pillow, she buried her face against it and finally wept.

She wept for the first time since she'd accepted that Dan was going to die. Since she'd discovered that the trust she'd given so freely had been violated not only by him but also by her best friend.

But tonight she wept because she would miss Cooper. Because she had hurt him and because her plan to save herself this kind of pain was as stupid as pretending she didn't love him.

An hour later, she'd cried herself out. Her nose was red, her eyes were swollen, and her head pounded. She was a total mess. And she couldn't do this anymore.

He'd blown it.

Coop lay on his sofa in the dark staring at the ceiling. He'd blown it big-time. He'd rushed her, and Rhonda Burns wasn't a woman who could be rushed.

He should have left her alone for a while longer. He shouldn't have pushed. He'd known she needed space and time to think and remember and digest everything that had happened between them.

So what had he done? Trapped her in her office like a cornered animal. Forced her to deal with both a current and a past trauma, when she'd just been through a life-or-death experience.

What a dumbass. Even without all the outside factors to push her to the edge, he'd known she couldn't be manipulated into like-minded thinking. He didn't know why he'd thought he could convince her of something she wasn't sure of. Something she was afraid of.

Temporary insanity was his best guess.

And now he didn't know how to fix things.

He hadn't seen Rhonda since the day they'd taken down Marjorie Reynolds.

"Leave of absence," Mike had told him when he'd asked where Rhonda was. "She's been through a helluva trial by fire, and I'd have been concerned if she hadn't asked for some time off. Glad she's taking care of herself. Speaking of which, you are officially on the DL. No arguments; take the rest of the week off. And consider yourself lucky I didn't fire your ass for being an idiot in the briefing room that day."

So he'd gone home. And there he'd stayed.

Brooding.

Accepting that for the first time in his life, he was in love and, because of his own stupidity, as alone as a lighthouse keeper at the North Pole.

"Pity party, your table is ready," he muttered.

When his doorbell rang, he almost didn't answer it. Probably Taggart, bent on harassing him—the big guy's method of showing a little love.

Fine. Maybe he could use some company. He turned on the end table light, then shuffled to the door on bare feet and opened it—and there stood Rhonda.

She didn't say a word.

He didn't do much better. "Um . . ."

"Can I come in?"

Like he was going to say no?

He stood back, and she stepped inside. That's when he noticed that her eyes were puffy and her nose was swollen and red. Even her lips looked sore.

"What—"

She held up her hand, cutting him off. "I don't know how yet, but I'm going to figure out how to deal with this, because I can't pretend anymore that I don't love you. But I swear to God, Jamie Cooper, if you let me down, I will seriously hurt you."

It took several nanoseconds for her announcement to kick in. "Seriously?"

"No. Of course, I could never hurt you." A tear trickled down her cheek. She swore and brushed it away. She was crying. And he was suddenly the happiest man on earth.

"So . . . just for clarification . . . was that a proposal, Buttercup?"

Tears matted her gorgeous lashes when she looked at him. "Do you want it to be?"

He pulled her against him with his good arm. "Oh, yeah."

"Then don't ever call me Buttercup again."

He kissed her. Then kissed her again. "Not even when I do that little thing that makes you scream?"

She finally gave him a watery smile.

"What brought about this change of heart?" he asked when they were naked and wrapped around each other in bed.

"With age comes wisdom," she said, nuzzling his neck.

"You've aged since Monday? Is that what you're saying?"

She touched her fingers to his cheek. "I'm sorry I hurt you. I was fighting for my life. At least, it felt like I was."

"So what happened? What changed your mind?"

She looked into his eyes. "Have you read the file on Marjorie Reynolds?"

That was the last thing he'd expected. "No. Should I?"

She nodded gravely.

"Any specific part?" he asked, still mystified.

"I'd say the part about humanity—but you won't find any in that file. All you'll find is abuse and betrayal and pain. Circumstances and bad choices made her into an emotionless monster. A shell of what she could have been."

"If you're trying to make some parallel between her and you—"

"No." She shook her head, the silk of her hair tickling his chin. "I'm trying to say that all of us get a raw deal at some time or another. Marjorie Reynolds got more than her share. She could have used those experiences to help others who suffered the kind of abuse she had. Instead, she chose to be a killer. Alone, most likely afraid, and an outcast." She took a deep breath. "I don't want to be alone and afraid and an outcast."

"Aw, baby," he whispered, stroking her hair. "You could never be that. Never."

"But I almost was. I let myself get mired in a decision that I'd carved in stone years ago. A decision that had nothing to do with now. Nothing to do with us. And not believing in us would have been the biggest mistake of my life."

"Do you honestly think that I was going to let you brush me off like that?"

"I wouldn't have blamed you."

"My mother didn't raise a fool. I was *so* not through working on you."

She laughed and kissed him sweetly, deeply, and then slid her hand down between their bodies. "What about tonight? Are you through working on me tonight?"

He groaned when she touched him, tangled a hand in her hair, and brought her mouth down to his. "Trust me—I've barely gotten started."

A New Day

Life is sweet.

—Jamison Cooper

43

Three months later, the teams resumed their monthly breakfast get-togethers.

Coop sat with his back to the wall of a new restaurant Rhonda had found. She'd checked it out personally, booked the reservation personally, and, despite protocol, did not log their true whereabouts anywhere at work. That lesson had been learned the hard way. No one but the Black Ops and ITAP team members knew where they were gathered this beautiful April morning.

Soon the rest of the teams would start to show up, but the Bombshell was the only reason he'd gotten up early. He just loved watching her walk into a room. And *ba-da-bing*, there she was now.

Her golden hair gently ruffled by the morning breeze, her blue eyes sparkling, her soft pink angora sweater hugging her like a lover.

"What's the deal?" she asked, joining him at the table. "I woke up, and you were gone."

"I wanted to get here early."

"Didn't trust my recon?"

"Didn't want to miss your entrance. Woman, you sure know how to wear a sweater."

"Why can't you just have a foot fetish?" She poured herself a cup of coffee.

He laughed, then leaned over and kissed her. "Oh, I've got one of those, too. I'm trying not to overwhelm you with all my little quirks at once."

"Speaking of quirks," she said, looking toward the door, "what's with Bobby lately?"

Coop watched as Taggart walked toward them. "What do you mean? He looks like the same Neanderthal I've grown to know and love."

"I heard that, Hondo." Taggart sat down beside Rhonda. "How are you, sweetheart? Come to your senses yet? This guy's not good enough for you. Tell me you left him."

She kissed his cheek. "You'll be the first to know if that happens."

Taggart looked disgusted. "He really told you why we call him Hondo, and that didn't send you running for the door?"

"Careful," Coop warned him with a grin. "Or I'll tell her why we call you Boom Boom."

"I thought it was because he's a munitions expert," Rhonda said.

"And you'd be right," Taggart assured her, glaring at Cooper.

Coop laughed. "It's his story. Guess I'll let him tell

it his way . . . for now." Then he made a big show of whispering to Rhonda, "Beans."

She laughed, and he continued, "And don't even think about threatening me, big guy, or I'll tell the Bombshell here that you were the one who gave her that name. Whoops. There goes another cat out of the bag."

Rhonda scowled at Taggart. "*You're* responsible for that?"

"What does it feel like to be hooked up with a squealer?" Taggart asked her.

She shook her head. "You're both a couple of big kids, you know that?"

Coop lifted his coffee. Taggart did the same. Then they clinked mugs and toasted in unison, "Growing old is mandatory. Growing up is optional."

"It's a good thing," Rhonda muttered into her cup, but she was smiling, and Coop knew she loved their silliness as much as she loved him.

Life was sweet.

But Coop had also noticed that something was off with Taggart. Just a beat here or there. Or a moment when he'd catch Taggart in deep thought, as if he was a million miles away. Whatever it was, it would come out eventually. It always did.

Rhonda waved as Stephanie and Joe Green arrived, and it wasn't long before almost every member of the Black Ops and ITAP teams showed up. Proof to the bad guys that if anyone messed with them, they'd only come out stronger.

"Oh, my gosh." Rhonda pressed a hand over her heart, and tears pooled in her eyes as she looked toward the door. "Eva."

Coop walked over to meet Eva and Mike, who stood protectively beside her.

"Are you . . . should you . . . can I . . . ?"

Eva smiled. "Yes, I'm ready to be out. Yes, I should be here. And yes, you can hug me."

Coop carefully folded her in his arms. "Welcome back, stranger."

"Thank you."

They were both teary-eyed when he gently returned her to her husband.

"Let's get this show on the road," Mike said cheerily. "I'm hungry."

After they'd all caught up with their lives and finished their breakfasts, Mike reached into his pocket for his jack of hearts. "Well, I guess it's that time."

"You don't need to get your cards out, boys," Rhonda said as the three men reached into their pockets. "Cooper's paying for breakfast today. He insists."

"Hey." Coop grinned at her. "You're not the boss of me."

Chuckles and a few hoots echoed around the table.

She leaned in and kissed him. "You do realize that you're the only one who actually believes that."

Keep reading for a sneak peek
of Cindy Gerard's next military romantic suspense
set in the world of the One-Eyed Jacks series

TAKING FIRE

Coming Spring 2016 from Pocket Books!

1

~~~

"Lord love a duck." Looking shocked and pleased, Ted Jensen pushed back his desk chair and stood when he saw Bobby Taggart in his doorway. "Look what the cat dragged in."

Though Jensen was the security chief at the American embassy in Oman, the grin splitting his face revealed the Alabama boy Bobby knew well and loved to hassle.

"Thought someone woulda killed you by now," Jensen added, his grin widening.

Bobby gripped the rough hand his old friend extended across the sleek walnut desk. "Trust me, it's not for lack of trying on their part."

Jensen laughed, rounded his desk, and trapped Bobby in a hard bear hug.

Bobby hugged him tight, glad to see him. Back in the day, when both were Special Forces, they'd served together on many deployments. Saved each other's asses more than once, too. Jensen had retired from the military and used his spotless record to get this gig in the Diplomatic Service. Bobby had hired on for private contract work in Afghanistan, but now worked for the Department of Defense.

"It's good to see you, man." Jensen finally released him. "I really was afraid you were dead."

"Highly exaggerated rumors," Bobby told him.

"You look damn good, given that ugly mug of yours."

"Says the man with the face like a waffle iron."

Jensen chuckled. "So how've you been, Boom Boom? I heard about the exoneration. Always knew those charges were bogus. What never made sense was why they charged you in the first place." His look promised a sympathetic ear if Bobby needed it.

Maybe if he were good and drunk, he'd indulge in a little info share. But sober, Operation Slam Dunk and the debacle that followed was a subject he never talked about.

"Water. Bridge," he said with a dismissive shrug, then made an appreciative scan of the lavishly furnished office. "You're clearly top dog in these parts."

"Don't let the fancy digs fool you." Jensen gestured toward a chair before sinking down in his own. "The dog house may be top drawer, but I'm still guarding a junkyard."

"So I've heard. And that's why I'm here."

"No shit?" Jensen narrowed his brows. "*You're* the big shot badass the DOD sent to bust my chops?"

"Drew the short straw."

"Huh." Thoughtful, Jensen reached into the top drawer of his desk and pulled out two glasses and a bottle of scotch. He gave Bobby an expectant look and when he nodded, poured them each two fingers.

"All the straws seem to come up short these days," Bobby added after tossing back the scotch. "You okay with me trying to poke holes in your operation?"

Oman wasn't exactly a hotbed of terrorist activity, but given their strategically important position at the mouth of the Persian Gulf, their shared borders with UAE, Saudi Arabia, and Yemen, plus their common marine borders with Iran and Pakistan, Oman's stability and that of the U.S. Embassy were paramount. Add in the ISIS threat and the volatility of the entire Middle East, and the State Department wasn't taking any chances.

So Bobby had been assigned to assess the security, recommend upgrades if necessary, and authorize the resources to get it done. Since Jensen was in charge of that security, Bobby was going to be tromping all over his dance floor.

Jensen said, "I've got a good team here. We've got a solid plan in place. But if I've got holes, I want them found. I don't want another Benghazi on my watch."

Neither did Bobby. The September 11, 2012, terrorist attack on the U.S. Embassy in Benghazi, Libya, had left more than the ambassador tragically and needlessly dead. Three other U.S. nationals—their brothers-in-arms—had died protecting American interests, because bureaucrats and politicians had ignored repeated concerns about the lack of adequate security at the compound.

"At least the Benghazi debacle brought attention to the need and opened the government's wallet," Bobby said. "So where do you want me to start?"

"You mean right this minute? Hell, no. It's almost six p.m., and we haven't seen each other in years. You can attack the defenses first thing in the morning. Right now, we're gonna go tie one on for old times' sake."

Bobby sank back in his chair with a grin. Maybe Ted was right. Maybe a stiff drink, some good ole days conversation, and a good night's sleep were in order. Especially after the ridiculously long flight with all its delays and jet lag.

"All right," he agreed. "I'm in."

Then he heard a voice from the hallway—a voice he hadn't heard in six years but had never forgotten. And whatever Ted had in mind for tonight faded like a freighter sinking into a deep ocean fog.

He stood. Hesitated. Then walked to the doorway and stepped into the hall.

And there she was, heading toward him. Head down, she focused on the sheath of papers clutched in her hand as she walked.

She hadn't spotted him yet. But she would if he didn't unglue his boots from the polished marble floor and beat his feet back into Jensen's office.

Yet there he stood. Unable to move. Barely able to breathe.

She looked the same. Knockout gorgeous and kick-ass cool. Still slim and sleek and in total control. Back then she'd worn camo or khaki, and usually twisted her hair into a thick black braid. Today it was a black power suit, crisp white blouse, and black heels. And her hair was pulled back into an elegant and sexy knot at her nape. Even before she looked up, he knew that the face he'd memorized by sight, touch, and taste would be as golden and lovely as when she'd been his.

Damn. He'd thought he was over her.

He'd figured they'd meet up again someday, but he hadn't thought that seeing her again would make him feel like a turtle lumbering across a busy freeway. Nowhere to go to escape the inevitable collision. Unable to move fast enough to avoid certain disaster.

She'd almost reached him when she finally raised her head to talk to the aide walking alongside her. Her dark eyes landed briefly on his face, then moved on past him.

An instant later she stopped, stood motionless for a long, humming second, and then turned slowly to look at him.

All the blood drained from her face when she realized it was him.

All the breath left his body.

After six years and countless regrets, he had the same reaction to her as he'd had the first time he'd seen her in Afghanistan. A searing connection, a sizzling electricity that wasn't only sexual, but intensely soulful and deep.

Oh, God. Not again. He could not survive her again.

Their eyes were still locked—stunned, disbelieving—when a massive explosion rocked the building.

Shattering glass, falling concrete, and the acrid stench of billowing smoke were joined by horrified screams; then hideous pain consumed him as the blast knocked him off his feet. He fell facedown on the floor, eyes glazed, head pounding, ears ringing.

The last thing he saw before he passed out was a black high heel flying across the broken glass that littered the embassy floor.

2

Kabul, Afghanistan
Six years earlier

Looking in the mirror behind the bar, Talia Levine
studied her assignment in the dimly lit room of the
Mustafa Hotel in Kabul. All the Americans in the bar
were a long way from home. All were lonely. But none
were easy—especially this man she'd singled out.

No matter. When she found the right tactical advantage, he would help her. He'd never know it, of
course, but if all worked as planned, she'd deliver the
goods to her commander within a week. Two, tops.

Even if she hadn't read his file, she'd have known
that he'd once been U.S. Army, Special Ops, just like
the other three men with him, who were now private
military contractors with the Fargis Group. He and his
kind had a battle-hardened look. This man in particular had a coiled readiness, an underplayed situational
awareness that allowed him to assess every detail of
his surroundings without blinking an eye. No one was

going to get the drop on him. Anyone coming after him was going to die. No hesitation. No regret.

She'd known coming into this assignment that she was going to have to be very careful. And for three nights straight, she'd played it cool, kept her distance, and waited for the right moment to approach him. Tonight might be the night.

His back was to the wall, his eyes were on his whiskey, yet she sensed that he knew she'd been watching him. Just as she'd sensed over the past few nights, making herself visible at the bar, that he was attracted to her but was deciding how things were going to play out between them.

She looked away, tipped her wine to her lips, and let him think about it some more—while she thought about getting what she wanted.

"Buy you another?"

For a big man, he moved like a cat. And while she wasn't surprised that he'd managed to slip into her personal space without so much as rippling the air between them, she couldn't help feeling a little unsettled.

She glanced up at him, then smiled. "Sure. If you don't make me drink alone."

He got the bartender's attention, made a circle in the air with his finger to indicate another round, and eased onto the bar stool beside her.

"Come here often?" His smile surprised her as much as the corny line.

She'd made certain that he knew this was her watering hole. Just as she knew it was his—along with all the other private contractors, mercenaries, spooks, and journalists who hung out here, searching for some like-minded company and a relatively quiet place to drink away the physical and emotional dirt from the day.

"Can't seem to stay away. Must be the homey atmosphere."

"Right." He made a cursory glance around the room's smoke-stained orange and yellow walls and worn, cracked marble floors. "That must be it. Or the cheap booze. Any port in a storm, I guess."

"What about you?" She nodded her thanks to the bartender when he slid a fresh glass of wine in front of her.

"When the pickings are slim, you take what you can get." He smiled again, surprising her again. He looked hard, this American, and what she knew of his background supported that. But when he smiled, there was nothing hard about him.

"Are we still talking about the hotel?" she asked reacting to that smile.

He laughed. "Well, we're not talking about you, ma'am. You class up the place."

"Ma'am?" The old-fashioned endearment charmed her more than it should have.

"Best I could do, since I don't know your name. Mine's Bobby. Bobby Taggart."

Robert Andrew Taggart, to be exact. Known to his coworkers as Bobby or Boom Boom. It was the Boom she had to be careful of. It was his military history and his fall from grace that would work for her. That, and simply his one X and one Y chromosome. She needed information; he had it. And she'd do whatever she had to do to get it out of him.

"Talia Levine. You're American, right?"

"What gave it away?"

She pushed out a flirty laugh. "Only everything about you."

He leaned a little closer. "Guess I'd better work on that. And you? Can't place the accent."

"I was hoping I didn't have one." She smiled. "Florida, actually. But of late, Israel, followed by London, Baghdad, and anywhere else my assignments take me. Journalist," she supplied, when he cocked a brow.

"I should have guessed. Why else would a beautiful woman spend time in a dive like this unless she was forced to?"

"Not forced," she corrected. "Volunteered."

"Ah. You're one of those." He sipped his whiskey, studying her face in a way that made her feel a bit like a mouse in a trap, when *she* was supposed to be doing the trapping.

She crinkled her brow, playing to his statement. "One of *those?*"

"An 'all for the sake of her career' woman. You take reckless chances to get your story."

"How would you know if I was reckless?"

"Not to point out the obvious, but you're in Kabul. And you're coming on to a stranger in a bar."

"Wow." She feigned insult. "That's harsh."

"That's life. No insult intended. But maybe a little wishful thinking. You *were* coming on to me, right?"

She sipped her wine. "I was still deciding."

He chuckled. "And now?"

"And now, I need to know more about you."

"Me? I'm an open book."

"Of course you are," she said, letting him know that he wasn't fooling her. He was good at this game. But not as good as she was.

"Are you really any different than I am in the reckless department?" she asked, now that the door was open. "You were military, right? Probably served more than one deployment in the hot zones. And now you're a civilian contractor."

She wasn't stating anything that wasn't general knowledge around Kabul. The Americans who ended up here all had military backgrounds, and most were employed by civilian contractors. "You also take reckless chances just by being here."

He lifted his glass. "That I do. So, it's settled. We're both a little crazy."

"Maybe. But you can't say it's not exciting."

"Yeah. This is definitely my idea of excitement. Watching the paint peel off the walls of this bar."

She toyed with the stem of her wineglass, then tilted him a coy smile. "You're not watching the paint peel now, are you?"

He perked up a little bit at that, because she'd just let him know she'd made her decision. "No, ma'am. I certainly am not."

Though this was just business on her part, an unsettling awareness zipped between them. And for a moment she let herself see the man, not the assignment.

Square jaw, military haircut, watchful green eyes. Attractive, especially when he smiled. She could picture him in another era, crossing the Atlantic on a tall sailing ship, landing at Ellis Island with his German, French, and Irish ancestry. He was big and muscular, this Bronx, New York, native, and had been a bit of a street brawler in his teens. According to his file, he was a man who kept to himself.

But judging by his expectant look now, that wasn't altogether true.

An electric silence had stretched out between them before she managed to fall back into her role. She glanced up at him. "Just so you know . . . I don't make a habit of picking up strangers in bars."

His gaze was intense but not judgmental as he shifted toward her. "So why me? And why now?"

She looked away, and when she looked back at him she had tears in her eyes. All she had to do was call up today's horrible memory to provoke them. "Why you? Because you look about as lonely as I feel. Why now? Because life—this life—*is* risky, and today I narrowly escaped with mine. Today, I need human contact."

He watched her with cool green eyes that had warmed just enough to tell her she'd struck a chord with him, and she felt an unaccustomed twinge of guilt.

"To remind you that you're human?"

She shook her head. "To remind me that humanity isn't dead . . . even in the midst of this inhumane war."

He studied her face, then studied his whiskey before tossing the rest of it down. "My room or yours?"

She'd surprised him, this Talia Levine or whatever her real name was. He'd been certain that his crude and direct invitation would have had her bolting with second thoughts. That she would've told him this was a bad idea, before telling him good-night.

But here he was. Following her and her exceptional ass up three flights of stairs. The question was why. Why was she lying to him? And why go to the trouble of staking him out in a bar for three nights running? If she was a journalist, he was a freakin' nanny.

Except, oh wait—he was as American as a Chevy truck, and she clearly wanted something from him.

How far will you go to get it, sweetheart? How far would he let her go?

One thing she hadn't lied about: Afghanistan was a hellhole. Every day was a crapshoot. And yeah, the need for human contact in the midst of all this brutality sometimes got you by the balls and wouldn't let go.

So he followed her out of the elevator, down the dim hallway, and stopped when she did at room 309. Three was his lucky number, and he could make four threes out of that room number—which quadrupled his luck, good or bad.

She fitted the key into an antiquated lock, turned it, and pushed the door open.

"Home sweet home," she said, flipping on the overhead light and stepping aside for him to follow her in.

He glanced around the room. A double bed. Two side tables. An open laptop sat on one of them. A camera with a bulky lens sat beside it, along with a notepad filled with scribbled notes.

Nicely done, he thought, and walked to the closet, opened the door, and checked inside. Empty except for her clothes. Same thing with the bathroom—no terrorist lying in wait to whack an American.

"Do we call this paranoia, or a basic distrust in women?" she asked after he'd checked under the bed.

"Call it anything you want," he said agreeably. "Mostly, it's called life lessons."

She nodded slowly, clearly entertained. "Do I pass inspection?"

"Well," he said with a smile as he walked toward her, "the room does. I haven't thoroughly inspected you yet. Got any explosive devises hidden under that horribly drab shirt?"

"Sorry I didn't dress for the occasion," she said as he gripped her hips and pulled her against him.

She didn't resist him. Didn't exactly melt against him, either. So he pushed a little further to see how far she'd let this go.

"Dressing is highly overrated," he replied. "Now, undressing—that's something I could get into."

"No surprises there," she said, but still made no effort to get on with the festivities.

Which told him she *was* having second thoughts. "It's not too late to back out, Talia—if that's really your name," he added just to see how she'd respond.

"Ah," she said, and looped her arms around his neck. "You really don't trust me."

"With my heart? You're going to steal it, for sure. And I'm okay with that." His smile quickly faded. "With my life? Not so much. What do you want from me?"

"I told you what I wanted," she said, suddenly sober. Playing no more. Suddenly shaken.

She could act. He'd give her that.

"Look. I told you I'd never done this before. Clearly I'm no good at it. Maybe you should leave."

She pushed away from him, walked toward the door, and opened it.

He'd detected a hint of a limp when she'd slid off the bar stool, but had been too busy watching her ass and wondering what she was up to, to process it. Now he wanted to know.

"Why are you limping?"

"I told you," she said still gripping the handle of the open door. "I had a close call today."

He walked across the room. Closed the door. "Let me see."

"Why? Because you don't believe me?"

"Because I want to see."

He was angry now, and not sure why. Just like he wasn't sure why he grabbed her arm, dragged her to the bed, and pushed her down on it.

"Take 'em off," he ordered as she lay there, looking up at him like a defiant bunny.

Evidently his look told her that either she do it or

he would, because she finally lowered her hands, un-buttoned her khaki pants, and undid the zipper.

"Where?" he demanded.

"Right leg. My calf."

He lifted her leg by her foot, undid the laces on her boot, and slipped both it and the sock off. Then he helped her tug the pants down so her entire right leg was exposed—except for the white bandage that wrapped around her leg from below the knee to her ankle.

She said nothing during this process. She just lay there, her eyes a little wide, her ugly shirt open just above her naval, revealing a smooth expanse of olive skin between the shirt hem and the band of her bikini panties. Flesh-colored. Practical. Sexy as hell without meaning to be.

He jerked his attention back to her bandaged leg. "Roll over."

She considered balking, but finally muttered under her breath and rolled onto her stomach. He slowly undid the gauze wrap, schooling his gaze away from one of the finest asses he'd ever seen. Then he closed his eyes on a hiss when he saw her injury.

That pretty olive skin had a jagged three-inch wound. Clumsy stitches bit into the angry red flesh.

"What the hell happened? And what quack stitched you up?" He sat down on the bed, helping her get more comfortable, then lay his hand over the wound. It didn't appear to be infected. The flesh was cool to the touch but clearly sore, because she winced as he continued his examination.

"I told you, I had a close call today. A corpsman stitched it and field dressed it for me."

He lay on the bed beside her, crossed his hands behind his head, and stared at the ceiling. "You were there? At the school?"

He'd heard about the ambush. A dozen Taliban bastards had opened fire on a group of children. Specifically, girls who dared to go to school. The death toll was staggering.

He felt her body shift beside him, sensed her gaze on his face. And he knew before he turned to look at her what he'd see.

"They killed them," she whispered through her tears. "They killed those beautiful children."

Without a second thought, he gathered her in his arms, replaying their words in his mind.

Because today, I need human contact.

To remind you that you're human?

To remind me that humanity isn't dead . . . even in the midst of this inhumane war.

And what had his response been? *My room or yours?*

He was a calloused, cynical bastard.

Was she who she said she was? Hell, he didn't know. And at this moment, he didn't care. He just cared about holding her as she wept, her body shaking, her grief as real as it gets.

And when he woke up in the middle of the night, he was still holding her. Him in his dusty fatigues, her half-dressed, his shoulder damp with her tears.